Pride, Prejudice, & Turkish Delight

KC McCormick Çiftçi

One

Eliza Britt sighed as she unlocked her office door. Today's classes had been a challenge, and the stack of essays to grade on her desk was sure to eat up her free time for the rest of the week. She released her brown hair from the ponytail that was threatening to give her a headache and rolled her shoulders. She was too young to be this tired, but she supposed it came along with the territory of being on her feet all day in her ESL classroom.

Eliza flicked on the electric kettle on her windowsill and placed a tea bag in her unwashed mug. While she waited for the water to boil, she checked her text messages.

"I don't know about you, but I'm too exhausted to think about cooking. How does Seoul Garden delivery sound?" her roommate Crystal had written.

A genuine smile broke through Eliza's exhaustion. At least they weren't going to argue about what to eat tonight because she didn't have the mental energy to convince her roommate that her taste in takeout restaurants was, in fact, *wrong*. "Sure! I'll be home late—midterms..." she wrote, throwing in an eye roll emoji. Crystal Kim was also an ESL teacher, so Eliza was sure she'd be able to feel the pain in that message. Crystal tutored private students in one-on-one lessons, while Eliza was overworked and underpaid at the local community college. Still, both of them felt the pinch of exam time, when many of their students realized the frustrating gap between the English they needed to learn to survive and function in American society and the English they needed to learn to ace their standardized tests and move on in their academic careers.

Remembering the panic on the faces of the students who'd clearly forgotten their midterm essays were due today brought a wicked laugh from deep in Eliza's belly. "Serves you right," she said to herself. "If only you'd paid attention in class or, I don't know, bothered to write it down in a planner?" She wasn't completely heartless, but she would deduct ten percent from the grade for every day it was turned in late. And maybe grade the procrastinators ever so slightly more harshly, but who could say for sure?

Not that Eliza didn't have students she loved, too. Many of the ESL students at West Community College were refugees, finding themselves navigating both the emotional upheaval of leaving their homes behind and the cognitive overwhelm of learning English spelling and grammar at the same time.

With her freshly steeped cup of peppermint tea, Eliza flicked open the top essay on her pile. *Hmm, actually. Maybe if I divide this enormous pile into a few smaller ones, it won't be quite so daunting.* As she made four smaller piles, one for each remaining day of the week, Eliza counted 68 essays. *Okay, actually I wish I didn't know there were that many. Maybe I'll forget and then be pleasantly surprised later on when the stack is half that size.*

She put them all in one big stack again and sipped her tea. Back to the first essay. Eliza's eyes landed on a sentence: "I miss my life in Syria very much, but I am happy to be safe with my family."

Oof. There were going to be some hard pages to read coming. Eliza had, maybe foolishly, she now realized, assigned her students to write essays that might double as their personal statements for their upcoming university applications. She had given examples of how to write about overcoming hardships, something many of the students in her class didn't seem to think was the most interesting thing about themselves, and she realized now that some stoicism would serve her well if she was going to work her way through the stack of essays without covering them all in tears.

How do I even begin to grade someone on how well they share their heartbreak? I don't want to censor or edit anyone, and I'm not sure that distilling their experiences down to appeal to our American sensibilities is really in the best interest of the students or of the admissions advisers who will ultimately read these things.

Eliza picked up her phone to text Crystal again. "Just kidding about my last message. I'm packing up now and I'll grade at home after dinner. Order me some bulgogi, please. See you soon!"

Yes, she knew she was procrastinating. But sometimes it actually was easier to grade at home. *These are the most crucial decisions I make—grade at this desk or at the dining room table? It's no wonder I can't relate to my students and their life or death decisions.*

Eliza headed out of her office, messenger bag full of to-be-graded essays slung across her shoulder. The bag was heavy and awkwardly balanced, slamming into her right hip with every other step and pulling sharply on her left shoulder. Her chiropractor mother had finally stopped trying to convince Eliza that a backpack would be a more sensible choice, and as she glimpsed her reflection in a nearby office, she smiled. Even if she had a little discomfort—and a crick in her neck that never went away—at least she looked the part of the college professor, just like she'd always dreamed.

She passed the reception area and was nearly out the door when the department secretary caught up with her. "Ms. Britt, I didn't realize you hadn't left yet. You had a visitor from State University drop by when you were in class. I don't know why he didn't just email you, but he left a note with me at the desk."

"That's strange," Eliza said, berating herself that her professional demeanor had vanished in a flash of sweaty palms and breathy words. "I hate surprises," she said by way of explanation, gesturing to the shakiness in her fingers as she took the note the secretary offered her.

The older woman patted Eliza's arm. "I'm sure it's nothing bad, dear. Surprises can be good sometimes, you know."

Eliza shook her head. "That's never true. I wish it were, but I've been right about this too many times."

With widened eyes, the secretary recoiled. "Aren't you a little young to be this jaded?"

"Not jaded. Just perceptive. If you pay close enough attention to what's going on around you, you never actually have to be surprised."

Eliza was almost sure she heard the woman mutter, "That's no way to live," to herself as she walked away, but she shook it off. She didn't have time to cater to anyone's feelings today. Not with that stack of essays weighing down her shoulder and not with this note weighing on her like the most unwelcome task on her to-do list.

She turned it over now, examining the source of her sudden influx of stress. It was from Dr. Bennett, her former advisor, and it merely said he'd be calling her later. *Great. Something to look forward to.* But as much as Eliza didn't like surprises—and as much as the phrase "we need to talk" made her break into a cold sweat—she'd never turn down Dr. B. His leadership, even if it was a bit eccentric at times, had already helped her get a great teaching job fresh after graduating from his program, and Eliza knew that if she wanted to keep building the career she so desperately wanted, connections like Dr. Bennett meant everything.

Eliza walked across the small campus towards the faculty parking lot. These end-of-summer days were special, with just a tinge of crispness to the air and the days getting ever so slightly shorter. She wondered briefly if she should feel some sort of sadness about the fact that she'd spent all summer working and hadn't made the journey to Lake Michigan even once...but then she remembered the career she was trying to advance and smiled to herself. There would be time for beaches and vacations when she was a tenured professor. Or even better, the director of her own program.

The door of Eliza's old black Jetta unlocked with a turn of her key. Her key fob hadn't remotely locked or unlocked a door in years, but apart from that, the 15-year-old car was holding up well and reliable to a fault. Eliza patted the steering wheel as the engine roared to life. "That's a good boy, Jets. I can always count on you, more than any other man in my life."

Twenty minutes later, Eliza pulled in to the parking lot of her apartment, sliding her car into the spot next to Crystal's BMW. The two cars made a funny pair, not unlike Eliza and Crystal, but there was a charming sort of rightness in their odd couple nature.

"I'm home! Please tell me my bulgogi's waiting!" Eliza called as she slid off her shoes by the door.

"Just got here, perfect timing!" came Crystal's reply. She poked her head out of the kitchen, paper bag in hand. "Let's eat!"

The two roommates plopped onto the old sofa in their living room, Korean food in hand.

As Crystal flipped on the television, she asked how Eliza's essay stack was going.

"Ugh, don't remind me. It's going to be the bane of my existence for at least the next few days." Eliza answered. "Hey! Let's watch that new detective show. It looks pretty good..."

"Oh yeah, another retelling of Sherlock Holmes. How could we possibly live with ourselves if we didn't get one of those at least every couple of years?" Crystal asked, dead-pan.

"Whatever, it's not like you don't enjoy them. It's just such a classic story, and I love seeing the new ways that it gets retold—"

"Okay, fine! We both know you won't drop this until you win, so I'll just opt for whatever will stop you from giving me that lecture about Sir Arthur Conan Doyle's relevancy in the 21st century again!"

Eliza tossed a pillow at Crystal's head as she settled in, takeout container in one hand and chopsticks in the other.

The two women had been friends since middle school, and in many ways, they were more like sisters. A friendship that blooms at the same time as puberty and survives the roller-coastering hormones, crushes (of both the unrequited and the competitive varieties), family drama, school stress, college applications, and four years of being roommates was cemented for life.

While many well-meaning friends and family members had advised the girls, back when they were high school seniors, to not even consider sharing a dorm room in college with their best friend, Eliza and Crystal hadn't given it a second thought. At first they were polite when offered this unsolicited advice, but by graduation time they had resorted to eye rolling, scoffing, and a sarcastic, "Gee, thanks, I never thought about that." They knew they would get on each other's nerves (heck, they already did), and they also felt pretty confident that they'd be fine. After all, they were more like sisters, and living under the same roof seemed to work just fine for all the sisters they knew.

"How were your lessons today?" Eliza asked Crystal. Crystal taught private English lessons online to students in other countries, a job she liked well enough but which got a little tiresome and repetitive.

"Fine," Crystal said with her mouth full. "I had a couple TOEFL prep classes, and then one lesson with a kid whose parents want to make sure he gets into the best high school. He was five years old, so we mostly focused on sentences like, 'Please take your fingers out of your mouth; I can't understand you when you do that.'"

Crystal had a lot of patience, which Eliza admired. "Yikes. I think that's probably better than the little ones who prefer to pick their noses, though."

"Um, yes. Of course. If we could NOT talk about that during dinner, that'd be just super."

"Sorry sorry sorry. Anyway, how were the TOEFL lessons? Do you think they're prepared for the test?" TOEFL, or the Test of English as a Foreign Language, was a requirement for students applying to graduate programs in the US.

"Yeah, I think we'll get there soon. We've got another class or two before they take it. But anyway, isn't that enough shop talk? Don't we have other interests besides what we get paid to do all day long?" Crystal glared at Eliza. "I'm pretty sure all those work-life balance experts out there don't actually encourage you to talk about work with your roommate all night until you eventually burn out from stress and then die of exhaustion."

Eliza laughed. "You're right. You're *dramatic* as hell, but you're right. Just this once. But speaking of work..." She winced. "No, I swear this is important." She dug through the pockets of her blazer before she found the note that had been left for her. "Someone left me a note at the front desk. Isn't that bizarre? It was dropped off by somebody from State...want to make a guess who it was?" Eliza asked.

"Hmm...well, it better not be that shitty ex-boyfriend of yours. I'm going to hope it was Dr. Bennett, just stopping by to say how much he misses you and your genius brain."

"Ding ding ding! You are correct!" Eliza exclaimed. "He just said he was going to call me later, and I'm not going to lie, that made me a little nervous."

"Gosh, I sure hope it's a pyramid scheme," laughed Crystal. "Maybe he's got an exciting opportunity that's going to make you a ton of money with almost no effort, as long as you recruit everyone you know to be a part of it. Let me be the first to say, 'Not it!'"

Eliza rolled her eyes at Crystal. She never took things like this, Eliza's *career* above all, as seriously as Eliza did. Just then, she felt her phone vibrate in her pocket. When she looked at the screen, she smiled at the synchronicity of it. "Speak of the devil," she said, as she showed Crystal the phone screen: Alfred Bennett.

"Hi, Dr. Benn—" Eliza answered.

"Lizzy! I've got the most exciting news!" Dr. Bennett interrupted. "We're establishing a partnership with a university in TURKEY, of all places, and I know just who's going to lead our side of things. I can't go, of course. You know I'm not good on a long flight. But I thought you, you would be a natural! We're starting right away. You'd need to be there next week. But of course that's no problem for you, you're young and unattached, and it's just SUCH a special, once-in-a-lifetime opportunity! What do you say, Lizzy?"

Eliza stared at Crystal, wishing she could hear what was happening on the other end of the line. She directed her next sentence to both of the people listening to her, asking incredulously, "You want ME to move to Turkey next week?"

Two

"What in the actual...?" As soon as Eliza hung up the phone, Crystal pounced. "Did that just happen?"

Eliza was too shocked to do more than nod as she sank deep into the couch. "I...I don't even know what just happened. I mean, I know Dr. B. is a bit flakey sometimes—"

Crystal interrupted with a laugh. "Just a bit, huh?" Off Eliza's look, her laughter stopped. "Okay, okay. I know the guy is, like, your career sherpa or whatever, but that doesn't mean he's not a drama king. Or that he doesn't take full advantage of the fact that you respect him. Anyway. What the heck? I only heard your side, so..."

Eliza groaned. "Well, if it sounded like he was trying to convince me to move to Turkey in a week, then that's exactly what it was. I can't believe he would do this to me! I've just settled in to my rhythm at WCC, I'm happy, and now he's expecting me to just throw that all away. This doesn't make any sense!"

"It does take Dr. Bennett's nonsensical ideas to a whole new level. Are you really not even going to consider it?"

"Of course not! I could never. What about my students? What about our lease? What about the fact that I don't speak any Turkish?"

"Eliza, come on. Not speaking Turkish is hardly the biggest point of concern here, though I'm sure my mom would be happy to teach you a phrase or two if you decided to go," replied Crystal. Crystal's mom had grown up in Greece, immigrating to the US as a young woman, after meeting Crystal's dad when the two of them were studying abroad in Germany at the same time.

Eliza forced a smile. "I can always count on Mama Kim." She shook her head then. "But no. That's not going to be necessary. Because I just can't do it. It's not going to happen. It might be a great opportunity, but I can't leave everything and everyone behind here!"

"Doesn't it sound a little exciting, though?" asked Crystal. "I mean, you could finally taste some real Turkish delight. Find out if it's worth selling your soul for."

"For sure." Eliza was distracted, which a lesser trained eye than Crystal's might not notice. But after a decade of friendship, Crystal could read her better than anyone.

"Come on, Eliza. What's the problem? Why aren't you excited about Turkey? About the job?" Crystal asked her roommate.

"It's not about Turkey. I'd definitely love to visit there. But it's the job. It just sounds like biting off way too much responsibility." Eliza said, her tone rising.

"Do you really think it's too much for you to handle? And do you really think Dr. Bennett would ask you to do something he didn't think you were perfectly capable of?" responded Crystal.

"That's the thing. I don't think he sees me realistically. I may have been a great student, but performing well in class—and even teaching well, as I like to think I do—doesn't mean I'm cut out for leadership. I mean, Crystal, this is basically administration! It's just what I've always wanted to do, the next logical step for my career. I'm just not ready for it to happen so soon. This wasn't the plan."

Eliza saw Crystal's eyes roll before she heard her friend's exasperated sigh. "Right, because *that's* what's most concerning. The fact that you're straying from your ten-year plan—by accelerating it, I might add—is the best reason not to do this. It's not like you wouldn't be teaching at all, right?"

"Of course I'd be teaching a class or two as well, but the responsibility for building the program and getting all the teachers standardized would be totally on me. I'm getting all sweaty just thinking about it."

"I hear you. Let's slow down for a moment and think, though." Crystal said. "You haven't accepted the job yet, and he's giving you a few days to consider it before he asks anyone else. So there's no need to get sweaty about it yet. Would you feel better if you made a Rory Gilmore-style pro and con chart?"

"Ugh, shut up." Eliza smiled as she folded her knees up to her chest. "But also, don't knock the pro/con chart. It's an indisputably effective way of making a rational decision. I don't have any chart paper lying around, though..."

"Okay, so what if we don't actually draw it? Let's just talk about it. What would happen if you *did* take this job?" Crystal asked.

"Well, I'd definitely learn a lot. I'd have a new experience, learn some new skills, meet new people. I like all of those things, but that doesn't mean I want to move to the other side of the world—"

"Aha! Stop right there, don't start answering what I didn't ask. What would happen if you *didn't* take this job?"

"Hmm. I guess nothing different, really. I might feel a bit like I'm missing out on something or like I wasn't brave enough to have an adventure that I really wanted." Eliza answered.

"What *won't* happen if you take this job?"

"Wait a second. Are you using one of your coaching techniques on me?" Eliza asked. Crystal had always been one to chase down unexpected hobbies in her free time, at least for as long as they kept her interest. One of those unexpected hobbies of hers had taken her all the way to nearly completing her certification to become a life coach.

"Whatever, they're good questions. Answer it." Crystal pouted.

"What won't happen if I take this job? Well, I guess I won't finish my semester here...I probably won't be around for all the holidays I like to spend with my family..."

"Anything else?"

"Hmm...well, I definitely won't get back together with Alec. And I'm not saying that would be a major loss or anything."

Crystal rolled her eyes. She had never been a fan of Alec and that was no secret. "Good riddance. Okay, last one: what won't happen if you *don't* take this job?

"That's a different way of looking at it. I guess I won't have that adventure. I won't test my limits professionally or personally. I'll miss out..." Eliza trailed off, a faraway look in her eyes.

Crystal gave her a minute to process before she started talking again. "What are you thinking? You got awfully quiet there."

"I don't know...I'm thinking about it," Eliza answered, surprising herself. "I can't believe I'm even saying that, and I'm probably going to talk myself out of it again before I even go to sleep tonight, but...yeah. I'm thinking about it."

"What city is the job in?" Crystal asked, pulling out her phone.

"Antalya," said Eliza. "I've never heard of it, have you?"

Crystal gasped as she held out her phone to Eliza. "This should definitely figure into your pro/con chart, friend. It's *gorgeous.*"

The phone's screen was covered in images of turquoise water, a coastline that seemed to stretch for miles, ancient ruins, mountains...Eliza found herself speechless as her hand dropped to her lap with the phone in it. "This can't be real."

"The pictures? Some of them are probably enhanced with a filter or two, but I'm sure they didn't Photoshop a whole city."

"You know what I mean," said Eliza. "This chance falling into my lap. It can't be real, can it?"

"Why not?" asked Crystal. "Why shouldn't something like this happen to you? Why shouldn't you have your world rocked by a once-in-a-lifetime opportunity?"

Eliza shook her head. "I just can't shake the feeling that it's a dream or a trick or something. That, even if I accepted the job, I'd show up there and find out it wasn't real. That Dr. Bennett invented this whole thing in his mind."

"Nah," said Crystal. "He may be a bit of an odd duck, but he'd never go that far."

Eliza wasn't so sure. Trusting anyone but herself to make the right decision for her future was a terrifying prospect, and she was glad she had some time to think about it before Dr. Bennett needed her final answer.

"I can't think about this anymore right now," she told Crystal. "I need a distraction."

Crystal picked the remote back up from where she'd dropped it on the coffee table. She pointed it towards the TV, ready to resume the episode of *Baker Street* they'd just begun when the phone rang. "As you wish. Though you and I both know you're going to be thinking about this constantly, no matter what else is distracting you."

It took Eliza a few moments the next morning to realize the whole thing hadn't been a dream. She'd fallen into a restless sleep late at night, tossing and turning and weighing the possibilities before her. If she took the job, she'd be leaving behind her current students, her friends, her family, her entire life as she knew it."

But if she didn't take the job, would she always wonder what she had missed out on?

In the middle of the night, she'd nearly convinced herself that she was the kind of adventurous soul who could throw caution to the wind and change her entire life plan overnight. But in the light of day, she knew that wasn't true.

"Who would I be if I didn't honor the commitments I've already made?" she asked herself. After all, she had rent to pay, courses to teach, and people who she'd already decided were worthy of her respect. She couldn't change her mind and let them down now.

She left her bedroom to find Crystal in the kitchen, making coffee. As soon as their eyes met, Crystal groaned.

"I knew it," she said, shaking her head. "You talked yourself out of it, didn't you?"

Eliza rushed into explanation mode without so much as a "good morning."

"It's not that I talked myself out of anything," she explained. "I just don't think I can justify going back on the commitments I've already made. Commitments to WCC, to you..."

Crystal waved her hand dismissively. "Don't you use me to justify your decision. I could find a sublessee in a heartbeat if I needed to. And it's still early enough in the semester that WCC could replace you or rearrange the teachers' schedules. What is it really?"

"That's really what it is, Crys." Eliza was exasperated. "Not everything has a deeper meaning, okay? I just can't take the job, and that's that."

The two friends waited in tense silence for the coffee to finish brewing. It wasn't often that they snapped at each other, and the unfamiliar feeling was uncomfortable.

Finally, Eliza broke the silence. "I'm sorry, I just..."

"It's fine," said Crystal. "I know you've been stressed. I didn't mean to push. I just didn't want to see you miss out on something special."

Eliza nodded. "And I appreciate that, I really do. I just think it's for the best."

Before Crystal could respond, they were interrupted by Eliza's phone buzzing in her hand. Out of force of habit, she glanced down at the notification—even though she would judge anyone else who got distracted by their phone while talking to her, she couldn't help doing it herself from time to time—and gasped.

"Oh my God," she said, her phone slipping through her fingers and landing on the counter. Eliza dropped onto a stool, already feeling her head start to swirl with anxious thoughts, her heart begin to race, and her palms begin to sweat.

"What is it?" Crystal rushed around the counter, one hand on Eliza's shoulder as they both reached towards the phone.

There on the screen was the message from Dr. Bennett that had just changed everything.

"I couldn't wait any longer for your response, my dear. This offer is too good to pass up, so I accepted the Antalya job on your behalf. Just sent your letter of resignation to WCC. Call me later to talk about your flight preferences. So exciting, isn't it?"

Three

*H*ere goes nothing, I guess. It's been a hell of a week since Dr. Bennett first told me about the job in Turkey. My flight leaves tomorrow. I can't imagine how I'm going to sleep tonight.

Eliza set down her journal. She knew it would be nice to look back at this experience documented in as much detail as possible...and yet she couldn't bring herself to sit down and write it out. The pre-flight jitters, pre-move jitters, were very, very real.

She walked back into the living room, where Crystal was flipping through channels on the television. She didn't seem too bothered by any of this.

"Did you get all packed up?" Crystal asked her room-mate. "Ready for the big flight tomorrow?"

"It's totally overwhelming." Eliza sighed. "I've got all my professional clothes, of course, but I think since I'm moving there for work, I can't even begin to think about anything else. What am I going to do on the weekends? Never mind that, what am I going to wear? And how do people dress in Turkey, anyway?"

Crystal laughed. "For how much you just *love* to know things, I'd have thought you would have done some research about that."

"Of course I have! I know Antalya is a very touristy city, so I'm sure there's a wide range of ways that people dress. Hey, at least I didn't ask if I'd have to wear a burqa."

Crystal rolled her eyes. "You say that as a joke, I know, but I'm sure people have been asking you, right? I wonder how many of them could even find Turkey on a map."

"No joke. People have asked me everything from if I'll be safe in a war zone to if I'll go to India on vacation since it's right next door. A great reminder that whatever jokes people make in other countries about Americans being ignorant about geography and the world are, as it turns out, funny because they are true."

"Sad as that is, I think you're right." Crystal answered. "Anyway, enough about packing. I'm sure the last minute panic of an empty suitcase will provide all sorts of inspiration for you. Want to watch a movie with me? Or do you need to talk about all the feelings you're feeling about tomorrow?" She asked that without a trace of irony, and for that Eliza felt grateful.

"If we could talk, at least a bit, that would be great. I've been trying to write in my journal, but that's going about as well as you'd imagine." Eliza's habit of writing in journals for only a week until she got frustrated with their lack of accuracy and perfection and went out and bought a new one was a running joke between the roommates.

"Sure, fire away. What's on your mind?" Crystal asked.

"Well, obviously, I've never done anything like this. I know someone is going to meet me at the airport, but what if there's a problem? What if I can't get through customs, or the person who is meeting me gets stuck in traffic? And even if that all goes well, I just can't help but think that my not speaking Turkish is going to be, like, a huge problem and inconvenience. What if I have a problem with my apartment? Or heck, even grocery shopping? I'm feeling so stressed about this, and I'm honestly having second thoughts."

"Well, first off, what about all the Turkish phrases you've learned lately? You've done such a good job. Pop quiz: you walk into my home and I say *'hoş geldiniz'*...how do you respond?" Crystal asked.

"Hmm. *'Hoş geldiniz'* means 'welcome'...so I would say *'hoş bulduk,'* right?"

"Exactly! 'It's good to be here,' though that isn't an exact translation. But whatever. Yes! Say that, and I'm sure you'll get a great reaction every time. It's polite, people might not expect you to know it, especially since you kind of stick out as a foreigner, and it's a great starting point." Crystal answered. Thanks to Crystal's mom, the two of them had been working together through a list of essential words. Even with just a few solid phrases under her belt (it had only been a week, after all), Eliza at least had the basics of polite interaction: greetings, please and thank you, and the ever-important welcome/it's good to be here exchange that was unique to Turkish culture.

Eliza snuggled closer to Crystal. After all the time they'd known each other and been roommates, she was going to miss her best friend. Crystal made her feel braver and stronger than she felt on her own, though that wasn't something she expressed to her in words. "When are you going to come visit me, again?" she asked, hoping against hope that it was sooner than she remembered.

"I told you, I've got to take care of a few things here and make sure I've got a day or two off in my schedule first. Plus I've got to wait until you've got internet set up in your new place, or else how will I teach my classes? But yeah, I'm looking for someone to come stay here in the apartment and water the plants. Then I can come and stay until you get sick of me."

Eliza smiled. It was reassuring to think of having Crystal there with her. They were such old friends and so close that people often assumed they were a couple. She didn't mind the confusion, and sometimes thought that it would truly make sense if they fell in love with each other. But they were already friends, confidants, roommates, and sisters. Apart from the obvious problem that Eliza was only attracted to men, the idea of having one person occupy all of those roles and be your lover just seemed impractical and irresponsible. And Eliza was nothing if not responsible.

"I know you're going to miss me, but you'll be just fine." Crystal reassured Eliza. "I'll take you to the airport tomorrow, and then before you know it, you'll be picking me up at the airport in Antalya. Deal?"

"Deal." Eliza smiled.

Crystal shifted forward on the couch suddenly. "Oh shoot, I almost forgot." She pulled a small gift bag out of the basket at the end of the couch where they kept throw blankets, magazines, and anything else that needed to be tidied up in a hurry when visitors came.

"What's this?" Eliza asked as she accepted the package. "You didn't have to get me something! You know that, right? I didn't think I needed to tell you…"

"It's not from me," Crystal cut her off. "My mom," she said by way of explanation. "Obviously she's excited you're moving to Turkey, but well…oh, just open it."

Inside the package was a square velvet jewelry box, and Eliza opened it to find a delicate silver bracelet full of small blue beads. They were royal blue with a lighter blue circle in the center of each one, looking almost like eyes.

"It's an evil eye bracelet," said Crystal. "It's called *nazar boncuğu*. You'll see that all over Turkey, and I guess my mom figured you needed one of your own for protection."

"It's beautiful," said Eliza, her fingers traveling along the bracelet. "I don't exactly understand, though. What's evil about it?"

Crystal laughed. "It's not evil. It's more like it catches any evil eyes that are sent your way. You know, like if someone's jealous of something you have, they'll try to send you some bad vibes, but the vibes will get caught in the beads instead." She shrugged. "You'll see them all over the place in Turkey, I'm pretty sure. Maybe it'll make more sense then."

Eliza hugged Crystal. "Pass that hug onto your mom for me, please. It's a bit late for Mama Kim, so I'll text her tomorrow to thank her." She closed the bracelet's clasp and leaned back on the sofa. "Now, what are we going to watch tonight?"

Thirty-six hours later, Eliza was in Antalya. A driver from the university met her at the airport, holding a sign that said "Eliza Britt" outside the arrivals exit. He presented her with a note from her new boss, Dr. Çelik, apologizing for being unable to meet her. The note stated that tomorrow afternoon, after she'd had some time to rest and adjust to the time difference, she would come to her hotel to meet her and take her to the university.

Eliza's driver dropped her off at a hotel near the beach where the administration had rented her a room. It was dark by the time she got there, so the drive from the airport to the hotel hadn't been quite as scenic as she'd hoped. She saw several large stores and shopping malls, and there was a stretch of road that seemed quite empty to one side. She assumed that was where the Mediterranean was, but she'd have to wait until morning to confirm.

In her hotel room, Eliza kicked off her shoes and looked longingly at the bed. The flight had been long, longer than any flight she'd ever been on for her few and far between vacations. Considering she'd never flown across an ocean, she supposed she shouldn't be that surprised that sleep had turned out to be an impossibility for her. A couple hours in, when the cabin lights dimmed and the other passengers fell still under their blankets and eye masks, Eliza felt a familiar anxiety. She was the only one awake, at least as far as she could see, and she suddenly felt like a nervous child again, staring at the clock in her bedroom, thinking, "If I fall asleep right now, I'll get six hours before the alarm goes off. And if I fall asleep right *now*, I'll get five hours and 59 minutes…" She worried that she'd feel so tired she'd miss her driver at the airport or say the wrong thing at customs.

But eventually she gave up, opting to trust herself and the pure excitement and adrenaline she was sure to be running on once her plane landed in Istanbul. She scrolled through screen after screen of available movies on the personal entertainment system in front of her seat, settling on a cheesy romantic comedy she would never have watched back home for fear of the merciless teasing Crystal would have given her.

In Istanbul, she found her way easily from the international terminal to the domestic one, where her flight to Antalya was waiting. The line to have her passport checked was long and didn't move that quickly, so she was happy to have a long layover. She wasn't surprised to find that the agent who checked her passport spoke English, but she was still relieved. The announcements on the flight and the signs in the airport, all of which were in both English and Turkish, were shaking her confidence in her ability to learn the language. She had had decent success with both Spanish and German in college, but as she stared at the Turkish words with some new unfamiliar letters, she saw that her prior knowledge was no help at all. If she was going to learn Turkish, she would be starting from scratch.

Back in her hotel room, Eliza prepared to take a quick shower. As much as she wanted to sleep, she knew she needed to wash the day and a half of travel off herself first. Otherwise, she feared she'd wake up with an oil and sweat imprint of herself (and especially her face) left on the sheets and pillowcase. Eliza recoiled at the mental image she'd created, then dug through her bag for a pair of comfy shorts and an old t-shirt from her alma mater. After her shower, she'd try to stay awake long enough to brush her teeth, but she made no promises.

Four

The morning of Eliza's first full day in Antalya, she woke up to the sun streaming in through her window. She had been too tired the night before to realize that her window faced the sea, and as she gained consciousness, she became aware of the vast blue that stretched as far as she could see. She climbed out of bed and walked to the window, pulling back the curtains to reveal a beautiful view of the water and the beach. To the left, she could see cliffs and the buildings of the city, and to the right, she could see mountains dropping into the blue. She recalled photos she'd seen of Rio de Janeiro, and wondered to herself why no one had ever told her Turkey was this beautiful.

She had hours until she would meet Dr. Çelik from the university, so she opted for caffeine and sea air to help her wake up and speed along the time zone adjustment her body was undergoing. She was pleased to see there was a coffee machine in her hotel room, as she didn't yet feel confident in her ability to form a coherent sentence in English, never mind attempting to do it in Turkish. While the machine brewed, she washed her face and found clothes for the day in her suitcase.

She saw a few messages on her phone, responses from her mom and from Crystal to whatever babbling mess she had sent them last night. As she scrolled back now, she saw that apparently her way of telling them she had arrived safe and sound was to text, "Here. So tiredd. Talk tomoro." Not her finest work, but it seemed to have gotten the job done.

Her mom had written, "Thank you so much for the update, sweetie. You are having an amazing adventure, and I am so, so proud of you. Mom."

Crystal had written, "Cool beans! (Do people still say that?)"

Eliza smiled to herself. She felt grounded knowing that even though everything that waited for her outside the room was unfamiliar and new, on the other side of the world, there was unchanging love and affection sent her way. She wondered how people had ever been brave enough to leave home for parts unknown in the days prior to smart phones and the internet, and she doubted she would have been one of those brave souls.

For some reason, the thought of going outside was daunting to her, and she hesitated, finding one more reason to check something in the mirror or get something out of her bag before braving the world outside. There was a vulnerability to being a foreigner in a new place, and she wanted to avoid that vulnerability as much as possible. If she could plot out her exact plan of attack and orient herself from this room, then she could exit the hotel and walk with such confidence that maybe no one would even know she wasn't from here. She laughed at herself then—who cared if she was a tourist or an outsider, anyway? The fact was that without leaving her hotel room she would have none of the adventure that she claimed to crave, and if she looked a little lost or bumbling along the way, well, then that would just have to make for some good stories. Plus, in her preliminary (albeit brief) research about Antalya, she'd learned that it was a highly popular tourist destination. While she was surprised, since she'd never heard of it and neither had any of her American friends, she fully expected to see plenty of German and Russian visitors in the same places she'd be going.

In the hallway, she locked her door and walked down to the elevator. This hotel was big, bigger than she had realized. In the lobby, she saw a blonde family, and her immediate thought was that perhaps they were from the US and had come in on the same flight as her. As she moved closer, she heard them speaking with the concierge, and she realized she couldn't understand a word. She presumed they were speaking Russian, or at least it sounded vaguely familiar from movies she'd watched, though it was possible that they were speaking Turkish and her ears just hadn't been conditioned to recognize it yet.

"*Günaydın!* Good morning!" a uniformed employee greeted Eliza.

"Good morning," smiled Eliza. "Can you tell me the best way to get downtown?" She hoped to do some exploring later on today, so why not get some information now to help make that a reality?

"I can!" he answered. "Are you interested in shopping or visiting the old city? You can take the KC-06 bus or the KL-08 bus, and depending on where you are going, you will need to walk maybe half a kilometer." He pulled out a map and started marking places on it with bold Xs. "This is Üçkapılar, Hadrian's gate, and this area is Kaleiçi, the old city. If you want to shop, the mall Mark Antalya is very close here, though there are also many, many stores in Lara..."

"Thank you so much. I don't think I will be shopping today. I just arrived yesterday, and I'd love to see the old city—"

"Welcome to Turkey! *Hoş geldiniz!*" he smiled. "I hope you will love our beautiful country and you will come back soon!"

"*Hoş bulduk,*" Eliza grinned to see his surprise that she knew the phrase. If only he knew that was all she knew how to say in Turkish. "I'm actually going to be working here for the next year, and I'm sure I will love it."

"Very good! Would you like a cup of tea before you set out for the day? Come, have a cup—it's Turkish hospitality, you can't say no!" He gestured towards a small table in the lobby for her to sit, then returned with a small glass shaped almost like a vase. It was set in a beautiful saucer, painted like tiles, and it was filled with a dark amber liquid that was steaming. There was a small spoon inside, too. "Would you like some sugar?" He set a small bowl full of individually wrapped sugar cubes in front of her.

Eliza thanked him as she unwrapped a sugar cube and stirred it into her tea. The sound of the metal spoon clinking against the glass was soothing and melodious, and she realized it was blending with the same sound coming from a nearby table where the blond family was sitting, also stirring sugar in their tea.

The hotel employee came back with another small dish, this one full of colorful cubes covered in white dust. "Turkish delight!" he announced.

Eliza had never even seen Turkish delight before, unless you counted that scene in *The Lion, The Witch, and The Wardrobe*. She picked up a piece and put it in her mouth. It was delicious, and the chewy texture was delightful. She loved it, though she wasn't sure that Edmund's betrayal of his siblings was quite worth it.

"Thank you so much!" she said to the employee, who nodded and placed his right hand over his heart. "What is your name?"

"I am Emre," he answered, "and I am at your service if you need anything else in your stay here."

"Thank you so much, Emre. You made me feel very welcome, and you are very good at your job." They both smiled. She added, "I am so impressed at how well you speak English, I must say! I am an English teacher, that's why I came here."

Emre was nodding. "Not many Turks of my age speak English that well, it's true. When I was a young man, I went to live in Germany. I was there for twenty years, and I learned both German and English. I came back to Turkey to retire, but I missed speaking with so many people from different countries and using my languages. That is why I come to this hotel."

"Wait, you don't work here?" Eliza asked, surprised.

Emre laughed. "My niece manages the hotel, and we live very near. I come here to help her and to welcome the new visitors to Turkey. Though some are not visitors, like you, but will stay much longer."

He held out his hand to Eliza. "I must go, Miss...?"

"Eliza." She smiled, showing her teeth.

"Miss Eliza. Welcome again to Turkey. I wish you a good day." He cleared her empty tea glass from the table and started towards the kitchen.

Outside the hotel, Eliza blinked in the bright sunlight. It was late August, still hot enough for the beaches to be full of sunbathers, and the heat was a welcome treat for Eliza. Back home in Michigan, it had been a beautiful summer, to be sure, but she had already begun to brace herself for a long, sunless winter ahead before she'd accepted this job.

She crossed the street separating her from the beach, jogging to make it across before the quick pedestrian walk light changed. As she neared the beach, which was lower than the road, she could see that it was covered not in sand but in smooth blue and gray stones. She found a set of stairs, slipped off her shoes and held them in her hand, and walked down to the beach. The stones felt cool beneath her feet, though their shape and texture made her jerk and pull as she walked towards the water's edge. It was like getting a reflexology treatment, and she'd always had ticklish feet. She tried her best not to react, already feeling embarrassed that anyone might see her.

The waves were gentle, and as she stood at the edge with her feet in the water, she enjoyed the grounding feeling of the cool water rushing over her feet and pulling away from under them. She sank lower into the small stones at the edge with each wave. She had always loved that feeling, though it felt different to be experiencing it in the Mediterranean and not in yet another vacation to Lake Michigan. As she stared at the vast expanse of water, the fact that she was here, in Turkey, sinking into the Mediterranean Sea, became real to her at last, and a grin spread across her face.

"Wow. This...this is amazing!" She pulled out her phone to snap a few photos, including some selfies for good measure, and after that, she sent a text to Crystal. "Definitely not Photoshopped!" complete with a few photos she had just taken for proof.

From the beach, she could see downtown Antalya to the left. She was determined to find her way to the old city and walk through—in the in-flight magazine, she had seen photos of the shops and restaurants, complete with impressive views from the cliffs. She knew it would be the place that would most impress anyone back home, and she also expected that her new coworkers would be shocked if she told them she hadn't yet seen it. Practical to a fault, she had her heart and mind set on making it there today. Let people be jealous of her and impressed by her adventurous spirit in a new country, but let no one pity or look down on her for sleeping through her whole first day in the hotel.

She pulled out the map Emre had given her from her bag and looked over the Xs he had made. Unfortunately, he hadn't written down the numbers of busses she could take, and she wasn't so sure about them anymore. KT-08?

KL-06? She couldn't be sure, and she couldn't remember which one of the Xs actually marked the spot where she was to catch the bus. As she looked at the map, however, it didn't seem like it was that far to the old city. Surely she could walk! She started talking herself into why this was such a brilliant plan, conveniently overlooking the fact that it would spare her from embarrassing herself by talking to a bus or taxi driver. *It will be great for my jet lag—don't they always say you should exercise? Plus, I'll get to know the city more than if I just looked out the window of a bus. And I'll have more control over where I go. I'm pretty sure Emre said I'd have to walk from the bus stop to the old city, anyway. Yes, it's decided. This just makes the most sense.*

A full hour later, Eliza Britt was sweating and out of breath at the top of a cliff. As far as she could tell from the map, Kaleiçi, the old city, was close, at last. She had walked along the beach for a while, enjoying the views, but the closer she'd gotten to downtown Antalya, the more it dawned on her that there was a significant change in elevation between where she was and where she was going. Now that she had climbed upwards at a steady grade for the last five minutes, she was more than ready to sit down at a nice cafe with a magnificent view and drink a lemonade. Honestly, she felt ready for a nap. If only she weren't so far away from the hotel...

Eliza walked down a street lined with shops and restaurants, with many of the doors occupied by a friendly face beckoning her inside. *"Buyurun!* Yes, please!" She smiled as she made eye contact, but she kept walking. The smells from the restaurants were enticing, though she wasn't quite ready to stop or to brave deciphering a menu and ordering a plate in a language she was so unskilled in.

Further up the road, she stopped, awed, in front of Üçkapılar, Hadrian's Gate. The bricks forming the gate with three arched openings looked ancient, as they should—if she remembered correctly, this was a remnant from ancient Roman times. And there it was, just standing there for all the city to see, to walk through, to touch. She made a mental note to tell her dad that this was nothing like the way artifacts would be treated back home. "It's not guarded or anything. It's like it's just there for everyone to enjoy."

She walked down the steps, through the gate, up the steps on the other side, and emerged into Kaleiçi, the old city. The narrow marble street ahead was lined with shop keepers, massive bougainvillea plants full of beautiful fuchsia and purple flowers, and tourists snapping photos. She walked slowly, peering through the open doors of the shops and nodding to the people who greeted her. She stopped to pet a cat basking in the sun, and she took photos of everything. When she went to cross another narrow cobblestone street, she jumped back with a start as a car drove through. *People are allowed to drive on these roads?! I would never—they seem too narrow!*

Finally, she arrived at the view she had been looking for: the street ended, and there, ahead, was the sea with the mountains behind it. She was near another ancient building. This one was round, with a smaller tower within it that went even higher, and there was a Turkish flag perched at the top. The building with the view behind made a perfect photo, one she fully expected to see on a postcard somewhere, and she snapped away.

Nearby, she found a place to sit at a cafe. As the waiter brought her a menu, she was relieved and grateful to see that it was in both English and Turkish. She ordered the lemonade she'd been craving, and as she sipped on it, she pulled out her journal and started to document her first day in Turkey. What a life this was.

Five

F riday morning, Eliza waited outside the hotel entrance for the shuttle that would take her to work. The day before, Dr. Çelik had come to collect her and show her around the university. It was a short drive to the campus, located just outside of the city, but Eliza had enjoyed the time getting to know Dr. Çelik regardless. She was in her early forties, and she spoke of the department and the new direction it was taking with such energy that Eliza couldn't help but feel her doubts melt away, replaced by optimism and pride over what they were building together.

The English department was located inside one of the buildings on campus, a three-story building that was bigger than Eliza had expected. It had its own auditorium, classroom after classroom that was loaded with the latest pedagogical technology, and a nice computer lab as well. Eliza saw the hallway with all the teachers' offices, and she was pleased to see that most of them had two teachers per room. In her old job, she had often felt isolated in her dark office, though the alternative (a communal space for teachers that was often crowded and noisy, full of colleagues complaining about the stresses of their classes) had hardly been preferable.

In the early morning light, Eliza saw several shuttle busses go by, and she started to feel anxious that she might not recognize hers. The cars were going fast on the coastal road, and the signs in the front windows identifying which business or school they were representing were too small for her to read. She wondered if she was expected to flag down the correct bus or if the driver would just know where to expect her and stop, no matter what her face or body language looked like.

As if in answer to her question, the next large bus began to slow down and huffed to a stop right in front of her as the driver opened the door. She saw the logo of the Mediterranean School of Languages in the front window as she double checked to make sure she was, in fact, about to go to the correct place. She greeted the driver as she stepped aboard, nodding and smiling in response to the rapid fire Turkish that he spoke.

Eliza made her way down the aisle, tripping a few feet as the bus lurched back into gear. She slid into the nearest empty seat, afraid she might trip and fall and embarrass herself if she didn't sit down pronto. She was sitting next to a young man, who had looked up and smiled as she slid into the seat. He had dark hair and dark eyes, and as she assumed he was Turkish, she greeted him with a tentative *"Merhaba"* and a smile.

"Hello!" He smiled back and reached out his hand to shake hers. "I'm Jack, and I'm one of the American teachers. You must be Eliza! We heard you were coming to help with this new partnership, and I have to say you arrived just in time. The program has been kind of a hot mess, and a number of us have been actually looking for jobs in other schools and other cities. It's so nice to meet you!"

Of course! *Of course the American teachers are here already, and of course everyone on this bus speaks English. What was I thinking?* Eliza berated herself. *Oh well, it's better to be polite and air on the side of being a good stranger in a strange land than to be the loud American who demands everyone speak English.* She looked at Jack, trying to recall all that he had just said while she was mentally scolding herself. "It's nice to meet you, too. How long have you been in Antalya?"

Jack told her he had arrived as a tourist just a few months prior and fallen in love with the city (and maybe with an attractive Turk, if the hints and eyebrow wiggles were any clue) and tried to find a way to stay. He had heard the university was hiring native English speakers, so he had done his very best to make a good impression and secure the job. "Long story short, I got the job, even if I ended up single again in the process."

Though his relationship with the hot Turkish guy seemed to have fallen apart, he had a warm, welcoming smile, and he seemed happy to be here. Eliza wondered how much training he had as an English teacher, but she decided not to ask at their first meeting, so as not to come off as a haughty new supervisor. He had been hired, after all, and even if there were still skills he needed to learn, wasn't that true for everyone? In fact, the less set in his ways an employee was, the more open he would be to the professional development she had planned down the road.

The shuttle stopped in front of the Mediterranean School of Languages, and Eliza stepped off to find Dr. Çelik waiting for her. "Come with me, Eliza," she said, hurrying her towards the auditorium. "We are going to have a presentation to welcome you to the program, and we've just got a couple of minutes to prepare before the teachers come in."

Eliza felt nervous, but she knew she was prepared. She hadn't expected to sit in the shadows and not be noticed, after all, so she had at least thought through a few things that she'd like to say to her new colleagues. While she didn't know she'd be on stage in an auditorium, she could fake confidence and fool the audience members—and maybe even herself.

As the teachers were settling into their seats, Dr. Çelik took to the stage. It was clear from the way she jumped right in while they were still milling about that she didn't believe in wasting any time.

Over the sound of chatter, Dr. Çelik introduced Eliza thus: "Welcome, friends. As you know, we have entered into a new partnership with State University in America, and today we are welcoming our new colleague, Eliza Britt. Eliza will help us transform this English department into a state-of-the-art facility with the best staff, graduating the best and brightest students in Turkey, and we are so glad to have her here. Please join me in welcoming Eliza to the Mediterranean School of Languages, or as we affectionately call it, Med School."

After some mild applause, Eliza smiled and began to speak. "Thank you all for welcoming me here today. I am looking forward to getting to know you, learning from you, and I hope we will have a very nice and rewarding time working together. Later on, I will share curriculum ideas with you, but in the meantime, I hope you can be the teachers and share with me all that you know."

She saw some confused looks in the audience, and Dr. Çelik seemed confused as well. "Eliza, don't you want to talk about the changes you're going to make? Isn't that why you're here?" she whispered.

Eliza stepped away from the microphone and off stage, effectively ending the meeting. "I don't mean any disrespect to you or to the staff, Dr. Çelik. I just don't want my time here to start with me dictating demands of the teachers before I even get to know them and learn where they already are. Let me just take this day to interview them, if that's alright with you."

Dr. Çelik nodded and dismissed the teachers to their offices. She pointed Eliza towards a conference room where she could conduct her meetings, then encouraged the teachers to join her there for the promised discussions. Eliza found herself sitting alone in that room for quite a few minutes, until she ventured out into the hallway, knocking on office doors and getting to know her new colleagues.

Over the course of the day, Eliza met all the English teaching staff, and she had started to notice a common thread in the stories and complaints they shared with her. The American teachers seemed inexperienced at best, apathetic at worst, and the Turkish teachers, all of whom were considerably more qualified for the position at hand, were embarrassed and resentful of their colleagues who didn't take the job seriously. They felt the burden of their lack of care falling on their own shoulders, and they were overworked and not getting enough respect from the administration to make it bearable. Eliza started thinking through the best way to share that with Dr. Çelik, already bracing for the fact that such a conversation wouldn't go well. After all, everyone knew no matter how much they might insist they wanted constructive feedback, it was rare that anyone could receive it without wanting to shoot the messenger.

Six

I n addition to moving her suitcases into a small apartment a few blocks from the beach, Eliza had a full weekend to prepare for broaching some sensitive workplace dynamics with Dr. Çelik, and for that she was grateful. She spent her days walking along the beach in Konyaaltı, taking the bus to Kaleiçi (now that she had figured it out and developed a bit of confidence) for another lemonade overlooking the cliff, and thinking and overthinking about the best way to bring up a difficult topic without stepping on any toes.

When she boarded the shuttle on Monday morning, she noticed Jack was dressed much more formally than he had been the previous time they shared a seat. "Jack! Why do you look so nice today?" she asked as she sat down.

"Um, didn't you hear? Today is the regional conference for English teachers in the greater Antalya area. Dr. Çelik must have forgotten to mention it to you!" Jack cried, concern written all over his face.

Great, just great. So I've got to go meet professionals from all over the area, and I'm dressed like a casual school teacher? And I don't even have business cards yet? Yikes! She turned to face Jack and said, "Oh great! That sounds like fun, actually. I wish I had known so I could have been a little more put together today, but there's not much I can do about it now." She pulled a mirror out of her purse and started patting down her hair.

Jack lifted himself out of his seat, not high enough for the driver to realize he was standing, but high enough to slide his head in between the two seats in front of them. "Hi!" he exclaimed to the two women sitting there. "Kat, Mira, you know Eliza, right? She just found out about the conference, and she needs a little confidence boost. Anything you can do to help her?"

Eliza had met the two teachers on their previous day at work. Kat, an American from Iowa, and Mira, a Turk who had grown up in Germany, both smiled at her and then started rifling through their purses. A few minutes later, they passed back to her a tube of lipstick, a few bobby pins, and the blazer Mira had been wearing moments ago. "Jack, switch seats with me!" Mira hissed.

The two switched seats with pure acrobatic talent, so quickly and unobtrusively that the driver (rightfully concerned with the safety of everyone on board his bus) was none the wiser.

"Mira, you don't have to give me your blazer!" cried Eliza. "I can't possibly take this from you!"

"Nonsense," Mira huffed, reaching around Eliza to place it on her shoulders. "In this dress, I am already ready to make a good impression. I just had the blazer for warmth, in case the air conditioning was cold inside, and you definitely need it more than I do. Where did you even get this blouse?"

Eliza looked down at her top, still wrinkled despite the fact that it had been hanging in the bathroom since she arrived. She had kept hoping that every steamy shower she took would be the one to shake out all the wrinkles, but it hadn't worked. She tried explaining that to Mira, who only shook her head.

"Try tucking it in. I know, I know, it's not meant to be worn that way, but desperate times and all that. Tuck it in and put on the blazer." Mira made a few minor adjustments. "Much better. Now let's do something about that hair."

As Mira pinned Eliza's hair back into a low bun, Eliza swiped on the lipstick. She glanced at her reflection in her compact mirror, already feeling more confident with what she saw there. "Thank you so much, Mira. You're a lifesaver," she said, as she turned around to give Mira a hug. "And thank you, too, Kat!" she called over the seat. "And of course you, Jack. I wouldn't have even known who to ask!"

The four of them smiled at each other. Eliza felt a sense of belonging for the first time since her arrival, and she was glad to have found this group of friends.

·♥·♥·♥·♥·♥·

The shuttle pulled up in front of the Akdeniz Hotel, a much shorter trip than the journey to campus. Eliza exited with Jack, Kat, and Mira, and she noticed other large busses unloading men and women in suits, coiffed to perfection. She felt grateful for her friends' intervention, though she couldn't help but note the Med School staff in comparison looked entirely less put together. She hoped that wouldn't be reflected in their professionalism as well, though there was no way to know that yet.

Inside the hotel, the participants were met by two smiling Turkish women, who directed them to the registration table and helped them find their nametags and schedules for the day. Eliza's badge said "Assistant Director" on it, and there was a purple star displayed on the front that, from the schedule, she could see granted her access to a few administration-specific meet and greets. One of those meet and greets was scheduled to start momentarily—it seemed all the participants would enjoy tea and pastries (buttery *poğaça* stuffed with olives or cheese, if Eliza's wishes came true—she couldn't get enough of them at the hotel breakfast), with the administration doing so ever so slightly removed from the instructors.

Eliza said goodbye to her friends and made her way to a small conference room that was marked with a purple star that matched the one on her nametag. Inside, she made her way through the buffet line (yes, there was *poğaça* to be had!), thanked the server who handed her a glass of tea, and carried her plate and glass to a nearby table, high enough that she could stand next to it as she rested her breakfast in front of her. She saw Dr. Çelik across the room, talking with a young man in a suit, and Eliza and her new boss nodded to each other in greeting.

Soon after, the man who had been talking with Dr. Çelik appeared at Eliza's table. "Hello there," he said. "Dr. Çelik told me you're the new assistant director, so that makes you my counterpart at Med School. I'm Deniz Aydem, assistant director at Antalya Technical Institute."

Eliza wiped her hand on her pant leg (why hadn't she grabbed a napkin?) and shook Deniz's hand. She had heard about the Antalya Technical Institute, though just enough to realize that, where Med School was still building its reputation, Antalya Tech was well-established and well-respected. She was surprised that their assistant director would even be standing here in front of her, and she fumbled over her words as a result. "Nice to meet you, Deniz." she said. "I'm Eliza Britt, and I'm brand new here. How long have you been at Antalya Tech?"

Deniz frowned. "Long enough," he said, changing the subject. "What plans do you have to shape up your department at Med School? We're very interested in having two well-respected universities in the area, and any attempts you make to rise to our level will, of course, be appreciated and supported."

"Thanks very much," Eliza said. He was blunt and to the point, but he seemed nice enough. "I've only just recently arrived in Antalya. Can you recommend one thing I must do while I'm here?"

"*Hoş geldiniz*, Eliza. I hope you are enjoying your time in Turkey. Is this your first time in our country?" he asked.

"It is, I'm sad to say! I've enjoyed it so much already, even just in these few days, that I can't believe I haven't come here sooner."

"Well, in that case, I highly recommend heading out into the country for a traditional Turkish breakfast in Çakırlar. It's a little difficult to get there—you have to find just the right bus or else you'll end up walking forever—but it's very worth it. Ask one of your coworkers to take you there." he said with a smile.

"Ça-kır-lar..." Eliza said as she jotted down a note on a scrap of paper in her purse. "Thanks very much! I'll definitely check it out."

"Please do. The next time we meet, I'll expect you to have been there so you can report back to me," Deniz said.

At the lunch break, Eliza found herself in line next to Jack.

"Ugh, isn't this amazing?" he exclaimed. "I made some great connections this morning, and I'm not going to lie, this day has already turned out way better than I expected."

Eliza was surprised to see Jack so excited about a professional conference, but her surprise soon evaporated when a handsome Turkish man asked if he could sit in one of the remaining empty chairs at their table.

"Eliza, this is Barış. Barış, this is Eliza," Jack introduced them. "Barış is an instructor at Antalya Tech, and he's doing some really interesting work with student motivation."

"It's nice to meet you, Barış," Eliza said as she shook his hand. "That does sound interesting. Can you tell me about it?"

"Absolutely." Barış shot a grateful, playful smile at Jack. "In my years of teaching, I've often found students unmotivated because they are learning English as a foreign language. They are not able to see the practical need to learn it, and because their only incentive is to pass an exam or get a decent grade, they often do the bare minimum. And it is nearly impossible to get them to speak."

"That's a great point," Eliza answered. In her old job, motivation had never been a challenge. Her students truly wanted to learn English so that they could have an improved quality of life in their new home, but she had often heard Crystal complain about just that. "What is your idea of how to increase their motivation?"

Barış smiled. "Well, that's where it gets kind of fun. We are using social media—something tame, not Tinder or anything like that—to connect them with friends who are native English speakers. The idea is that when they meet a cute girl—or a cute guy—who they can't communicate with unless they get better and better at English that we'll see their learning improve significantly."

"Wow, that's an interesting concept to explore, especially in a traditionally religiously conservative country," said Eliza. "Doesn't the university object to it?"

"That's the great thing about Antalya Tech," answered Barış. "In a public university that has to toe the government line, I'd never even be able to suggest something like this. But Antalya Tech is respected, despite or because of its more liberal faculty and viewpoints. I certainly couldn't be out and proud at a government university, but Antalya Tech doesn't care."

Eliza appreciated having her suspicions confirmed, and Barış's openness strengthened her presupposition that there might be more to the connection between Jack and Barış than just mutual academic interests. She'd be asking Jack about it on the bus back home at the end of the day.

"So, are you going to come with us?" Jack asked Eliza as soon as she slid into the seat next to him on the shuttle. He had grabbed her arm in the hall as they passed each other a few hours prior and whispered a cryptic message about drinks in Kaleiçi with some of the Antalya Tech teachers.

"Maybe. Where are you going exactly? I have to pick up my friend from the airport after work, so it's going to depend on how she feels, anyway." Eliza answered. Crystal's flight was due to arrive in the next hour, so Eliza was planning to take the shuttle to a different stop. She'd get off downtown, where it would be a cheaper taxi ride to the airport—or maybe she could try out the tram she'd heard so much about, but since she hadn't taken it yet, she didn't feel that confident that she wouldn't miss her stop.

"Oh, fun! Bring your friend, it'll be a great welcome to Turkey for her!" Jack exclaimed. "We are going to meet at Hadrian's Gate—you know where that is, right? And then from there we'll probably argue about the best bars or clubs to go to until someone finally convinces us all. Look, I haven't put a ton of thought into this, but I just know I want to go out, and I'm excited to see Barış again."

"Okay, tell me about that. What's going on there? Is it really his research that's so interesting, or...?" Eliza trailed off as she wiggled her eyebrows at Jack.

"Oh shut it!" Jack laughed, checking her with his elbow. "Obviously he's totally fine and sexy as hell, but yes, believe it or not, I do actually think his research is interesting, too. I mean, if I could get something like that going at Med School, it might really help turn around our student motivation issues, too. Anyway, Barış is like the whole package, and I definitely want to talk to him some more."

"Fair enough. I don't mean to tease or pry; I was just curious. I really liked him too, and I think if you guys do some work together or start dating or all of the above—whatever happens—I support you. Though maybe I should get to know him a little better before I give you my unequivocal blessing."

"Um, yes, you should—not that I need it." Jack teased. "Who's this friend that's coming, anyway? Are we talking like a 'special friend' or the regular kind?"

"That's a fair question—give me a taste of my own medicine!" laughed Eliza. "She's my best friend, my roommate actually, and no, that's not a euphemism. Actually, why do we keep using the word roommate? It was appropriate in college when dorm room space was a commodity and we actually slept in bunk beds, but we've had separate rooms ever since. If anything, she's my apartment mate. Eh, that sounds weird, too."

"Okay, okay, I get it. You don't have a lady lover, or at least this person isn't occupying that role. Anyone catch your eye today in that department?"

"Well, if you can believe it, Jack, I wasn't exactly scoping around for hotties today." Eliza rolled her eyes. "I spent a bit of time talking with a guy named Deniz, who's the assistant director at Antalya Tech, but apart from that I didn't have a lot of one-on-one conversations."

"Hmm, I think Barış mentioned Deniz—they're friends, if I'm not mistaking him for someone else. Was Deniz hot? Maybe he'll come out with us tonight, too!"

"Jack! I don't feel comfortable—nor do I think it's appropriate—judging my Antalya Tech counterpart based on his looks or as a potential love match. I mean, he was definitely not bad to look at, but that is as far as I will go."

"Ooh! Sounds like someone's got a little crush..." Jack teased. "Okay, okay, I know. I'll stop." He pouted.

"Not to change the subject...but okay, actually, let's change the subject." Eliza said. "How do I get to the airport, anyway?"

Eliza exited the tram and made her way to the domestic arrivals gate, where Crystal's flight from Istanbul would be exiting. She had almost resigned herself to just paying extra for a taxi, but Jack had scolded her until she accepted that maybe (just maybe) taking the tram was straightforward enough that she could handle it. It had turned out to be just that—there was only one tram line, and it only went in two directions. The airport was the last stop in this direction, so as long as she got on the way that said *"havalimanı"*—the word for airport that she had just learned—she was all set.

The tram had made good time getting to the airport, faster than a taxi would have been, so Eliza was there before Crystal's flight had even landed. She found a place to stand where she would have a clear view of the doors, not too close to all the chauffeurs with signs, and pulled a novel out of her bag. She loved people watching, but she'd been reading a new story that was so enthralling she could hardly put it down to go to bed at a reasonable time.

True to form, she was entranced in her story when a shadow fell over the pages.

"Um, hi? Is this how you meet your best friend at the airport?" Crystal's eyes were tired but full of laughter. "I don't think you even noticed all the people swarming around you—that flight was full!"

Eliza pulled Crystal in for a hug. "It's really you! Welcome, I'm so glad you're here!" She shoved her book back in her bag, wishing she could finish the chapter she was reading, but knowing that it wasn't every day your best friend flew halfway across the world to see you.

"Dude, chill! It's been like two weeks. Surely you managed without me?" Crystal was teasing, but Eliza was still happy to have her here. Her new friends were great, but there was nothing that could compare with your oldest, best friend. She grabbed the handle of Crystal's suitcase and started rolling it towards the tram line.

"So, how are you feeling? Tired? Hungry? We could head back to my apartment, eat something there, take it easy, and start exploring tomorrow. Or, if you were interested, no pressure, we could go downtown and meet some colleagues of mine for drinks. We could get you something to eat there too, but if you're too tired, my apartment is pretty nice and we can go there."

"Are you seriously trying to use me to get out of going out?" Crystal scoffed. "I know you aren't a big nightlife fan, but there's no need to pawn that off on me. I'm tired, sure, but I'm way more interested in adventure than I am in going to bed at a reasonable hour. Plus, who are these coworkers anyway? Anyone interesting? Anyone cute?"

"How did I know you were going to say that?" laughed Eliza. "Do you at least want to go back to my apartment first so we aren't carrying your suitcases around?"

"Not a chance!" said Crystal. "If we go back, I'll sit down and get cozy for a second, the tiredness will hit me, and before I know it, I'll be waking up in the morning feeling well-rested. No thank you! Now answer my question. Who are we going to meet?"

"Alright, have it your way! We're going to meet up with Jack. He's one of the Americans I'm working with and you'll really like him. Kat and Mira will be there too, I think, and some teachers from the other local university, Antalya Technical Institute. Technically, they'd be like our competition, but their program is so vastly superior to ours that I don't think any of us would use the word 'competition' without making it into a joke."

By now they had gotten onto the tram heading in the other direction, back towards the old city. They were on track to be at Hadrian's Gate right about the time everyone else would arrive there, and Eliza was relieved about that. She still didn't know her way around well enough to find anyone out and about, and she knew she had a much better chance of connecting with the group if she started off with them from the very beginning.

Once the tram stopped, they made their way towards the ancient gate, both Eliza and Crystal wheeling a suitcase behind them. Crystal's stay was indefinite, and Eliza was glad not to have an end date to be counting down towards just yet. They might tire of each other's company now that they would be sharing a small space again, but for at least the next few weeks, Eliza was grateful to have the security blanket of her old roommate again.

Eliza spotted Jack and Barış standing together, having an animated conversation. As she approached them to introduce Crystal, Deniz appeared in the group as well, walking up from the side opposite to hers. Eliza introduced Crystal to the three men, and Jack suggested they head towards a rooftop bar he knew. The others who were going to meet them had decided to come later on, so they planned to meet up whenever they got downtown.

On their way to the bar, Deniz and Barış walked ahead, and Jack dropped back to pepper Crystal with questions. In the middle of their banter, Crystal turned to Eliza. "I like this one!" she said, smiling at Jack. "You've met some cool people here—and hot ones too!" She gestured her head towards Deniz and Barış.

"Oh we know!" interjected Jack. "I called dibs on Barış, but Deniz is up for grabs as far as I know."

"Jack!" Eliza rolled her eyes. "First of all, keep your voice down. We do not need them to hear that we're talking about them. And second of all...come on! They're human men, not playthings for us to claim."

Crystal and Jack started to speak at the same time.

"Always a party pooper!" called Crystal.

"Ugh, I know! Just let me have my fun, okay?" said Jack.

"I'm sorry, guys." said Eliza. "I'm really not trying to ruin your fun. I just get a little sensitive about us being Americans here in a foreign country. We don't exactly have a great reputation for respecting local people as, you know, people, and any objectification that we do makes me worry that we're heading in that obnoxious American tourist direction."

"I know, hun." answered Jack. "I feel the same way deep down, but that isn't going to stop me from having my fun and saying my outrageous things. It's a test. If someone can't handle the way I talk and behave, we probably aren't really going to be great friends."

"Hear hear!" called Crystal. "I think you and I will be great friends, Jack."

Eliza smiled at the two of them. She had a feeling they were all in for a great night.

Seven

Monday morning, Eliza exited Dr. Çelik's office, feeling sure of herself and ready for the week ahead. She had just shared her plan with Dr. Çelik for how they would turn the program around, and it had been received well overall. Her plan required some additional hours from the teachers, professional development which would unfortunately be unpaid, but Eliza believed that if they felt as strongly as she did about turning the department around, they'd be on board with it. The natural consequences of hiring inexperienced teachers who just happened to be local foreigners who spoke English as a first language was that those teachers would need both training and experience before they could even dream of competing with teachers who had been recruited from abroad—as the case had been at Antalya Tech, of course.

Back in her office, Eliza saw that Dr. Çelik had already sent an email out about Eliza's program. Or at least, the email announced a meeting to discuss the program. Eliza could see that Dr. Çelik didn't want to be the bearer of unwanted news, and she suspected that the burden to do so would fall on herself. It was her idea, after all, and if she wasn't confident enough in it to announce it to the full staff, then she should have come up with a different plan.

The meeting was scheduled for the second half of the lunch hour, so Eliza took the rest of her morning to prepare for it. She created a few PowerPoint slides, practiced a few talking points to make sure she had the wording just right, and took a few walks around campus to calm her nerves—and peek in the windows of a few classrooms. By the time lunch arrived, she had worked out her apprehension and was able to enjoy her meal while chatting with Jack, Kat, Mira, and a few more teachers. She spilled a bit of salad dressing, some pomegranate sauce (or *nar ekşisi*) down the front of her white shirt, which rattled her confidence before the meeting only the slightest amount.

In the conference room, she welcomed everyone. "Thank you all for taking some time from your lunch break to join me here. I know you probably have papers to grade or would like to use this time to prepare for your afternoon classes, so I'll try to keep it short." She looked around the room and saw that a post-lunch lull was setting in.

"As you know, the partnership between the Mediterranean School of Languages and State University should help Med School take its place at the forefront of English language education for the region. In order to get there, we will have to make some sacrifices, but I firmly believe we can do it. We have a new cohort of qualified English teachers, recent graduates from the Master's TESOL education program at State, coming to join us here next semester, which will be incredibly helpful. For right now, though, we have an unusual mix of highly qualified Turkish teachers and, no offense intended by this, American teachers with limited experience and training. I am developing a series of professional development workshops which will help all of us improve our teaching skills, which will take place weekly on Saturdays." She stopped there to let the teachers express what was written all over their faces.

"Excuse me," spoke up a Turkish teacher named Ayşegül. "Are these Saturday workshops going to be mandatory? I have children and I usually spend my weekends with them."

Kat chimed in more loudly and with considerably less diplomacy. "What the heck? Is this extra time even going to be paid? And what happens if we don't go?"

"Yeah, I think there are a lot of questions about who exactly this is for," said Jack with an apologetic smile on his face. "I mean, I know I could use some extra training, but you said yourself that the Turkish teachers are highly qualified. It hardly seems like they need to be coming to these workshops, too."

"I hear and appreciate all of your concerns." answered Eliza. "And I've been pondering many of those same questions myself in the days leading up to this meeting. I believe one of the biggest additional benefits of these trainings, beyond the skills you'll be learning and practicing, is the opportunity for team building. For that reason, it is important that all of us attend them, regardless of your personal levels of education and experience. When I make an exception for one teacher, then suddenly we all want to have exceptions made for us, and it just won't work that way."

Everyone was talking now, and Eliza could tell from the faces around the room that this news had not been received as favorably as she would have liked. She realized now she had overlooked the teachers who had families—and especially children—by generalizing her own experience as a young, single, childless professional who had only moved to the city for her career. What could she say now to win them back over?

"For those of you who have children, we can work together to find the best solution. If we have the trainings here, maybe your spouses and children can come and enjoy spending a sunny morning out on the playground?" she asked. "And we will absolutely respect your time and keep the trainings short and efficient. I imagine they will take half a day—three or four hours, max."

Eliza realized that whatever goodwill she had been building up with her colleagues was likely gone now. She understood why Dr. Çelik hadn't announced the news herself, and she hoped that in the future she'd be able to get back in their good graces. For now, though, she needed their respect (and their willingness to attend the trainings and take them seriously) more than she needed a friend or even someone to sit with at lunch. She was still human, though, and rejection didn't feel good. She made eye contact with Jack and was relieved to see he didn't look away. There was a playfulness in his eyes that made her think they'd weather this just fine.

$\cdot\heartsuit\cdot\heartsuit\cdot\heartsuit\cdot\heartsuit\cdot\heartsuit\cdot$

Crystal and Eliza met after work for dinner at a soup restaurant. Eliza had been skeptical of the idea of a soup restaurant, but Crystal had insisted that the restaurant she stumbled into the morning after their night out had been something Eliza couldn't possibly miss. When the waiter brought over the skillet of browned butter to pour into her creamy, savory lentil soup and the smell rose through the room, Eliza knew what Crystal was talking about.

"You were right about how my plan would go over with the teachers. I don't know why I didn't see it." Eliza said, taking a bite of fresh, warm bread. "Of course, no one else is feeling as excited as I am about professional development. Half of them are more qualified than I am and the other half haven't found they've needed any qualifications yet—and if they didn't need them to get the job, why should they need them to keep it? It's a mess. I don't know what I was thinking."

"Eh, you're new. Who can expect you to have it all figured out your first couple of weeks on the job?" Crystal answered. "The admin in most schools can't be expected to understand the needs of the teachers for years, heck, or even never! Anyway, isn't this soup great? I know you had your doubts, but I think I won this one."

"You sure did," agreed Eliza. She'd eaten plenty of soup in her lifetime, but she'd never had lentil soup like this before, with its flavors of chicken broth, rich butter, hearty lentils, and a splash of lemon juice all blending together into a mouthful of bliss. "Let this be my lesson to never underestimate soup again!"

The friends laughed together. It felt good to have at least one person in her life that Eliza couldn't disappoint too terribly. Just then, her phone buzzed with a text message. It was Jack, and he wrote: "Getting together a few of us (and some of the Antalya Tech staff too) for a happy hour on Wednesday. You're invited!"

"Ugh!" groaned Eliza. "I seriously can't bear the thought of making Jack mad at me. This text doesn't sound like him at all." She showed the phone to Crystal.

"Yeah, that's almost cold for him," agreed Crystal. "Would you even want to go, though? Aren't happy hours for, like, complaining about work? It kind of seems like they might not exactly welcome you with open arms."

"I mean, yeah, of course that's what would happen. I hadn't even let myself wonder if I'd want to go." Eliza hung her head lower. "Though maybe with the Antalya Tech guys coming, that would keep the dynamic from getting too specific with the workplace gossip."

"Aw man, I almost forgot about those guys," said Crystal. "And good riddance! Why does Jack keep inviting them along?"

"What's the problem?" asked Eliza. "I thought you liked Barış, at least."

"Barış is nice, and he and Jack are definitely very cute together," said Crystal. "I forgot about it until this morning when I was finally recovered from my two-day hangover, but Deniz was kind of a jerk to you that night."

"He was?" Eliza was surprised. "I don't even remember the two of us talking!"

"It wasn't *to* you, it was about you." explained Crystal. "I had stepped outside for some fresh air—don't look at me like that, I swear I wasn't smoking—and I overheard Deniz talking to one of the other American teachers about you. He was saying what a joke the program at Med School is and how you're a fool if you think you can actually make a difference. The other teacher was trying to defend you, and Deniz just said that you're nice enough, but you're naïve and you won't last long. I'm sorry, Eliza. I wish I hadn't heard any of it."

"Wow. No, I'm glad you did," replied Eliza, stunned. "I definitely thought he and I were friendlier than that, but I'm honestly glad to know the truth. If I see him again, I'll be a lot more mindful of how much I share, or, honestly, if I even talk to him again. He sounds like such a jerk. I mean, who even asked him what he thought about our program or about me? I'm sure that other teacher didn't!"

"I'm sure you're right," said Crystal. "And it's definitely better to know than not. No need to see him as a friend and make the mistake of asking for his advice or, God forbid, being vulnerable. That's what friends like me are for, anyway!"

Eliza's face brightened. "It's true! There's nothing I could say to you that would turn you away—we've got way too much blackmail material, anyway."

Eight

Where there used to be friendly greetings in the hallway, now there were coworkers avoiding eye contact. Eliza sighed as she shut herself into her office. It had been a long week already, and it was only 10:00 in the morning on Tuesday. She was tempted to regret her desire to make changes—but she also knew that it was why she had been hired. It was true that stepping into an administrative role wasn't a good way to make friends, and it was also true that she was losing touch with how it felt to be a teacher. There was a way (surely there was!) to do an admin role well and with integrity, and she could only hope that she would figure out what it was soon, while she still had any friends left at work.

There was a knock on the door then. "Come in!" called Eliza, willing her voice to sound as friendly as possible.

Ayşegül entered with a tentative smile. "Excuse me, Ms. Britt, but I wanted to talk with you about this Saturday's training."

"Of course, take a seat. You can call me Eliza, you know."

"Okay, Eliza *Hanım*," Ayşegül answered, using the Turkish word for "missus" or "ma'am" to convey a level of respect. She clearly wasn't comfortable being on a first-name basis, Eliza noted, and that wasn't going to help her break down any distance between them.

"What can I help you with, Ayşegül?" asked Eliza, taking out her planner and a pen to jot down any notes.

"This Saturday, I will have my children with me. My husband works on the weekends, and I have asked my parents and his parents, but no one is able to take the children. I don't know what to do, but I know the training is mandatory, so I think I have no choice but to bring them with me."

"I understand, and I'm sorry that you're having this problem." responded Eliza. "Of course you can bring them to the training. May I ask how old they are?"

"Oh, thank you! I have a little boy who is two years old and my daughter is four years old."

Eliza stopped her face from registering her surprise just in time. These children would not be self sufficient, content wandering around campus or coloring in their mom's office. They were going to need supervision and entertainment, and Eliza didn't have the first clue of how they would get that while their mother could still get her professional development in. "Is there anyone who could help out during the day and come here with you? Even an older cousin who could play with the kids so that you can still come to the session...?" Her question trailed off.

"There is no one that day, ma'am. My younger sister's wedding party is happening in the evening, so all the family will be busy with it. I hope we will finish in time that I will be able to attend as well."

Eliza's heart was in her throat. It was becoming clear now that she had been too harsh with her requirements of mandatory attendance for all the teachers. Surely, there was no way that missing time with her family on her sister's wedding day was in Ayşegül's best interest.

"Ayşegül, it's your sister's wedding! Of course you should be there—family is more important than career, and I insist that you take the day off from our training."

"Oh really, Eliza? Thank you so much, that is amazing news!" Ayşegül smiled for the first time since entering the office. "I'm so happy to know that I can be there for every part of my sister's special day."

"Of course!" answered Eliza. "We will have to come up with a plan for you to make up the training that you miss, so that the other teachers don't feel too resentful, okay? Would you be able to stay late one day or meet with me during lunch breaks?"

"Yes, Ms. Eliza, that makes sense," answered Ayşegül, some of the smile melting from her face. "Whatever you need, I can make it work. I really appreciate your help."

As Ayşegül stood and left, Eliza felt better. She had made headway with one colleague, at least. Perhaps this was just the first in a series of dominoes and soon they'd all be on friendly terms.

♥ · ♥ · ♥ · ♥ · ♥

Eliza shouldn't have been surprised when the knocks started. First, it was Kat, asking if she could come for just half of the day on Saturday so she wouldn't have to miss a dinner out of town where she was meeting her boyfriend's family for the first time. Twenty minutes later, it was Elif, one of the most senior teachers, wondering if it would be alright for her to miss the trainings because on the weekends she was working on her PhD. They both made good points, and it felt impossible for Eliza to say no.

Soon after that, a group of five first-year teachers arrived, textbooks and syllabuses in tow, to discuss in detail with Eliza all that they had learned in their last year of university. For every topic on Eliza's intended program, they could show that they had covered it and then some. She didn't feel comfortable excusing them all from attending—so she asked them if they would be interested in taking on some teaching or assisting responsibilities during the trainings. One or two of the first-year teachers seemed flattered by this offer, but the others had clearly been hoping that they'd be excused for the duration.

Just before the shuttle came to take them all home, there was one last knock on her door. Jack. "Come in, Jack!" Eliza exclaimed. "It seems like it's been ages since we talked last."

"I swear I haven't been avoiding you or anything," he answered. "This new training thing you're creating isn't exactly making you Miss Popular, though, and I'm trying to play my cards right so I don't get ostracized, too. I mean…" His smile suggested he was at least partially kidding, but Eliza couldn't be sure.

"All right, all right." Eliza was happy to let that sentence end there. "What can I do for you, Jack?"

"I actually wanted your advice," he replied. "Barış asked me to help him with his research, and—"

"Let me guess." Eliza barely stopped herself from rolling her eyes. "This research is happening on Saturdays, and you won't be able to come to the trainings if you work with him?"

"Oh honey, no. If I wanted out of your precious trainings, I would just tell you—as I believe I've done a couple of times now." Jack smiled. "Actually, I wanted your input on whether it was a good idea to do this or not."

"Ah. Sorry about that, Jack." Eliza was sheepish. "I'm a little defensive after the day I've had, and I shouldn't take that out on you."

"You definitely shouldn't, and I'm glad you know it," smiled Jack. "But anyway! What do I do? The work sounds interesting—and you know I'd love an excuse to spend more time with Barış, but…"

"But what?" asked Eliza. "If you want to spend more time with him, what's stopping you?"

"I just don't know if it's a good idea. Liking someone like that and also trying to work with them. What if something goes wrong? Like, what if we start dating or something and then we break up and then it's awkward to be working together?"

"Whoa whoa whoa." Eliza waved her hands. "I think you're getting a little ahead of yourself, don't you? You two haven't even admitted that you like each other yet, and you're already thinking about an awkward breakup."

"Guilty." Jack hung his head. "It's just that things haven't really worked out for me that well in the past romantically, and I'm a little wary of getting burned again."

"Well, I definitely get that," Eliza noted Jack's raised eyebrows, "and that's a story for another time. Why don't you try something different this time? You and Barış could work together, focus on your friendship—keep it platonic for as long as the project lasts—and if at the end of all that you still really like him, then ask him out!"

"That's not a bad idea. Play it cool, huh?"

"Exactly. It might be good for you, and you might even like it." Eliza smiled at Jack. "I'm glad you found someone you really like, and I hope this will be a great experience for you. You deserve it."

"Thank you." Jack took her hand in his. "Don't think I forgot what you said about your own romantic misfortunes, though. We will definitely be getting into that later and finding you your own Prince Charming before the year is up."

"Ugh!" groaned Eliza. "That's the last thing I need to be worrying about now. I appreciate your concern, though. Let's not worry about it just yet. For now, I need to keep my teachers from staging a full-on mutiny…"

Eliza took a break from the exams she was marking to check her email. She had made good work of the stack on her desk, but there were at least a few more hours to go before she would be finished. This pile would likely be going home with her in her messenger bag, so why not head out sooner than later?

At the top of her inbox, she spotted Dr. Bennett's name and the subject *"What do you think about this?"* Well, that could mean anything, from a cute video of a water skiing squirrel to the best name for his first grandchild. It wouldn't be dull, of that Eliza was sure.

She sighed and clicked, and before she could even start reading the email from top to bottom, her eyes fell on the phrase *"this could justify leaving Med School"* and her heart leaped in her chest. What in the world? She was just getting started here. How could he even suggest it might be time to leave already? No, this couldn't be happening.

Eliza took a deep breath and started reading from the beginning.

Dear Eliza,

I hope your first week is going well at Med School. I am looking forward to our video call next week to hear the full update from you. I can't say I'm surprised that your professional development initiative hasn't exactly been a big hit, but I'm hopeful for you that it has the potential to be a game changer.

I'm writing because I just got an interesting message from someone named Nathaniel Collins, and I need a favor from you. Mr.

Collins is a Canadian entrepreneur, and apparently his specialty is language schools. He is in Antalya right now, scoping it out as a setting for a language school, not just for local Turks, but also as a destination setting for tourists from Germany, Russia, or anywhere else who are looking to learn English. He saw a billboard announcing our partnership with the Mediterranean School of Languages, so he did a little snooping online and reached out to me. I think he had hoped I was in Antalya right now, but since I'm not (you know I won't be getting on a flight like that anytime soon), I am going to need you to meet with him on behalf of me.

His school sounds interesting. Honestly, part of me thinks that if it's a robust program that this could justify leaving Med School, but I know I'm getting ahead of myself. Just look him up and meet with him, alright? He's based downtown—Kaleeci? Something like that? The school is called Collins Language Training. You have my blessing to handle this however it needs to be handled, and I trust your judgment.

Talk soon,
Bennett

Eliza's shoulders dropped. This wasn't the cause for alarm she was afraid of—but it was still a distraction from the work she needed to do. She owed her education, her career, and every opportunity that had come her way to Dr. Bennett, so how could she possibly say no to him?

Resigned, she typed "Collins Language Training" into the search bar on her laptop's open browser. The results popped up with a photo of Nathaniel Collins, as well as a phone number for the school. At first glance, Mr. Collins looked nice enough—sandy blond hair in need of a hair cut, thick glasses, and a tight-lipped smile on his face. He had a "taking himself seriously" vibe about him, and Eliza wasn't convinced having a cup of coffee with him would be a barrel of laughs. Shaking her head, she typed his number into her cell phone and lifted it to her ear as it started to ring.

"Collins Language Training, Nathaniel Collins speaking," a monotone voice answered.

"Mr. Collins, hello. My name is Eliza Britt, and I'm calling from the Mediterranean School of Languages." Eliza said. "My boss at State University, Dr. Bennett, asked me to reach out to you."

"Miss Bennett, so nice to hear from you!" the voice on the other end of the line chirped, rising in expression. "I am eager to talk about our potential future together—"

"Ahem, sorry, it's Britt, not Bennett." Eliza coughed. "Dr. Bennett is my employer, but we aren't actually related—"

"Ahh, my mistake, Miss Britt." Mr. Collins answered. "I got ahead of myself in my excitement. Are you currently in

Antalya, Miss Britt? Are you available to meet for a cup of coffee this evening?"

"Yes, I'm in Antalya now. But I've got a stack of student exams to mark this evening, unfortunately. Could we meet tomorrow evening instead?" Eliza asked.

"Absolutely, we can." Mr. Collins replied. "Could you please give me your email address, and I'll send you the address of my favorite cafe? They make an excellent flat white, and most other places here, you know they've really mastered Turkish coffee, but they haven't quite caught on to the Australian specialties."

"That's fine, Mr. Collins," Eliza smiled to herself. "Here's my email address..."

·❤·❤·❤·❤·❤·

While Eliza was waiting for the shuttle bus to depart, Jack plopped into the seat next to her. "Are you excited for happy hour tomorrow?" he asked.

Eliza groaned. "I totally forgot. I just made plans to meet Mr. Collins after work tomorrow, and now I don't know if I can make it. Dang it! I need that time to get myself back into everyone's good graces."

"Wait wait wait," Jack breathed. "Who is this Mr. Collins person? Spill, please!"

"Don't get ahead of yourself, buddy," Eliza chuckled. "This is definitely not a romantic sort of meetup. He's someone Dr. Bennett asked me to meet with, and I don't think even you can spin him into a romantic lead."

Jack's face fell for a second before he stopped himself. "Got it. So he's not a hottie on the Eliza Britt scale, but that doesn't mean he's not someone's dream guy. What are you two meeting about, anyway?"

Eliza didn't know how much she could say. "I'm not entirely sure. Dr. Bennett was a little vague. He has a language school of his own as far as I know, so if nothing else, it's good for us to have that connection in our network."

"Got it. Boring stuff," Jack teased. "But come on, that can't possibly take hours and hours. Why don't you still come meet us afterwards? A little socializing, a beverage or two...it's the perfect Wednesday evening!"

Eliza laughed. "Am I getting old, or what? A 'beverage or two' on a Wednesday evening doesn't sound like fun at all anymore. But hanging out with you and seeing Barış again sounds great. He'll be there?"

A hint of pink flashed on Jack's cheeks. "Yeah, he'll be there. I'm glad you like him."

Nine

Eliza made herself comfortable at the small round table. Keyif Cafe was bigger than she had expected, with a small seating area in the front and a large patio in the back. Her table had an umbrella to block the Mediterranean sun, and it was just the right size to set up her laptop and catch up on some of the emails in her inbox, messages from students eager to learn (or negotiate) their exam scores.

She had arrived early for her meeting with Mr. Collins on purpose. If she was going to go out socializing this evening, she may as well take care of her administrative tasks beforehand. And arriving before Mr. Collins felt like an advantage. Like it gave her the high ground, staking this table as her territory, not that it mattered. They weren't in a dispute or a negotiation, so why did it feel like it?

"Excuse me, Miss Britt?" a voice called over her shoulder.

Eliza spun around. Who knew her here? A student? Had the emails in her inbox suddenly materialized into a physical being, hoping to earn a few more points on his essay?

Then her eyes fell on a man who looked vaguely familiar—Nathaniel Collins. His hair and glasses were the same as the photo she had seen online, though of course she hadn't been able to guess at his height or physical presence from the two-dimensional image.

He was tall, but he carried himself in a hesitant, unsure way. Even now, when he was trying to get her attention, it seemed like he was apologizing for it.

"Nathaniel?" she asked. Then, at the look on his face, she clarified, "Mr. Collins?"

"That's right," he smiled. "Nice to meet you, Miss Britt."

Eliza accepted his extended hand and shook it. "Nice to meet you, too. I'm surprised you're here so early!"

"I could say the same to you, Miss Britt." he replied. "I have been working from this cafe for the afternoon, and when you came in, I noticed you immediately. When I saw the State University sticker on your laptop, it was enough confirmation for me to come over and say hello. In the worst-case scenario, if you weren't actually Eliza Britt, there would be a good enough chance that you work with her or at least know who she is."

Eliza bit back a chuckle at his justification. Mr. Collins was thorough and careful, and this only confirmed her expectations that he wasn't a man to jump into anything without carefully thinking it through and considering it from all angles. She was even more curious now about the nature of today's meeting. What was she actually doing here?

"Would you like to join me, Mr. Collins?" she asked, gesturing to the seat next to hers.

"If you don't mind, Miss Britt," he replied, ducking his head, "I've got a table for us just over there. I can help you carry your things if you'd like."

Eliza let him take her laptop as she gathered up her purse and her messenger bag, full of yet another batch of student essays she had deluded herself into thinking she would start grading tonight. There was no way that was going to happen, especially if she actually managed to make it to the happy hour with the other teachers today.

Settled at their new table—which looked identical to where Eliza had been sitting, making her wonder again why the move had been necessary—Mr. Collins looked expectantly into Eliza's eyes.

"Well, Miss Britt," he began, "You must have some questions for me. I will explain everything today, but so I know where to begin, would you mind telling me what you already know about the proposal I've shared with Dr. Bennett?"

"Proposal?" Eliza jolted. "Well, for starters, I suppose I hadn't realized there was an actual proposal on the table."

Mr. Collins's cheeks colored. Before he could apologize and explain, Eliza interjected, "But that's not the point. Anyway, what I know so far is that you have language schools all over the world and you're looking to start one here in Antalya. I know there was some interest in collaboration, but I don't know the details of it. And I know Dr. Bennett wanted me to meet with you, I assumed, because the professional English language teaching community here in Antalya is small, and there's no need to see each other as competition."

Mr. Collins let out the breath he had been holding while she spoke, and he smiled. "Yes, that sounds right so far, Miss Britt. Now, if you don't mind, I'll share the proposal I had in mind with you. Long story short, I want you to come work with me and run the program."

Eliza balked. "You can't be serious! I've barely been in Antalya a month, at the request of Dr. Bennett, and you're coming with a new offer? Can you imagine the look on Dr. Çelik's face if I told her I had a new job offer? Or what my colleagues would say to me leaving before I've even implemented any of the changes I came here to make—"

"Ah yes, Miss Britt," Mr. Collins interjected. "That's part of the reason why I sought you out in the first place. A few of my part-time instructors also work at Med School as English teachers. I may have overheard them grumbling to each other about this Saturday professional development that you're instating. It sounded like such an unfavorable reception to the idea that I imagined you might rather appreciate having a new opportunity swoop in and rescue you from the chagrin and judgment of your new coworkers."

"I'm sorry, rescue me?" Eliza asked. "That seems awfully presumptuous, considering we hadn't even met yet when you had that idea."

"Well, yes, but..." Mr. Collins looked down. "I may have already talked about this with Dr. Bennett."

"Dr. Bennett?!" Eliza shrieked. "Here I was thinking I was having this meeting on his behalf, but it turns out to be an ambush? My God, there has to be a better way of doing these kinds of things."

"I reached out to Dr. Bennett at first simply to make the connection." Mr. Collins explained. "We exchanged a couple emails, but after I overheard those teachers complaining, I asked more pointed questions about who was in charge here, what their experience had been like, and then I made my proposal."

"And what did Dr. Bennett say to the proposal?" Eliza asked. "Am I expected to leave this meeting as an employee of Collins Language Training? Have I been married off with no say in the matter whatsoever?"

"Nothing like that, Miss Britt. Dr. Bennett seemed interested, but he did unequivocally state that the decision was yours and he could not and would not decide on your behalf."

Douglas Bennett, that flaky scoundrel. If Eliza knew him as well as she thought she did, none of this was going to be up to her. She'd bet her VW Jetta there was already an email waiting for her, outlining all the reasons she should take this offer. But why had he sent her to run this program if he was going to give up on it so soon? They had a lot to talk about when Eliza got back to her apartment, that much was clear.

"Mr. Collins, thank you for meeting with me today," Eliza stood and held out her hand. "At the moment, I am not able to make a decision about your proposal. I will speak with Dr. Bennett and get back to you."

·❤·❤·❤·❤·❤·

As Eliza left Keyif Cafe, she pulled out her cell phone and fired off a quick text to Jack.

"Where are you all right now? I'm done with my meeting, and I could use a little stress relief."

While she waited for his reply, she took a deep breath and stared at the screen of her phone. The idea of dealing with Dr. Bennett right now felt about as appealing as getting a wisdom tooth pulled with no anesthesia, but it wouldn't get any better the longer she put it off. She checked the time: 8pm in Turkey, which meant it was noon at State. There was a chance she'd be able to catch him on the phone, so she gritted her teeth and dialed.

"TESOL Department, this is Larry Smith speaking. How may I help you?" trilled through the phone to her ear.

"Larry, hi! It's Eliza Britt. Is Dr. Bennett available?"

"Hi Lizzy!" Larry answered. She winced at the pet name that only Dr. Bennett was allowed to use, but willed herself to listen to the rest of what he was saying. "Dr. B. is in meetings all afternoon. Is there anything I can do to help you?"

"Thanks, Larry, but I don't think so." Eliza sighed. "I just wanted to update him on a meeting I had today that he was rather insistent about. I'll send him an email and try calling again later."

"Ooh, was this the meeting with Mr. Collins?" Larry breathed. "How did it go? Are you going to take the job? Are you leaving that university job with all the stubborn Turks?"

Eliza bristled for one reason after another. How did he know? And what did he know about her current job or the talented, highly skilled teachers she was working with? She asked him exactly that, toning down the words in her mind ever so slightly. "I'm sorry, Larry. How did you know about my meeting today? And what have you heard about my current role? This is all a bit of a shock."

"Sorry, Lizzy, you know Dr. Bennett and I love to get into some gossip from time to time," Larry explained. "I think he needs someone to talk to, with all the swirling thoughts going through his head at any moment, and, well, I'm definitely the most accessible person for him to chat with. I didn't realize you didn't know these things were common knowledge."

Eliza exhaled. "I mean, I think I get it, Larry. I care about Dr. Bennett too, and I know he has been lonely since Mrs. Bennett died. I'm just a private person, and it makes me uncomfortable with my frustrations and feelings being, as you said, common knowledge."

"Relax, Lizzy, it's not common knowledge like everyone knows it. I just mean, like, of course *I* do. That's the best perk of this job. I know all the things. Really. Test me. *All the things.*"

Eliza could hear the smirk in Larry's voice, and she couldn't resist asking her next question. "Alright then, humor me. Do you happen to know Dr. Bennett's thoughts about, say, the meeting I just had? Is there a particular outcome he's hoping for from me meeting with Mr. Collins?"

"There sure is, Lizzy my dear!" panted Larry. "He's been so excited about this meeting, and he's talking about it non-stop. *Larry, imagine how it would look on our alumni page. 'State University graduate Lizzy Britt is running her own language school in Antalya, Turkey.' I mean, the university gig sounds cool too, but it's been so much work. This might be just the prestige our department needs to kick up the alumni donations and finally get some of the respect we deserve. The foreign language department is constantly rubbing their graduates' successes in my face, and I'm really getting sick of it."*

While the impression of Dr. Bennett was on the nose enough that it almost made Eliza laugh, the content of it made her heart drop into her stomach. Was that what this was about? Prestige and bragging rights? And was Dr. Bennett really that willing to let go of the partnership with Med School, just because it had turned out to be a little more work than he bargained for? She was going to need to talk to him about this. Heart to heart.

"Thank you for the information, Larry. It's been really helpful." Eliza put a polite smile on her face, hoping it would come through in the tone of her voice. "Could you put a meeting on Dr. Bennett's calendar for the two of us to talk tomorrow? How about at this same time?"

"Sure thing, Lizzy. You're booked in, and I'll make sure he's free and expecting your call." Larry sounded overjoyed, and Eliza couldn't help but feel annoyed. "Have a great night!"

"Thanks, you too. I mean, have a great afternoon." Eliza hung up the phone in time to see a message pop up from Jack.

"We are back at Castle Bar. Upstairs on the balcony. I'll order you something—Efes okay?"

Eliza wasn't much of a beer drinker, but the desire to fit in and 'when in Turkey, do as the Turks do' prevailed. She could try a Turkish beer and see what she thought of it.

And then she could switch to water because, after all, it was a school night.

"Sounds great, Jack. Thanks! I'll be there soon."

As soon as she walked in the front door of Castle Bar, Eliza's eyes landed on Deniz. She sighed, wishing she could have caught Jack alone for a minute or two of commiseration, but that wasn't meant to be. She saw her friend engrossed in conversation with Barış while Deniz stood off to the side. Behind the three of them, she saw and waved at a few of her Med School colleagues, as well as a couple of people she didn't recognize—teachers at Antalya Tech, she guessed.

Deniz hadn't registered her presence yet, and without his stern expression trained on her, Eliza enjoyed a second of superficial appreciation for his appearance. If not for his personality, he would be considered a handsome man—he had all the attributes that usually caught her attention, after all. He was tall but not too tall (her days of making height her #1 requirement in a partner died an abrupt death when Alec broke her heart despite his godlike height). His dark hair and dark eyes gave him a look that was handsome and capable, like he wasn't just a pretty face. Eliza was wary of unapproachable handsomeness, but it wasn't his appearance that made Deniz unapproachable—it was just his personality and his icy feelings towards her.

As she'd been making this Deniz appraisal, she had continued walking towards the bar, sliding up next to Jack. Jack still hadn't registered that she was there at all, intent as he was listening to Barış, but Deniz gave her a tight-lipped smile.

"Eliza, nice to see you."

"You too, Deniz." Eliza answered. "I didn't realize you were going to be here tonight."

"I'm sorry to disappoint you," he responded.

Was that a hint of a smile on his face? Was that supposed to be some kind of joke? "I mean, I'm not disappointed," she stammered. "I just didn't expect to see you, that's all."

"It was a joke, Eliza." Deniz said. Yes, it was definitely, unmistakably, a smile creeping across his face. "How was your day?"

"It was fine. A little strange at the end, and that's why I'm here, actually. I really need to talk with Jack, but I don't want to tear him away from this conversation…" She trailed off.

Deniz laughed. "Oh, if you wait for this conversation to end, it'll never happen. When Barış starts talking about his research, you won't get him to stop. He's my best friend, and he's a brilliant teacher, but he's definitely not a succinct speech giver."

Deniz's laughter and the clear affection for his friend surprised Eliza. She hadn't realized he could feel that warm towards someone, and she wasn't sure what to think about it. But she listened to his advice that she shouldn't wait for Barış to stop talking and gave him a small smile as she tugged on Jack's sleeve.

"Well hello there, buddy!" Jack crowed. He pulled her in for a hug, glowing from within. "I'm so glad you made it! Barış, can you excuse me for a bit? I promised Eliza that I'd be her shoulder to cry on, and it looks like she's come to collect on that promise."

Without waiting for an answer, Jack pulled Eliza toward a table on the balcony as he handed her the drink in his hand. "Spill, friend. What's going on?"

"Ugh, Jack. Everything is a mess. That guy I met with this evening?"

"What, was he hot? Did he mess up your plan to be career-focused Eliza Britt because he made you want to quit your job and have a bunch of babies and never look back?"

Eliza jolted. "Jack, what the heck? No, not even a little. For starters, that was a professional meeting, not a personal one. And no, I know what you're about to say, and even though professional meetings are allowed to involve attractive people and romance and careers put on hold, this one definitely didn't."

Jack's face fell, just a touch. "Whatever, I can dream. Then what was so terrible at your professional meeting?"

"Honestly, I don't know how much I can tell you...but I also really need to talk about this with someone. All I can say right now is that I'm confused about what I'm supposed to do, what Dr. Bennett wants me to do, and basically about my career in general. I'm sorry, I don't know why I came here. I should go find Crystal and unload all this on her."

"Wow, lucky Crystal." Jack's eyes widened. "I wouldn't phrase it quite like that to her if I were you. But yeah, hon, drink a beer with us. Let yourself think about anything else in the world other than work for a minute and then go home and talk with Crystal with a fresh perspective."

"I can do that." Eliza smiled. "Thanks for the pep talk, Jack. I'm sorry I tore you away from Barış."

"It's okay," responded Jack, a twinkle in his eyes.

"You really like him, don't you?" asked Eliza.

"I feel like the answer to that is pretty obvious."

"Have you told him that?"

"Do I need to? Like I said, I think it's pretty obvious—I'd try to hide it, but I think we both know my heart is written all over my face."

Eliza smiled. "I mean, I definitely can see it. But it still might not hurt for him to hear it from you yourself, bud."

Ten

Crystal was waiting at the kitchen table when Eliza got back to her apartment.

"I guess you got my text, huh?" Eliza asked, face grim.

"Yeah, that didn't sound good at all. I ran downstairs to the market to get some reinforcements." Crystal said, leaning over to the chair next to her and pulling chips, chocolate, and a bottle of wine out of the bag she had stashed there.

Eliza laughed. "I can always count on you, Crys. But let's not get sugar and wine drunk just yet. I need to think my way through this with a clear head. I wish you had been at the bar tonight and we could have talked about this an hour ago. Now we'd already be a glass deep in that wine bottle and nearly finished with the chips."

"I told you, goofy. I would have been there if I could have, but I've been so darn busy with my students. The time difference here is good in some ways...you know I like to sleep in...but sometimes my classes just go later and later into the evening, and honestly, I'm kind of getting exhausted from it. Is it Saturday yet?"

Eliza hadn't even asked Crystal how she was doing. Yikes. Maybe Jack had been doing that whole "all truth is said in jest" thing when he gave her a hard time about unloading on Crystal. Eliza made a mental note to at least try to be a better friend. Was their relationship as one-sided as it sounded when Jack teased her about it?

"Earth to Eliza..." Crystal said. "Where are you right now? What are you thinking?"

"Sorry, I got distracted. Am I a terrible friend? Do I ask you how you are? Do I actually listen to you? Why do you like me? Why are you here?"

"Whoa whoa whoa. You, my friend, are spiraling. For starters, there is nothing terrible about you. I've had plenty of opportunities to dump you in the decade plus that we've been friends, and I never have, because I like you so darn much. You are fun and caring and compassionate, and you listen to me just as much as I need to be listened to. You know I'm not usually used to being in any role other than the coach/therapist's role...if you suddenly expected me to be the patient while you grab the clipboard and start taking notes, I'd flip."

Eliza sighed. "I mean, I'm glad to hear you feel that way. I just don't want to let you down."

"Is that what this is about? You're afraid of letting someone down?"

"I think so, yeah. God, you're wise. You got right to the root of it, and I haven't even taken my shoes off yet." Eliza exhaled.

"Wait, you're still wearing your shoes?!" Crystal screeched. "Damn it, Eliza, you've been in Turkey long enough to know that's a no go! Why didn't you leave them outside with mine in the hallway?"

Eliza gave her friend an "are we really talking about this right now" look and slumped her shoulders. She reached down, slipped off her shoes and nudged them out of both of their eyelines.

Crystal spoke again, softer this time. "Who are you afraid of letting down? What happened with Mr. Collins?"

"Mr. Collins definitely wants me to come work with him. I know!" she exclaimed in response to Crystal's widened eyes. "And worst of all, I called Dr. Bennett and Larry made it pretty clear that Dr. B. is, like, totally on board with this."

"What the hell does Larry know? Why did you talk to him about it?" Crystal asked.

"Trust me, I wasn't trying to talk to him about it. But in the process of, I don't know, leaving a message, I guess Larry thought he should interject the bits of gossip he'd been hearing around the office. Dr. Bennett really needs a friend—maybe even a girlfriend—so he can stop thinking so much about my life, my career...I feel like I'm just a piece on his chess board, and I'm still in the middle of the last move he made and here he comes, expecting me to make a new one. Like, what happened to the strategy we were working on literally two days ago?"

"Eliza, you're going to have to stop with the chess metaphors if you want me to keep listening to you," Crystal warned. "But I think I kind of know what you mean, even apart from the terrible reference to that boring ass game. Dr. Bennett has changed his mind about your work at Med School and now he wants you to go work with Mr. Collins?"

"That's what it sounds like."

"But why? Why throw in the towel with Med School so soon?"

"Honestly, I think it's about the prestige of having me run my own language school, and—"

"Wait, what?! *Run* your own language school? You didn't mention that..." Crystal trailed off, shock written across her face.

"Oh yeah, that's what makes it so prestigious and appealing. It's not like I'd be leaving to work for Mr. Collins and do the same thing I'm already doing at Med School. It would be a ton more responsibility, a ton more autonomy...I'd be the one hiring, setting the curriculum, running the show. I can see how Dr. Bennett would be enticed by the idea of being able to say, you know, 'Look what one of our graduates is doing!'...I would just feel so lousy about abandoning Dr. Çelik, my colleagues, and the students at Med School. My God, the students..."

"Well, my dear friend, it sounds like you know what you need to do," Crystal said, nudging Eliza's elbow with her own. "So how are you going to tell Dr. Bennett?"

"You're right, that's all there is for it. I know what feels right to me, and I don't need to waste any more time thinking about it." Eliza pulled out her laptop, tapping open the email icon.

"Whoa whoa, are you, like, writing it right now? I didn't intend to communicate *that* level of action taking. Especially when you've been out at the bar and surely had an Efes or two. What about drafting a note in Word rather than composing an email you might accidentally send before it's ready?"

"You're right," Eliza smiled. "Plus, I'm talking with Dr. Bennett tomorrow evening. It doesn't make total sense to email him before I've even heard his side of the story...God knows if Larry actually got it right, after all."

"Thatta girl," answered Crystal, reaching out for a high five. "Now let's eat and talk about literally anything else. Who was at the bar tonight?"

"Surprisingly, Deniz was. Apart from Jack, he was the only person I chatted with. And he wasn't 100 percent annoying this time—or at least, he wouldn't have been if I didn't know how he secretly felt about me."

"Ugh, he's hot." Crystal groaned. "Why are the hot ones always jerks?"

Eliza chuckled to herself. Hadn't she just been thinking tonight about how his unique brand of hotness wasn't the intimidating kind? Well, apparently it wasn't the kind that disqualified him from being a jerk, either. "I'm guessing it has something to do with missing out on the character building that comes from growing up a little awkward...and having an ugly phase or two. You know, I credit my middle school years for my sense of humor and empathy entirely. There was nothing easy about being a greasy, bespectacled weirdo in braces."

"Oh for sure," snorted Crystal. "And that's definitely why we became friends then, too. It was like 'the hottie within me, buried beneath all these layers of awkwardness, recognizes the hottie within you, buried beneath all those layers of awkwardness.' Real 'namaste' shit."

Eliza had to laugh at that. "That's not exactly how I would have phrased it, but yeah, we did put in our time with each other during those lonely, pubescent years in hopes of there being a light at the end of the tunnel. Cheers to coming out the other side of that wild and wacky journey."

Crystal met Eliza's raised glass with hers. "Cheers, hon. I wouldn't want to be doing this life thing with anyone else. And thank you for turning my day around, too. Seriously. Today wasn't fun, and it wasn't pretty either."

"I'm sorry, Crys," said Eliza. "What happened?"

"Ugh, it's just the usual," she groaned. "One-on-one classes are exhausting, especially when you teach a bunch of them back to back. And when one kid has an attitude, it seems like they all do. I know that isn't really fair...it's probably more like one of them has an attitude and that messes with my mood and leaves me expecting the same from all the rest of them. And then, because I'm expecting it, I create that reality. The power of the subconscious mind can be so damn annoying!"

Eliza snickered at that. "Wow, I would have happily worked through that with you, but it seems like you just life coached yourself. Feel better?"

Crystal hung her head. "The reframe helps, but it doesn't change that feeling of dread I get thinking about another day of back-to-back-to-back classes. If I'm not careful, I could drive myself right into burnout. I think I need a day off—ooh, or a weekend away! Yes yes yes, let's do it!"

"I'm not sure—" Eliza began.

"Come on, Eliza!" wheedled Crystal. "You know I need this! I've been here for weeks now and barely been outside of Antalya proper. You do know Antalya is a whole ass province, right? With cute little towns all up and down the coast? How many of them have you seen, miss? You know I'm right, and you know you need this too!"

"Fine," Eliza admitted. "I can see when I've been outwitted. Want to turn it into a weekend with friends? I can ask Jack and a few others if they'd be interested...and maybe tomorrow morning you can look around online and figure out which town you want to go to? Oh, and where you want to stay? Preferably someplace with lots of available rooms, because I'm not exactly looking to turn this into a slumber party."

"Spoilsport." Crystal smiled. "Of course. This should be a vacation for everyone, not a mandatory rave whether you like it or not. I'm thinking about Adrasan...or maybe Kaş...ooh, this is fun! Thanks, buddy!" She leaned in for a hug and rested her head on Eliza's shoulder.

The next afternoon, Eliza breezed into her office and dropped into her chair with a hard exhale. She had finished her last class and had ten minutes until this week's professional development meeting. This was one compromise she had agreed to with Dr. Çelik and the rest of the teaching staff. Rather than Saturday mornings, she had forty minutes every Thursday afternoon. This week they were going to be talking about correction techniques for speaking exercises, and she had a feeling they might need to turn this particular topic into a series of workshops.

After the workshop finished, Eliza and Crystal were meeting with Jack and a few other teachers—Jack had been in charge of the invitations, so Eliza could only guess who that might include—about the weekend getaway to Kaş. Kaş was the destination Crystal had settled on, and Eliza admitted to herself that she was actually a little excited about it. From the photos she had seen, she expected a quiet weekend with lots of beach time and clear skies at night to see all the stars she missed in the city center. This might be just what she needed.

Her stomach sank when she remembered the call waiting for her after tonight's social meeting with the teachers. Dr. Bennett. Eight o'clock. Eliza groaned just thinking about it. Since she had some time to spare before the professional development meeting started, now seemed as good a time as any to review the document she had typed up last night with her notes for today's conversation.

> Be sure to thank him for always having my career and my best interest at heart. Too soon to pull the plug on the Med School partnership—what if we take a different approach? Try the professional development thing for at least three months. Host our own conference next year? Incentives for teachers to continue improving their teaching skills. Some way to encourage American teachers to get additional qualifications—perhaps a

Master's program that is built in to their
schedule? Free of charge and no extra time.
How could they say no? What would it look
like to get accreditation here for that? Does
that even make sense? Could they get it long
distance from State? That might make the
most sense. Also, emphasis on the refugee
support program. That's State-led, so if I
leave there's a good chance it will crumble.
If I leave, if the partnership dissolves, what
happens with the other American teachers'
contracts? No offense, but what in the world
are you thinking?

Okay, calling it a document was putting it loosely. This
was a stream-of-consciousness rant about all the things
on her mind, and Eliza knew she'd need to be a lot less
scattered if she was going to convince Dr. Bennett that she
knew what she was talking about.

Eliza and Jack claimed a spot on the beach, spreading their
towels and holding down the corners with shoes and bags
of snacks.

"This was a great idea to meet here. It's quiet and relax-
ing, and I'm a lot closer to home for my phone call. Thanks
for looking out for me, Jack." Eliza smiled.

"Of course! If I can sneak in an early evening swim, it's
a good day for me." he responded. "Actually, I might hop

in right now. Do you mind? It's early enough that I'll have plenty of time to air dry before I need to head home."

"Go for it! I wish I had brought a suit and could join you," rued Eliza.

"Next time!" crowed Jack as he peeled off his shirt and started jogged towards the shore.

Eliza chucked as she watched her friend rush in to the wavy water at full speed, his head disappearing under the waves before popping back up with a wide grin across his face. She felt light, almost relaxed, for the first time, maybe even since she arrived in Turkey. Going away this weekend—and soaking up even more of this relaxation—was going to be just the medicine she needed to screw her head back on right.

She heard a throat clearing behind her and turned to see Deniz approaching, a towel over his shoulder and a bag from the market in his hand.

"Eliza? Is Jack with you?" he asked.

Eliza nodded. She hadn't been expecting this—him—tonight, but knowing Jack and his penchant for being nice to every-freaking-one, she couldn't say she was entirely surprised. "Yeah, he's with me. He went in for a quick swim, and I'm holding down the towels while we wait for the others to show up."

"Wonderful." Deniz smiled. "I think I'll join him in the water."

Eliza felt relieved. She couldn't see any more familiar faces on the horizon behind Deniz, and the prospect of making small talk with him while they waited for Jack to return or anyone else to arrive was daunting, to say the least. "Sounds good," she answered.

Deniz spread his large beach towel next to Eliza's, depositing his own bag on the corner. He reached for the hem of his shirt and as he started to remove it, Eliza abruptly turned her head, squinting out at the sea in an exaggerated effort to see where Jack was right now. She felt oddly uncomfortable, aware that she had never seen Deniz out of his work clothes before. To go from buttoned up shirts and jackets to t-shirts and shorts was one thing, but to see him naked from the waist up? That would just be too weird, and she couldn't count on herself not to make it awkward for everyone. God only knew what expression her face was making right now just thinking of it.

"See you later!" Deniz's voice called. Eliza turned just in time to see his bare back slipping into the sea. Deniz waved to Jack, but he didn't venture far from the shore. Her eyes took in his sun-kissed muscles, broad shoulders, biceps...she stopped herself. This wasn't the time to appreciate the physical specimen that was Deniz Aydem. If and when that time ever would come was another story.

Eliza gulped as realization washed over her. If Deniz was here tonight, that must mean Jack had invited him to join them in Kaş. *Crap!* she thought. *I guess I should have given Jack a little more guidance. As in, don't invite anyone who talks shit about me behind my back, regardless of how hot that person is.*

·❤·❤·❤·❤·❤·

An hour later, Eliza gathered her towel, shook it off, and stuck it in the bag she had carried with her. She waved to Crystal, who was listening to Kat and Mira relate a story to the others about their last weekend trip together. If the parts of the story that Eliza had heard were true, they were all in for a wild weekend. "See you at home," she mouthed to Crystal, smiling at the others as they waved.

As Eliza opened the door of her apartment, her phone started to ring in her pocket. "Right on time," she said to herself, though the time on the screen showed she had ten minutes to go until her scheduled call with Dr. Bennett.

"Hi Dr. B., you're nice and early," Eliza smiled into the phone. "How's your day going?"

"Lizzy dear, it's been a wonderful day, and it's quickly becoming an even better one now that I'm hearing your voice. My dear girl, I've missed you so since you left. Isn't it time for you to come back yet?"

Eliza couldn't help but laugh. "It's good to hear your voice, too. And yes, I miss you too. Though it's not like we saw each other daily or even weekly when I was teaching at WCC. Can't you just pretend that's where I am right now? It might help you not miss me so much."

"Ahh, that's the problem though," Dr. Bennett replied, chagrin in his voice. "I'm too observant and tuned in for my own good. I could tell myself those lies all I want, but I'd never believe it. I'm too clever. Oh, Lizzy, it's not easy to be me, I tell you."

"Fair enough," Eliza admitted. "I'm all out of ideas for how to help you not miss me so much. But do you have some free time now so we can talk about my meeting with Mr. Collins?"

"Absolutely, Lizzy," said Dr. Bennett. "I'm all ears. Larry told me he gave you a little inside scoop, so you might already know how positively thrilled I am that this opportunity has come your way. In fact, I was just imagining how it would look to have you and Mr. Collins, maybe a photo from the ribbon cutting ceremony if that's still a thing that happens, with the Mediterranean as a backdrop on the cover of the alumni magazine. My goodness, the colors alone would positively pop! I could see that issue of the magazine flying off the shelves, if you know what I mean. It's not as if it's actually sold on shelves, but…"

"If you don't mind, Dr. Bennett," Eliza winced. "I think you may be getting a bit ahead of yourself. I haven't actually told you—or Mr. Collins, for that matter—that I'm going to accept the offer."

"Not accept the offer?! But Lizzy, this is the best thing to come your way! Ever! How could you even think of not accepting it? My dear girl, take it from me. I've been in this field much longer than you, and opportunities like this don't just fall into your lap. And perhaps they're even less likely to fall into your lap after you turn one down. The community of international language schools is fairly close-knit, you know. If word gets around—"

"Dr. Bennett, please let me finish." Lizzy intoned. "I'm not at all comfortable stepping away from my responsibilities at the Mediterranean School of Languages. This job is what I moved to Antalya for, after all, and there is a great deal of unfinished business here that I couldn't possibly give up on. For one thing, I am still determined to see this professional development endeavor through—no, no matter what you say, so let me stop you right there—I simply don't believe it's a waste of time. Above and beyond that, there is the partnership between Med School and State, and as I am the public-facing representative of it,

I think it would be toxic to that relationship if I up and left before my contract ended. Maybe I can't see the full picture from here, that's true, but I believe my professional reputation would suffer and I can't in good conscience make that decision. Furthermore, there is the matter of the Syrian refugee students and their dependency on this program for their residence status here..."

"Lizzy," Dr. Bennett sighed. "You've made your point, as always. You've got reason after reason to prove me wrong, and I can't help but feel like a foolish old man for ever getting excited about this. What was I thinking? How dare I?"

"Dr. Bennett, it's not like that," Eliza reassured him. "I know where your heart is, how much you care about the success of your former students, and I even understand how captivating this offer was. Trust me, I imagined at least once what it might look like to have a new business card that says I'm the director of the entire school."

"That would have been nice, Lizzy." Dr. Bennett pouted. "Now it will never happen. You'll be stuck under-earning, underachieving, underwhelmed by life just because of the goodness of your heart. What a disadvantage it is to be so selfless, so good, so—if I'm honest—boring. No offense, dear."

"None taken," Eliza bit back a chuckle. "I appreciate you understanding, and I hope you won't take this too hard. Is there anyone else you have in mind for the position? I'd be happy to welcome any other State graduates you send to Antalya...I can show them around, take them under my wing in a manner, help them get settled in."

"I'll think about it, Lizzy. No one compares to you, though. Of course, Mr. Collins probably won't agree. He'll be devastated. Have you told him yet? Oh dear Lizzy, please tell me you're not leaving that responsibility to me? I couldn't bear it..."

Eliza sighed. "I'll gracefully decline the position for myself. That's no problem. And perhaps you should wait and see if someone else comes to mind before you contact him again. If you can recommend someone after all, I'm sure there won't be any hard feelings."

"You're right, Lizzy. Well, I should be off. I'll need to use the rest of this lunch break to come back to myself a bit. Cheer up my spirits. It was nice to hear your voice, even if it was delivering bad news. Take care, my dear."

"You too, Dr. Bennett. Please do take care of yourself. Do something fun after work today if you can," said Lizzy. "Don't take this too hard. You know it isn't personal, and you know I adore you. Why don't you take yourself out for a movie tonight?"

She heard the corner of Dr. Bennett's smile raise in his voice. "I just might do that, Lizzy. Bye now."

As Eliza hung up her phone, she felt the tension release from her shoulders. That conversation could have gone better—but it would have had to have been someone else on the other end of the line. For Douglas Bennett, that was as relaxed and drama-free as that sort of news was ever going to go. Once again, Eliza found herself wishing that Dr. Bennett's tendency to get overly involved with his students—some might say micromanage, but not her—could be tempered by a little more fun and relaxation in his personal life. But she also couldn't imagine Dr. Bennett without a proverbial bee in his bonnet, and that thought brought a smile to her face. She had spoken her piece, it had been received, and now she was free to do the work she had come to Turkey to do—for herself, for her department, for her students, and for her career.

Eleven

Eliza relaxed into the beach lounge chair and sighed deeply. The minibus had dropped the six of them—Eliza, Crystal, Jack, Kat, Mira, and Barış—off in Kaş forty minutes earlier, and after checking into their rooms, they had agreed to meet at the beach after dropping off their bags and changing into their swimsuits. Eliza and Crystal were the first to arrive at the beach, claiming the two best chairs, an umbrella, and a table for their bottles of water and the books they had brought to read.

"Are you glad you came?" Crystal asked with a twinkle in her eye. "I mean, is it even possible that this is better than grading papers at our kitchen table?"

Eliza laughed. "It is much, much better, and I definitely deserve that sass. Please remind me to do this more often. Regularly, even."

"I'm going to hold you to that, Eliza," Crystal replied. "So next time you say you're too busy, I'm going to remind you of exactly what you said just then. If I could get it in writing, that would be even better."

"Shush, you," Eliza laughed, jabbing at Crystal's arm. "What do you think we should do first—read until we fall asleep in the sun, or take a dip in the sea?"

"We should give our sunblock a few more minutes to soak in before we emerge from under the umbrella—and definitely before we plunge ourselves in the sea, though waiting to do that feels like torture. Let's read. What did you bring?"

Eliza chuckled to herself at Crystal's precision sunblock management. If she made it through this summer without a severe burn, she would have only Crystal to thank for that. She reached into her bag and pulled out two books. "First, I have *Management Techniques for Educational Administration...*"

Crystal rolled her eyes so far up into her head Eliza could nearly hear it happening without looking. "I know, I know..." she continued. "I did also bring a fun little beach romance. Have you read this one?" She handed her copy of *Summer Loving* to Crystal.

"I have *not.*" Crystal's grin grew. "But it looks adorable!" She flipped a few pages in the middle of the book. "Okay, not just adorable. Also, *spicy.* I like it! Can I read this when you're done?"

"Of course," Eliza laughed. "Who am I to deprive you of spice?"

The two women settled into their seats, towels at their backs to keep their sunblock from getting on the chairs. They had gotten an early enough start—it had been a half day at school, so they had been able to catch the 1:00 Friday minibus, beat most of the weekend traffic, and arrive in Kaş just over three hours later. They had the afternoon and evening ahead of them, and they wouldn't be heading back to city life until 48 hours later. *This is the life*, thought Eliza. *This is why I came to Turkey in the first place, and I can't believe how quickly I forgot it.*

At the bar that evening, a handsome stranger caught Eliza's eye. His hair had a reddish tint to it, and his eyes looked hazel from this distance. She wondered if he was Turkish, because he was defying her expectations of what a "typical Turk" looked like. As he made eye contact and smiled, she kicked herself for the assumption that she knew anything at all about typical Turks, as immersed in her work as she had been.

The stranger had made his way over to Eliza's end of the bar now, and she turned away from her circle of friends to meet his eyes. He smiled and said, "Hello. I noticed you from across the room and I had to come over and introduce myself to such a beautiful woman. I'm Cem."

He held out his hand and waited for her to shake it. "I'm Eliza. It's nice to meet you, Cem." Eliza noted the Turkish name and berated herself once again for the "typical" thought she'd had just a moment before. "What brings you to Kaş, Cem?"

"I think maybe the same as you. I live in Antalya, but I made a plan to come here this weekend to enjoy the quiet a bit. Swim, relax, unwind, enjoy the beauty." He said those last three words while his eyes roamed over her face, and Eliza felt the heat rise in her cheeks.

"You're right, we're here for the same thing," she said, gesturing to her circle of friends. "The six of us came to get away from our work for a bit. We're all teachers, most of us at the Mediterranean School of Languages."

"Teachers! Wow, it's a small world. I'm in the education field too. What do you all teach?" Cem asked.

"English…I suppose it's fairly obvious that's what I teach, considering that you didn't even attempt to speak a single word of Turkish to me. Is it that obvious that I don't know more than a few phrases?" Eliza grimaced.

Cem laughed. "I admit I watched your little group for a bit, and when I saw this lovely gentleman here," he gestured to Barış, "helping a few of you with the menu I figured it had more to do with language proficiency than illiteracy."

Eliza couldn't help but chuckle back. That was some solid deduction on his part. "So Cem, where do you work?" she asked.

"I'm actually between jobs at the moment, as you Americans like to say. Or rather, I'm searching for a position while I'm in the process of finishing up my higher education."

"Are you a teacher as well?"

"Not exactly," Cem answered.

My goodness, it was like she had to pull the answers out of him. "So…" Eliza prompted.

"So what's your favorite thing about Turkey so far?" Cem asked, either failing to pick up what she was putting down or intentionally ignoring it. Whatever. If this guy wasn't interested in professional networking, then she supposed this would just have to be a purely personal connection. If she remembered how to have one of those.

"Well, I wish I could say I've explored more, but this is actually my first journey out of the city. Though I have to say so far I've absolutely loved it, so I doubt it will be my last. Any recommendations for places to go and things to do?"

"Depends what kinds of things you like…are you more into ancient ruins or night clubs?" Cem asked, bobbing his head to an imaginary beat.

His chicken impression made Eliza laugh. "I'm definitely more inclined towards ancient artifacts than sweaty dancing."

"That's a pity," he said, holding her gaze a beat too long before his eyes flicked down to her lips. "Though you're in luck. There are beautiful ruins all over the province. In fact, most Turks have become almost immune to their charms. You can only see so many amphitheaters before you just stop being impressed."

"I doubt that very much," answered Eliza. "Which one do you think is the most impressive?"

"Do you know Efes?" Cem asked. "And before you ask, I mean the city, not the beer."

"Like from the Bible? Ephesus?"

"Yes, I believe that's what you call it in English. It's definitely worth a visit. It's near Izmir, which is where my family lives. If you plan a trip there, let me know. Perhaps I can show you around."

"I'd like that," Eliza replied, just as Crystal tumbled into the bar next to her, elbow jabbing her in the side. "Ouch, Crys!"

"Sorry about that," giggled Crystal, her eyes glassier than they'd been the last time Eliza saw her. The stress she'd felt earlier this week was long gone, and Eliza was glad to see her friend relaxed and having fun, even if she'd be paying for it with a headache tomorrow.

"What's up?" Eliza asked in response to the probing stare Crystal was directing just south of her eyes.

"First of all, introduce me to your friend, please," Crystal grinned at Cem. "And second of all, did you hear Barış say that Deniz is joining us tomorrow? Ew." She scowled.

Eliza groaned. "Crystal, this is Cem, who I just had the pleasure of meeting. Cem, this is Crystal, one of my oldest friends. And thank you for the news, Crystal. This place is so magical, though I won't even let Deniz Aydem ruin it for me."

Crystal and Cem exchanged smiles and handshakes before Cem turned his gaze back to Eliza and raised his eyebrows. "Did you say Deniz Aydem? I wonder if it's the same Deniz I know...do you know him from work? The one I know doesn't work at Med School, so maybe I'm mistaken."

Eliza saw the hope in his eyes extinguish as she responded. "No, he doesn't work at the Mediterranean School of Languages. We met at a conference, and he works at the Antalya Technical Institute in the English department."

"Damn it," Cem muttered under his breath, "No escaping him anywhere."

"Ooh, spill!" Crystal squealed. "We aren't exactly in the Deniz fan club, so if you've got dirt to share, we are only too happy to listen."

"Let's just say we go way back—maybe not as far as the two of you—" Cem gestured between the two women, "—but far enough. We studied together once upon a time. Actually, we were even friends."

"You *were* friends?" Eliza asked. "Not anymore, I gather?"

"You gather correctly," Cem replied with chagrin in his voice. "But let's not talk about Deniz right now. He's not even here yet, so what right does he have to ruin this evening? He can do that tomorrow when he shows up."

"Fair enough," smiled Eliza. She could put her curiosity aside for now. And maybe in getting to know Cem better, he'd feel more comfortable sharing whatever he was keeping inside. Time would tell.

Saturday morning, Eliza and Crystal found their way to the hotel's dining room for Turkish breakfast. They walked past the spread as they made their way to claim a table with a view of the beach, and Eliza's stomach rumbled. Sliced tomatoes and cucumbers, salty cheeses and olives, *sigara böreği* and sausage...it all looked and smelled delicious. She greeted the owner of the hotel and answered his questions about what she'd like to drink (coffee, thank you) and how she wanted her eggs prepared (fried, please).

Once the two women were situated at their table, tucking into their plates, the expanse of time—and lack of responsibilities for the day—settled into Eliza's awareness. She was gloriously free this weekend, and she couldn't wait to spend the day swimming, exploring, and not thinking about work.

"Hi ladies," Barış's voice cut through her thoughts. She looked up to return his smile and noted that he wasn't alone. Deniz was at his elbow, smiling a tight-lipped smile of his own. "Do you mind if we join you?" Barış asked, gesturing to the two empty seats at their table.

"Go ahead," smiled Eliza. It was always nice to see Barış, even if it seemed unavoidable that Deniz would be with him.

The two men went to fill their plates, as Crystal hissed to Eliza. "Do you really believe what Cem said about Deniz? I just can't wrap my head around it. Barış is such a sweetie, and Deniz is his best friend. I don't want to believe that Barış has terrible taste in humans. What does that say about us?"

"Maybe he doesn't know, Crystal." Eliza responded. "Or maybe he just always sees the good in everyone. I can admit that I'm not perfect, so I fully believe it's possible for Barış to care about flawed humans."

"Can you really admit that?" Crystal scoffed. "That would be a novel experience."

"Shut it, you," smirked Eliza, sipping her coffee.

"We can keep gathering information, at least." Crystal said. "No need to jump to any conclusions yet."

When Barış and Deniz returned, the four discussed their plans for the day. The two women had been intending to camp out in a few beach chairs for the day, but when they learned about the rest of the group's plans to take a boat tour out to a beach on a nearby island, they were easily persuaded to join. They all planned to meet at 10 o'clock at the front of the hotel to make their way to the boat. Barış reminded them to wear their swimsuits under their shorts, and to bring sunblock and water for at least a few hours.

On the boat, with the wind blowing their hair, a new lightness settled over the group. Eliza could taste the salt in the air and feel its texture on her skin and in her hair. Her cares had melted away, and she felt so deeply happy to be with the others on this boat that even Deniz's serious presence couldn't bring her down.

The boat cruised next to a rocky island, and as it came around a corner, a sandy beach came into view. Eliza had forgotten how charming a sandy beach could be, having adjusted to the smooth stones on the beach in Antalya. It looked so enticing that she couldn't wait to jump off the boat and swim to shore.

She slipped off her tank top and shorts, placing them in her bag, then she made her way to the edge of the anchored boat. As she prepared to jump, she heard a throat clear and felt a hand at her elbow.

"Careful, Eliza," Deniz's baritone cut through the excited chatter around her. "It's quite deep here. Do you swim?"

"Of course!" Eliza's laugh was cut short by the serious look in Deniz's eyes. "Don't you?"

"I do, but not particularly well. I didn't grow up near the sea, so I just learned a couple of years ago."

Huh. There's a cultural difference for you, Eliza thought. She felt like an ass for laughing, but as she looked around and noticed the readily available life jackets and inflatable donuts that many people were picking up, she realized Deniz's experience was likely more universal than she realized. Of course, the rest of the world assumed all of Turkey was beachside; and, of course, the majority of the country's landmass wasn't actually on the coast.

"Where did you grow up?" Eliza asked Deniz.

"Isparta. It's known for roses. Do you know it?"

"I don't, sorry," Eliza responded. "I guess you didn't get to go to the sea a lot as a child then?"

"My parents are farmers. The summer is busy for them, so we didn't have a lot of opportunity to take vacations then. When we would go to another city, it was usually in the winter. Not much appeal to swimming then." he answered.

"No, I guess there wouldn't be." Eliza hadn't thought of what Antalya would be like in the winter. The idea of swimming year round appealed to her, but from what Deniz was saying, that didn't sound like it would be happening.

He smiled at her. "Be safe, Eliza. See you on shore."

"Thank you, Deniz," she answered, puzzled by the smile on his face and the way she was reacting to it. Then she jumped off the boat, letting the warm salt water bathe her body and empty her mind of all thought. This was heaven.

Twelve

The beach was glorious. The boat had anchored close enough to the beach that Jack, Barış, and Deniz had carried everyone's bags to shore, so Eliza rested on the sandy beach, sipping her water and nibbling on the trail mix she had slipped into her tote. Between the sun and the swimming, she was feeling deliciously relaxed and just tired enough to nod off right where she sat.

Mira and Kat appeared and plopped down into the sand next to her. Kat held out her hand for some nuts and dried fruit, which Eliza gave her. As Mira and Kat munched on them together, Eliza asked if they'd enjoyed the day so far.

"It's been great! A little low key for my taste, though," Mira replied. "I think I'll need a little dancing tonight to make up for all these old people's activities we're doing today."

Eliza laughed. "You're what...23? This must seem like a senior citizens' outing to you."

"It's fine," said Mira, "But yeah, I've got plenty more energy to burn off."

"Fair enough," Eliza nodded. "Let me know what you come up with, though no promises I'll join you." An early-ish night in bed sounded great. Certainly more appealing than a loud bar or...shudder...a night club.

"Oh no, you don't!" interjected Kat. "You're not getting out of whatever we plan, *even before we plan it.* We're on vacation, remember? And fun is on the menu for tonight, no matter how much you want to curl up in bed with a freaking book."

Damn. Was she that predictable? Eliza wondered. She chuckled to herself. "You caught me, Kat. Let's see what happens tonight."

That was all the promise of a good time the two young women needed, and they sprinted back to the water then, sending a blast of sand over Eliza as they did. She brushed herself off, laughing, and looked out at her friends in the sea. Kat and Mira were splashing and squealing, Barış and Jack were out a little farther and looked to be treading water and talking intently, and there, on the sandbar...was that Crystal with Deniz? And was she touching him? Helping him float? What in the actual hell?

A strange sensation went through Eliza just then, one she couldn't name. Disgust? Discomfort? It couldn't be jealousy. But there was something about Crystal touching Deniz that she didn't like, plain and simple. If those two were getting up to something, maybe she should intervene before it turned into a mess. She tucked her water bottle back into her tote bag, placed it out of the sun, and made her way back to the water's edge.

As the water flowed up Eliza's calves and over her thighs, she slowed down. Storming into the middle of a flirtation would only be awkward for everyone involved. She needed to cool off, screw her head on straight, and, if she was going to insert herself into that interaction at all, it had to be done in a way that wasn't abrasive, aggressive, or just plain weird.

She took a deep breath and ducked under the surface of the water, eyes screwed shut. Under the water, the noise of her friends' laughs and shrieks was almost nonexistent, and she felt cooler, calmer, more grounded. The water had that effect on her. If only she could have all of her work meetings at the edge of the sea, diving in any time things got tense or moods got elevated.

When Eliza popped back up and wiped her eyes, she saw Deniz and Crystal standing—apart—ten feet away. Crystal was beaming at her, gesturing her over, and Deniz softly asked, "Hey, Eliza. Coming to join us?"

Eliza smiled back. "Hey guys. What are you two up to?" She hoped her voice was light and the tension she had been feeling wasn't coming through.

Crystal's wide smile stretched even further across her face. "I was just using my old camp counselor skills on Deniz, helping him gain a little extra confidence in the water."

Deniz's smile was bashful. "It's not that I can't swim—I just get nervous about it. It's so unnatural. I'm not sure I'm meant to be in the water. Or that humans, in general, are."

"You might not be, Deniz," laughed Crystal. "Look at this, Eliza, he's like zero percent body fat. No wonder floating is such a challenge." Crystal reached for Deniz's hipbone just as he jumped to the side, out of her reach, his cheeks flushing red. Eliza felt a growl rise in the back of her throat and barely suppressed it. What had gotten into her today?

Crystal was unfazed. "Want to try again, Deniz?"

"Thanks, Crystal. I'll keep practicing on my own. Why don't you and Eliza go ahead without me?"

Eliza made eye contact with Crystal and gave her a stern nod. She wasn't going to play swimming instructor to Deniz, especially not if he didn't want it. "Why don't we swim over and check out that rock formation over there, Crys?" Eliza gestured to what looked like the entrance to a cave about 100 feet down along the island's shoreline. "You're sure you'll be alright?" she shot to Deniz.

"Yes, thanks. I promise I won't let myself drown while you're gone." Deniz affirmed. "Go on ahead."

The two women started swimming along the shoreline, doing an adapted breaststroke with their heads out of the water so they could chat while they swam. Eliza raised an eyebrow. "What was all that with Deniz?" she asked her friend.

"Just trying to give him some pointers on how to float a little more confidently," Crystal responded. As her eyes moved to Eliza's, her expression changed. "What? Is that jealousy I see there? I thought you hated him!"

"Ugh," Eliza growled. "Honestly, I don't even know. I think it's just always a little confusing when you see people, um, in their swimsuits and not at work. And maybe I'm being a prude, but touching each other while in swimsuits is, like, 'get a room' territory." She cleared her throat and tried to look cooler than she felt. "So, um, was there any of that sort of thing going on? Because I'm not opposed to it...I just need a little time to get on board, I think."

Crystal laughed at her. "Right, you are *so* cool with it. Relax, Eliza, I'm not about to mess up your little crush or *professional relationship* or whatever the hell it is. Things are complicated enough in that brain of yours without me bringing that hottie home for private swimming lessons. He's not exactly my type, you know."

It was Eliza's turn to laugh. "Um, remind me what exactly your type is then? Because that man is very attractive and I've never seen you turned off by that particular blend of muscles, dark hair, dark eyes...please enlighten me."

"If you must know," Crystal splashed Eliza in the face, "I tend to prefer men who are, you know, interested in *me*. When they spend every minute with me glancing around to see where *you* are, it sends a massive friend zone bat signal to my lady parts."

Eliza sputtered, choking on a mouthful of water. "What—? No, that's not right. He was probably just looking to see where his friends were. Maybe he's uncomfortable being up close and personal with attractive women in swimsuits, so he was looking to excuse himself politely and go rejoin Barış."

"Give me a little credit, Eliza," Crystal shook her head. "I'm not brand new to the human race, and I know how to read body language. That man had no problem with me or my body, he was definitely appreciative of the swimming lesson...*and* he was 100 percent aware of where you were at all times."

Huh. That was new and unexpected information, and Eliza didn't know what to do with it. She swallowed down a secret smile and changed the subject. "I'll believe that when I see it. Anyway, what are you up for doing tonight? The youngsters are trying to convince me that we need to 'go out clubbing' tonight, and I'm trying to figure out the most graceful and believable way to excuse myself without actually saying I just want to keep reading my book."

Crystal groaned. "Look, I'm not a club kind of gal either, but you are being ridiculous. Read on your breaks in between classes. Hell, read in the bathroom when we get home. Ignore me for a week and read your book at every meal. But if you don't come out tonight and actually have a little fun, I am going to dig up the most embarrassing middle school photos I can find and have t-shirts made for every single one of us."

"Fine," scowled Eliza. "I thought you would be on my side, but clearly I've had too much sun and fried my brain. Peer pressure wins. Looks like I'll be putting on my hot girl disguise and pretending to enjoy dancing in public tonight. Yippee."

They had arrived at the mouth of the cave, but one glance inside made it clear they wouldn't be venturing in. It was dark, and the gap above the water was just a few inches tall. Claustrophobia didn't feel like a great idea, especially not in a place where drowning was an actual possibility. The friends' raised eyebrows expressed all of this, no words necessary. When Crystal asked, "...so, turn around and swim back?" Eliza nodded.

As the beach came back into view, the two friends slowed their swimming. Kat and Mira were sunbathing on the beach, Jack and Barış were still engrossed in conversation and smiles, and Deniz was standing at the water's edge watching their approach. He reached up to wipe his wet hair out of his face and then, in one smooth motion, sat at the water's edge, resting his elbows on his knees. Crystal let out a breath. "Damn, that really is one hot man."

"Sure," was Eliza's tight-lipped reply. She had seen the muscles, and true, there was something about the water in his hair and his eyes that felt intimate and vulnerable, like they had just showered together. Holy shit, how had her mind gone there? "Isn't it just such a cliche, though, Crystal?"

"What's wrong with cliche hotness? Hotness is hotness, and I won't discriminate in my appreciation of it."

"It's not the hotness that's cliche, it's the drooling over the 'exotic' man from another country. You know, like sexy accents, tall, dark, handsome strangers, falling in love at the beach, for crying out loud."

"Whoa there, Eliza. Are you telling me you're only appreciating this man's hotness because he's Turkish? If we took away the accent and the sunset and the beach...you wouldn't give him a second glance? Didn't you notice he was attractive before today?"

"You're ridiculous. You know that, right?" Eliza asked. "Of course I could objectively appreciate his physical beauty the first time I saw him. Without even hearing him speak—I know, shock of all shocks. But is it wrong or cliche that after deciding I don't like him it's only now, in this setting, that I'm sort of maybe quasi tempted to give him a second chance at a first impression?"

"Well, hon, there are tons of reasons you might be inclined to change your mind this weekend. It could be the change of setting...or the swimsuits...or the vulnerability he showed by admitting he wasn't an Olympic swimmer. Does it really matter?"

"I guess not," admitted Eliza. "I just don't want to be *that* American girl who objectifies all the hot foreigners. It gives me flashbacks to college and the way some of the international students were treated."

"Hey, they didn't seem to mind," chuckled Crystal, then at the look Eliza sent her way she continued, "But I know what you mean. It's gross. So I get why you're sensitive to it. But that's not what you're doing, so ease up a bit, okay?"

"Eliza! Crystal!" came a shout from the beach. Kat was waving at them. "There's a boat leaving soon, and we're going to take that one so we can get ready for dinner and dancing. Hurry up!"

Eliza groaned. "There's no getting out of this, is there?"

"No, there absolutely isn't," Crystal smiled. "And you're going to have fun, damn it!"

Back at the hotel, the group parted ways as they all headed off to the showers and clean clothes that were waiting for them. They agreed to meet back in the hotel lobby at 8:00 and head out for a late dinner, moving on to the dancing portion of the evening from there. Everything was walking distance, but comfortable shoes would still be a good choice for the night they had planned.

Crystal and Eliza rummaged through their suitcases together, sharing accessories and trading clothes like they had since they first met over a decade ago. One of the first days they had bonded at school, Crystal had swapped her barrette for Eliza's headband. Confronting a shared fear of head lice while finishing off their outfits with much more fitting hair accessories had cemented their friendship that day. They'd been swapping and sharing ever since.

"Ooh, Eliza, what do you think of this?" crowed Crystal, holding up a delicate turquoise sundress she had packed. "You got a little sun today and this color would be absolutely perfect on you!"

Eliza hesitated. "It's beautiful, but what will you wear? You packed that for a special evening out, didn't you?"

"I packed it because vacation always makes me think I want to be more adventurous in how I dress—and then always reminds me that I dress the way I do because it's comfortable and I like it. Besides, I really like this outfit," she explained, holding up a pair of crisp white pants and a sexy green halter top.

"Alright, as long as you're not depriving yourself on my account," acquiesced Eliza. "A little sexiness might be just what I need to get in the mood for the evening ahead, eh?"

The restaurant where their group headed for dinner specialized in seafood, which made sense, considering the location. Rather than ordering main courses—there were so many delicious items on the menu—they ordered something of everything and shared it all. Over small plates, free-flowing drinks, and the dying sunlight, the connections among their group of coworkers turned friends forged themselves stronger. There was laughter, as incidents from just a few hours before were remembered and embellished, and the level of comfort and camaraderie grew stronger and stronger as the evening wore on.

When the fish, crab, octopus—and a few things Eliza still wasn't sure what to call, but that had tasted delicious—were cleared from the table, the group sat back and there was a collective exhale of satisfaction. Serenity. Contentment.

But Eliza should have known this moment couldn't last.

"Alright, who's ready for some dancing?" crowed Kat, wiggling her eyebrows. She and Mira were on their feet and ready to herd the group out the door before anyone else could even respond.

Groans could be heard around the table. Eliza noticed she wasn't the only one feeling hesitant—the same feeling was written all over the faces of Jack, Barış, and...Deniz? Well, that couldn't be. As confused as his vulnerability and overall attractiveness had made her feel today, she still wasn't sure she wanted to be a part of a group that he was also in. Time to rally.

"All right, all right," Eliza gave in. "You win, kids. Where are we going?" My God, were they really hopping up and down? Had she ever had that kind of energy and excitement—about dancing, of all things? That was hard to believe.

"There aren't a ton of clubs around here," Mira responded. "I mean, have you seen this place? I don't think the locals do a ton of dancing, but there was one place that looked cute and fun, if not super touristy. I think it's called Limonata. It's a short walk. Let's go!"

Standing with a barely muffled groan, Eliza's eye caught Jack's. Was he...trying to tell her something? Oh...there it was. She smiled. It looked like her friend needed a little support, a wingwoman perhaps, to make the plans he and Barış had in mind come to fruition without attracting too much attention. She could do that.

The yawn Jack gave was exaggerated, theatrical. "I'm going to head back to the room, I think. Too much sun today, you know. No, don't be disappointed, Kat. I promise I'll let you take me out clubbing all over Antalya next weekend."

"I'll walk you back," offered Barış. "These aren't good dancing shoes."

"Actually—" began Deniz.

Eliza cut him off. "Deniz, you have to come! We can't have all the men abandon us, can we? Who's going to help me keep an eye on all these rowdy youngsters? Be the fun police, if you will?"

Deniz's tight-lipped smirk told her he was on board, and Jack's grateful eye contact was all the reward Eliza needed. She mouthed, "Have fun," to him, winked, and turned on her heel to follow the younger women out of the restaurant.

Deniz caught up with her a moment later. "Do we really need to supervise Kat, Mira, and Crystal? That feels very out of character for you, anti-feminist or something like that."

"Oh, Deniz," she smiled, "Sweet, simple Deniz. Couldn't you tell Jack and Barış wanted to be alone? Did you really want to third wheel their in-the-room date?"

Deniz furrowed his brow. "Is that what that was? I swear I can't tell with them. I know Barış well enough to know what he's feeling, but I honestly can't figure Jack out. Do you think it was a *date* date, or like a 'talking about my research' date?"

Eliza laughed. "I doubt they'd need to be alone for the research date. Hell, I imagine we'd all happily leave them alone for that one, enthralling as it may be. No, I'm pretty sure there's a spark there and I'm not making it up. To be safe, let's keep you out of the room for at least a few hours. Sound good, Mr. Aydem?"

"Yeah, I can do that," Deniz answered. His smile disappeared as his lips thinned into a straight line. "Now, if only we had something to do for the next few hours that was anything but dancing."

"Not a fan?" Eliza asked. "I'm not judging, neither am I. I'm going to try to have some kind of out-of-body experience tonight. Pretend I'm someone other than me, someone who has fun doing this kind of thing. You can try it too!" She laughed, elbowing him in the ribs.

Deniz's lips quirked into a small smile. "I've never looked at it quite that way, but I'll give it a try. Time to be the kind of guy who loves this sort of shit."

Thirteen

The next morning, Eliza's headache woke up before the rest of her body did. As she came to, the light streaming through the window and into her tired eyes, she groaned. Fumbling at the bedside table, she found a lukewarm bottle of water and guzzled it down. Rookie mistake, having too much to drink and not hydrating herself. And how could she have forgotten preventative painkillers?

Her groan had woken up Crystal, who seemed to be in the same condition as Eliza. "Why do we do this to ourselves?" croaked Crystal's voice as she flopped over and buried her head under her pillow. "Do we hate ourselves? Or are we stupid and just don't remember that this is the consequence of a night of having too much fun?"

"A little of both?" asked Eliza. "Come on, get up. Let's get some water, some food. You know, all the old standby cures. Hair of the Dog, and all that."

The two of them moved like rusty robots with malfunctioning batteries as they stuffed their limbs into yesterday's clothes, tied up their hair, and brushed their teeth. Good enough. Now about that breakfast...

Stumbling out of their room, they ran into Deniz and Barış in the hallway. Or rather, they *collided* with Deniz and Barış because apparently Eliza had never bothered to learn to look both ways when crossing a street or merging into a hallway. In a particularly unfair twist of fate, Deniz and Barış both looked like they had slept for 10 hours and woken up in time this morning to go to the gym, get a massage, and have a healthy bowel movement. Eliza felt jealous rage bubble up in her. How dare they? Or was this just part of the unfairness of gender expectations, men looking great no matter how old or tired they were, while women were expected to be cover models even if they had just delivered a baby or been hit by a car?

"Good morning, boys," Crystal greeted their friends. "Don't expect any words, or at least any kind ones, out of Eliza for at least another 20 minutes. If you don't mind, steer me towards the breakfast room so I can get some caffeine and protein in her?"

Barış laughed, "Follow me," and the four of them fell into step together, Crystal and Eliza trailing behind the two men. Deniz shot a furtive look over his shoulder, turning his head back quickly when Eliza's eyes met his own. That was strange. Eliza wracked her scrambled egg brain to remember what the two of them had talked about last night and came up empty. She hoped whatever she had said—or done—hadn't been too embarrassing, and cringed at the thought. She'd ask Crystal about it once she could form sentences again.

Entering the dining room, she made a beeline for the buffet. Coffee would have to wait until the dining room manager emerged to ask for hot drink and egg preferences, just like yesterday, but in the meantime she could satisfy her body's craving for cheese, carbs, and fruit. Just what the doctor ordered. Plate full, she turned to scope out a table for their group and nearly collided with Cem.

"Cem?" Eliza squawked. "I didn't know you were staying here, too."

"Absolutely," he smiled. "I was sorry not to see you around last night. Where did you go?"

As Eliza opened her mouth to answer him, she caught a glimpse of Deniz at the table where he sat. He was staring at the back of Cem's head with disdain and rage, no attempt made to disguise his feelings. He must have sensed Eliza's gaze, because his eyes flicked to hers and then back again to Cem, with no change in his expression. There was definitely more to this story. Tempted as Eliza was to invite Cem to come sit with them and get it all out in the open, she suspected that would be an uncomfortable situation for everyone involved. And shouting and tension never cured anyone's hangover.

"Sorry about that," she told Cem. "We're heading back to Antalya this morning. Maybe when you're back in the city, we can meet up and hang out?"

"Oh, so you *would* like to see me again," smiled Cem. "I was wondering about that. Definitely. Just give me your phone number and I'll be in touch."

Cem handed over his phone and Eliza typed in her Turkish phone number. She could feel Deniz's eyes boring into her, as if willing her not to do what she was doing. When she looked up, his eyes darted away, downcast. Whatever. If he had been a dick to Cem, it made sense that he wouldn't like to have potential friends learn about that. Maybe he was about to be exposed to Barış and all the other people in Antalya who inexplicably liked him. *That sounds like karma to me*, she thought.

"I'll see you later," Eliza called to Cem as she went to join her friends at the table. The cafe manager came to take their drink and egg orders, and once Eliza's coffee was deposited in front of her, all was right in the world. Except for the nagging feeling that something was weird between her and Deniz. What in the world had happened last night?

When they had finished eating, Eliza and Crystal made their way back to the room to pack up their things. On the way, Eliza asked, "Um, do you know what the heck is going on with Deniz? He is looking at me strangely this morning and I can't, for the life of me, remember what we talked about last night."

Crystal's eyes widened. "Really? Wow, you definitely can't hold your liquor, can you? I don't know what the two of you *talked* about, but you were out on the dance floor with him, like, 90 percent of the time. Hell, when he excused himself to use the bathroom or take a break or something, you *dragged* him back out there."

"Oh God," Eliza felt the blush rising in her cheeks. "Ugh, Drunk Eliza, I hate you so much! I'm so embarrassed. How clingy and annoying and no wonder he is looking at me like I'm a freak this morning."

Crystal laughed. "He didn't exactly seem to mind last night, though. I mean, he's a big guy and he definitely could have stopped himself from being dragged if he wanted to. Not to mention, he had no problem saying no and scaring off the other girls who tried to get him to dance when you *finally* sat down for a goddamn minute. I think he had fun. Don't worry about it." Crystal rubbed Eliza's back. "You were cute. I don't know what got into you, but you were cute and fun and charming. It was weird."

"Shut up!" Eliza laughed. "Is it such a shock that I can be charming?"

"Yeah, actually," scoffed Crystal. "Have you met yourself?"

Eliza shoved her friend away and flopped back onto her bed, arm covering her eyes. "Alright, that's enough. Let's pack up and get the heck out of here. Back to the real world!"

"Yeah, about that..." came Crystal's reply. "Have you seen your phone today?" She was standing next to the table between their two twin beds, where Eliza's phone had been charging since they returned last night. Well done, Drunk Eliza, for remembering to plug it in.

"No, why do you sound concerned?" Eliza started, pulling her phone away from the outlet. "Shit..." she trailed off, scrolling through the countless notifications littering her home screen. Missed calls, text messages, and emails...all of them from one person.

"Dr. Bennett." Eliza grimaced. "He's been thinking more about Mr. Collins's offer, apparently. From the looks of it, he isn't too happy with me and my decision. I mean, 'Please reconsider, Eliza, this is *positively ridiculous*' doesn't exactly sound like he's on board with whatever I decide, does it?"

"You weren't kidding about 'back to the real world,' Eliza." Crystal's face was sympathetic. "Can it wait until tomorrow? It's Sunday. Surely he can't expect to hear back from you over the weekend."

"Crystal, you know as well as I do that isn't how Dr. Bennett works," Eliza smiled with chagrin. "Mercifully, it's way too early in Michigan for me to be expected to call him right now. But yeah, when we get back to the apartment, I'll owe him a phone call. Probably a long one, from the looks of these texts."

"Well, my dear," began Crystal, "There's only one thing I can suggest at a time like this—boundaries. Text him now, and tell him what time you can talk. But give him an end time too. Otherwise, you'll be on the phone until you pass out from hungover exhaustion."

"That's not a bad idea," answered Eliza, opening her text messages. "I'll tell him, 'I've been out of town, but I'll call you when I'm home this evening.'"

"Good start..." encouraged Crystal, "Now really set those limits. Seriously. You can do it."

"Okay," sighed Eliza, "How about, 'I'll be free from 8:00 until 8:30, so I'll call you then.'?"

"Well done," smiled Crystal. "The real challenge will come at 8:29 tonight when you have to decide if you're going to stick to your guns or let him continue talking your ear off."

❤ · ❤ · ❤ · ❤ · ❤

As Sunday morning wore on, it became clear their group had a couple of different agendas at play. Kat and Mira were happy to squeeze in as much beach time as possible before heading home, while Deniz and Barış were eager to get back to Antalya and prepare themselves for the new work week starting the next day. Jack and Eliza opted to join Deniz and Barış for the early bus home, while Crystal decided to stay and soak up a little more sun with Kat and Mira.

When they parted ways, Crystal gave Eliza an encouraging squeeze. "I'll try to be back before you have your big phone call, but no promises. You don't need me, anyway. Just stick to your guns and don't give in, no matter how much whining or manipulating he directs your way. You've got this."

Eliza thanked her friend and climbed into the minibus, planting herself next to Jack, in the seat in front of Barış and Deniz. Jack and Barış were both seated next to the windows, headphones secured over their ears, and Deniz was in the seat behind Eliza with a novel opened in his lap. The three men acknowledged Eliza's entrance with small nods before returning to their music, podcasts, and literature. Eliza sighed and pulled out her own beach read novel, wondering if Deniz—who was likely reading a classic work of highbrow literature—would judge her for her rom com selection. As if she cared.

The minibus made its way along the coast, and Eliza soon remembered that the stretch of road closest to Kaş had been full of twists and turns on the way there on Friday. In fact, while she had been able to read and relax for most of their previous journey, during the last 30 minutes, she had nearly been sick on the side of the road. Now, especially considering Drunk Eliza's irresponsible consumption the night before, she had better be careful. Vomiting on the side of the road wouldn't win her brownie points with anyone on the bus, and even Jack might not want to sit next to her after that. She set her book down in the seat next to her and closed her eyes.

Twenty minutes later, a tap on the shoulder startled Eliza out of her reverie. Deniz was leaning forward, holding out his hand to her. *Summer Loving* was in it, and he was asking her something, judging by the way his eyebrows were raised. She blinked twice to clear her head. "Sorry, did you say something?" she asked.

"Did you drop this, Eliza?" Deniz asked. "It slipped under the seat just now, and I thought it might be yours."

"Oh, yes, thanks," blushed Eliza, taking the book and covering the illustrated characters and their playful embrace on the cover. "I like to read something a little lighter when I'm at the beach." She refused to make eye contact with him, but she could feel the judgment in his eyes boring into her.

Deniz cleared his throat. "I know what you mean," he said meaningfully. When she looked up, his eyes darted from hers down to the second book he was holding out. The one he had been reading. Was that...another rom com? And by one of Eliza's favorite authors in the genre? This guy was full of surprises. As Eliza's eyes raised to his, he put a finger up to his lips. "No need to tell anyone about this," he said, darting an eye towards Barış. "My reputation is at stake if it gets out." There was laughter in his eyes, though, and Eliza couldn't imagine Deniz crumbling under anyone's perception of him.

"Fair enough," she laughed. "I love everything Cate Austen writes, too, for what it's worth. I haven't read that one, though."

"I'll let you know what I think of it," he responded, "And if you want to borrow it when I finish, you're more than welcome."

"Thank you," Eliza said, turning back around to face the front before her motion sickness could sabotage the rest of the journey and turn this conversation into something uncomfortable and disgusting.

After they parted ways at the bus station, Eliza made her way to her apartment. It was a few blocks from the bus station, and after sitting in the minibus for a few hours, it felt nice to stretch her legs. She stopped on the way to pick up a quick dinner, *çiğ köfte* from the stand near where she lived. The interplay of spicy bulgur, tangy pomegranate sauce, and zesty arugula sounded delicious. Once inside her apartment, she left the bag with her dinner in it on the coffee table while she took her suitcase into her bedroom. After a quick shower and change of clothes, she sat on the couch to eat and check her email while she waited for the time to call Dr. Bennett to arrive.

At 8:00 on the dot, her phone rang. "Right on time," she smiled as she greeted Dr. Bennett. "Did you have a nice weekend, Dr. B.?"

"Oh, it was terrible," he rushed, "I've been so preoccupied by this whole mess with Mr. Collins. Lizzy, I can't believe you haven't changed your mind. Think of the opportunity you're missing! And think of the boost you could give to State's reputation! I just think—"

Eliza interrupted, "Dr. Bennett, I know you're feeling stressed, and I'm sorry that it's affected your time to rest and relax over the weekend. I just got home myself from a couple of days spent out of the office, and it did me a world of good. Have you eaten? Slept? Taken more than fifteen minutes away from all of your work stress?"

"Eliza, you know I don't have the luxury of doing that," groaned Dr. Bennett. "There are entirely too many people depending on me, and if I'm not available, I really don't know what they will do."

"Dr. Bennett, I'm saying this with all the love and respect in the world," began Eliza, "But I really think stepping away for even a few hours would be huge for your mental health. You are excellent at your job, it's true, but you aren't a surgeon—you don't need to be on call 24/7. And maybe being so available for everyone all the time is just enabling them to continue to disrespect your boundaries—"

It was Dr. Bennett's turn to interrupt. "Oh, *boundaries*, I just hate that word. Boundaries keep people out, and I don't want that. I care about the students I work with, my advisees, and what would they do if I started shutting them out?"

"You might be thinking of boundaries a little too literally," Eliza said gently. "I'm not talking about borders between countries. I'm talking about emotional boundaries, setting limits so that people don't walk all over you. Taking care of your mental health first rather than everyone else all the time. You know, putting on your oxygen mask first before you help anyone else with theirs?"

"Yes, yes, that's all well and good," Dr. Bennett sounded exasperated. "We can talk about my mental health another time. Don't try to take my focus off of you, young lady. What can I do to get you to reconsider Mr. Collins's offer?"

"Nothing, I'm afraid," explained Eliza. "I'm committed to seeing this program at Med School through, and I can't be talked into abandoning the responsibility I have here. I have students who need me here, especially the international students. Did I tell you about the refugee community here?"

"You did, Lizzy, and you know I support all of your bleeding heart efforts." Eliza felt her eyes roll in response to Dr. Bennett's tone. "I just don't see why you can't do all of that *and* help Mr. Collins run his school, too."

Wow. Now that was a different approach. "I'm sorry, are you suggesting that I take on *two full-time jobs* at one time?" asked Eliza. "I have more than enough to keep me busy at Med School, and I absolutely could not give Mr. Collins's school the time, attention, and energy that it needs. No, I must categorically turn down the position. There's no way around it."

"Eliza, dear," Dr. Bennett's rueful tone reached her ears through the phone line, "We simply need to talk about this some more. Can you fly home and come to my office on Tuesday?"

"You know I can't, sir," said Eliza, "I've got a full load of courses this week, as well as Thursday's professional development workshop to lead. We'll just have to talk this through over the phone, and why shouldn't that suffice?"

"I need to speak with you face to face," explained Dr. Bennett, "Though of course I understand that you can't come here just in the same way that I can't come there." Well, it wasn't quite *the same* way. Dr. Bennett was terrified of flying, and Eliza's excuse was more about remaining gainfully employed than panicking over the ocean when the turbulence hit.

"I know!" Dr. Bennett interjected. "I've got it. I'll send Larry. He'll be my proxy. I'll inform him tomorrow, book a flight for him as soon as possible, and you can meet him at the airport when he arrives. It's a perfect solution."

Eliza's eyebrows reached unprecedented heights on her forehead. "Dr. Bennett, I'm sure that isn't necessary. It's a big expense for the department. Not to mention, surely there are more pressing tasks for Larry to be working on—"

"Nonsense," said Dr. Bennett, "I *need* to speak with you face to face, and this is the only way I can make even a semblance of that happen. It's settled. He'll be there sometime this week. And of course he will need to stay with you. If you're concerned about expense for the department, then we shouldn't put him up in a hotel on the foreign language school's dime."

Eliza swallowed. "How long do you imagine he'll be staying with me? My apartment is small, and I'll still have a full-time job, you know."

"As long as it takes, Eliza," Dr. Bennett responded. "As long as it takes."

Fourteen

The trip to Kaş had refreshed Eliza in more ways than she realized until she was back in her classroom on Monday morning. The energy with which she greeted her students, her patience while some of them were a bit hesitant to get back into "student mode," and the amount of fun they were able to have together...all of it suggested that a mere three days earlier she had been a different, more anxious version of herself. *Note to self: breaks from work are important if I want to continue to have a career rather than a burnout or a breakdown. Keep doing that from time to time.*

It was nearly time for her students to take their midterm exams, and the tension surrounding that assessment was palpable. Performance during this semester would determine the students' placement for the upcoming semester. All of them hoped to move up to the next level in the English program, and some extra ambitious students were working to skip a level by taking another placement test during the semester break. One of those students, Ahmad, was a part of the community of Syrian refugee students Eliza taught, and he came to her office during the lunch break to ask for some additional materials to support his efforts.

"Ahmad, this is a lot of work!" Eliza exclaimed. "I think it's awesome that you're so ambitious, but don't you want to take your time with the program in its regular pacing? What's the rush to get into your faculty department, anyway?"

Ahmad lowered his eyes, looking at his hands in his lap. "Miss Britt, my family needs me to start working. The longer it takes me to graduate, the longer they have to wait for me to start making money. I will do whatever I need to support my parents and my younger siblings."

"Are you the oldest, Ahmad?" Eliza asked. "Is that why you are expected to take this on?"

"I am the second born," Ahmad explained. "My older brother was killed before we left Aleppo, and now it is my responsibility even more to help my family. Please, can you help me prepare for this test?"

Eliza couldn't imagine the heart-rending grief Ahmad and his family had experienced. And who was she to suggest a more "balanced" teenage experience to this young man who had been forced to grow up before others in his generation would? "Of course I will help you. Your writing skills are excellent, so I think the best place for us to direct our energy would be on the speaking portion of the exam. Are there other students who are working towards this same goal?"

"Yes, Miss Britt," Ahmad nodded, "I believe there are about fifteen of us."

"Wow, that's great!" Eliza was surprised. "Could you help me organize a group, then? Ask around, and if there are other students who are interested, we can form an extracurricular group to practice the sample speaking questions. Find the students who are interested, and maybe get them to vote on a day and time that would be best for them to gather. I can help coordinate at least the first few sessions until you all get comfortable doing it yourselves."

"Thank you, Miss Britt," Ahmad smiled. "I will let you know shortly what I learn. I appreciate your help."

"You're welcome," Eliza said. "I'll do whatever I can to help."

When Ahmad had left her office, Eliza opened her laptop to look over her lesson plans for the afternoon. Taking another afternoon to work with students would cut into her time to work, both as a teacher and as an assistant director, but she couldn't imagine delegating this task to someone else. She had always enjoyed her work with international students and especially with those in the refugee community back home. If there was any way she could help them ease their transition to life in their new country—and get the support they needed in any other areas—she would do what she could to help. *Plus, it's not like they need me to hold their hands for the rest of the semester. These students are capable, and all they need from me is some specialized support about preparing for this specific exam.*

A notification popped up on Eliza's laptop then—she had a new email from Dr. Bennett with the subject line

"FWD: Flight confirmation for Larry Smith." Teeth gritted, Eliza opened the message...

...and then started in shock. Larry was arriving tomorrow morning. She checked her watch. He was probably already at the airport, waiting for his first flight to Frankfurt. After a few hours there, he'd be flying to Antalya and landing before lunch time on Tuesday. That was...rather soon, to say the least.

Eliza pulled out her phone to text Crystal. "Remember that Larry is coming to stay with us sometime? Apparently he's arriving TOMORROW."

Crystal's response came quickly, and it was a series of shocked emojis, followed by the word "WHAT."

Eliza laughed, her fingers already flying in response. "I know. Seriously. I know. I'll pick up some sheets for the couch tonight and maybe a better pillow, too. Can you do some grocery shopping today?" Their time to prepare for their unexpected—and frankly, unwanted—guest had gone from indefinite and open-ended to panic-inducing. *Damn it, Dr. Bennett,* Eliza thought, *you couldn't give me a little more warning?*

Then she noticed the few lines Dr. Bennett had typed above the forwarded message: *"Just a heads up. Larry will be expecting you at the airport. Hope you kids have fun together!!!"*

No, Dr. Bennett clearly couldn't give her a warning. Because he didn't think this was the kind of visit that warranted a warning or any sort of preparation. In his mind, this was just two long-time friends hanging out and enjoying the beach together. Never mind the fact that Eliza had an important job to do. And never mind the fact that one of Larry's main tasks on this visit was to convince her to leave that important job to satisfy someone else's wishes.

Eliza needed to let Dr. Çelik know about this. Not about Larry or Dr. Bennett's agenda, but about the fact that now she needed at least a few hours off tomorrow to pick him up from the airport and get him settled in. Ugh. She'd probably need the whole day off. *Time to figure out how substitute teachers work at Med School*, she groaned to herself.

Dr. Çelik was sympathetic to Eliza's dilemma, and it was arranged that Ayşegül would cover her first class of the day and Kat would take the second one. Thankfully, her Tuesday course load was the lowest of the week, so there was nothing of note happening after lunch. Regardless, she planned to return to her office in the afternoon, if possible, in order to stay on top of the assignments that needed to be graded and the Wednesday lessons that needed to be prepared.

When Dr. Çelik suggested Eliza leave after her last class finished today, rather than waiting until the work day ended at 4:00, Eliza nearly hugged her. "Thank you so much! I've got a lot of preparing to do, of course I didn't expect to have a visitor so soon—"

"I understand, I really do," Dr. Çelik stated. "And it is important to show hospitality to the person who is coming to stay with you. Perhaps your colleague can come visit us here during his stay. I imagine observing some lessons and getting to know some teachers here, as well as how we do things, would be very interesting to him."

Eliza groaned inwardly as a tight smile appeared on her face. "I'm sure he would like that," she said. She had been honest with Dr. Çelik that Larry was working closely with her and Dr. Bennett and that was why he was coming here. Of course, she hadn't been able to mention anything about Mr. Collins or Collins Language Training. But maybe having Larry come to Med School would help Eliza make her case for remaining in her current position, since she was not going to be budging on accepting the job with Mr. Collins.

When Eliza's Intermediate Listening and Speaking class was finished, she packed up her books and laptop and headed from her classroom straight out of the building. No need to return to her office or even check out at the main office; Dr. Çelik had given her permission to leave. Despite that, she felt guilty as she walked by the classrooms where lessons were just beginning and offices where teachers were decompressing. No one was even looking at her, and yet she felt like she couldn't escape from under the glare of guilt and judgment fast enough. Maybe there was something there to unpack later; for now, she had hospitality responsibilities.

Outside the school, Eliza texted Crystal. "Where are you now? I got out of work early."

Crystal's response came quickly. "Just got to the grocery store. Want to join?"

"I'll be there in 10."

Ten minutes later, Eliza found Crystal staring at the produce with a confused look on her face. Crystal turned to face her as she approached, and Eliza could see her shopping basket was nearly empty.

"Eliza, how the heck are we supposed to feed someone we barely know? Does he have allergies, dietary restrictions, things he likes or doesn't like? I've never even seen Larry eat!"

"I'm in the same boat, Crys." Eliza said. "I mean, I suppose I have seen him eat, but I don't think department lunches count since I never really paid attention to what anyone was eating. It's awfully intimate to go from workplace acquaintances to roommates while skipping the friend or drinking buddy stage."

"No joke," said Crystal, "Not to mention that we are now two ladies who are about to have a semi strange man sleeping on our couch. So long, no pants movie parties!"

Eliza laughed. "I think we'll live without them; this is just temporary. And he's not *strange*, we just don't know each other that well. I'm sure if we put a little effort into making him feel at home, this transition into roomies will feel a lot more natural and maybe even fun." Eliza's words conveyed hope, even if her insides didn't match that emotion.

"All right, all right," admitted Crystal, "I'm willing to give it a try. Let's get all the best Turkish snacks then to welcome him to his new—but please God, *temporary*—home. Turkish delight, *ayran*, hazelnuts...what else?"

Half an hour later, they left the store with four full shopping bags between them. They had breakfast foods—eggs, white cheese, breads and assorted spreads, Turkish coffee, and olives, as well as all the classic snacks and beverages they could remember enjoying during their first few weeks in Turkey. *Ayran* (a refreshing and salty yogurt drink) and *şalgam suyu* (hot purple carrot juice) were both a little interesting, but they had grown to enjoy them to varying degrees. Of course, they had a variety of

Turkish delight flavors, as well as *helva*, real Turkish ice cream, and even a frozen *künefe* to prepare at home. Maybe trying to recreate the sweet and cheesy dish—that was so unlike anything either of them had ever tasted—in an at-home instant version was ambitious, but they couldn't help it. The shopping had gotten them excited to try some new and different things, bound and determined to make Larry's first day here a treat from start to finish through every single morsel they served him.

Eliza and Crystal returned home to unpack their groceries and help create an environment for their guest to feel comfortable in. They each moved their belongings from the living room into their respective bedrooms, Crystal taking the laptop they usually watched Netflix around together into her room and placing it on her nightstand, while Eliza took a stack of books and put it next to her bed. They moved the couch to the far side of the living room, turning it to create a bit of a barrier between the dining table and the space where Larry would be sleeping.

In celebration of their last evening as just the two of them, the friends opted to go out for dinner and then settle in for a movie and some ice cream. Locking the front door behind her, Eliza linked her arm through Crystal's as they made their way to the *tantuni* restaurant downtown. "I'm glad you're here, Crystal," she said, "And I don't think I tell you that often enough."

Crystal smiled. "I know you're glad, and I am too. Don't worry about it. And I promise to help try to keep you sane during this visit with Larry. If there's anything I can do to help and I don't notice it right away, feel free to stomp on my foot or clue me in some other way."

Eliza laughed. "I promise I won't stomp on your foot, but I definitely will take you up on everything else you just said. We're in this together, after all."

Dinner was delicious—*tantuni* was one of the first Turkish foods Eliza had been truly enchanted by. When Eliza had first seen the chicken wrap, she hadn't expected anything special. It looked like any other dish made of thin bread wrapped around meat and a select few vegetables. But she had been in for a surprise. The combination of flavors, the juiciness of the chicken, the peppery arugula and sour lemon, the heat and flavor that permeated the cooking oil and dripped out of the wrap onto her face—wow. It was perfect, especially when enjoyed between sips of tangy *ayran*.

The friends ordered two chicken *tantuni* wraps each, as well as two bottles of *ayran*, and while they waited for their food to arrive, they reminisced about the time they had spent together in Turkey so far. "Are you glad you accepted this job?" Crystal asked Eliza.

"I really am," Eliza responded. "It's been a lot of work, of course, but I feel like I'm up to it, and I've really enjoyed the challenge so far. I hope the university would say the same about me, and I really deeply hope that by the time my contract ends I will have helped make this a great place to learn, to work and teach...we'll see what we can all create when we put our heads together."

"That's great," Crystal smiled. "I'm proud of what I've seen you doing here, and I'm so honored to have a front-row seat as your best friend."

Eliza noted the tightness in Crystal's expression. "Is there a 'but' coming? How has your work been going lately?"

Crystal let out a sad laugh. "That's always the thing, isn't it? I'm glad to be here with you, and of course I wouldn't trade this experience for anything. I just think I'm heading towards burnout with the work I'm doing. I've been teaching so many one-on-one lessons back-to-back-to-back...Some days it feels like a robot or even a recording could do the same job I do, if not better. A video wouldn't get impatient with the students when it has to explain itself over and over again."

"I had no idea." Eliza shook her head. "I thought you loved the one-on-one teaching."

"I do!" Crystal exclaimed. "Honestly, I think it's a better fit for me than being in the classroom all day like you are. But it still doesn't mean that I want to—or that it's even possible to—keep doing it day after day, teaching the same lessons I taught a year ago, confronting the same challenges with student comprehension that I've seen since the beginning."

"Is it just about the material?" Eliza asked, "Or is it something deeper?"

"Hmm, there's a question for you." Crystal looked thoughtful. "I think maybe if I had more freedom with the curriculum...if I could make changes where I see them being needed, or if I could create something entirely new and maybe more interesting to the students, I might find a second wind in the English tutoring career world. I never thought about it like that."

"Well, it's definitely worth exploring." Eliza confirmed. "With all the skills and experience you have, maybe you *could* even create video content. If you could explain things so well in one go that students could watch it over and over again...why not start your own English language learning YouTube channel?"

Crystal's eyes widened. "That sounds like fun...like a challenge...and like a *lot* of work. I suppose that could be something to do on the side—but I don't think I should quit my day job to pursue it just yet. No, I've got at least a few more months of this one-on-one teaching in me. I promise I won't work myself into a burnout on your watch, and maybe I'll even take off a day or two just to keep my mental health where it needs to be." Crystal smiled at Eliza. "Thanks for listening, and thanks for the perspective. That's enough of that kind of talk, though. Now let's come up with some ways to encourage Larry to keep his visit nice and short!"

Crystal's wicked smile made Eliza laugh. "No practical jokes, please. We'll make that happen with sheer reason and logic. I have no doubt he'll be on his way back to Dr. Bennett by the end of the week." She hoped those weren't famous last words.

Wednesday morning, Eliza was once again making her way to the airport to pick up one of her fellow Americans. She hadn't been to the airport since the day Crystal arrived, and she was surprised at how much more confident she felt this time around. She made her way to the international arrivals, and she found a place outside the exit beyond customs where she could stand with an eye on the door, visible to Larry on his way out of the building. This time, Eliza wouldn't bury her nose in a book—Larry was likely to be more disoriented and out of his element than Crystal had been, and as much as she resented him being there at all, Eliza didn't want him to feel unwelcome.

Eliza checked the arrivals screen and noted that Larry's connecting flight from Frankfurt had landed a few minutes early and was taxiing to the gate. *Here goes nothing*, she thought. Twenty minutes later, a steady stream of passengers were making their way out of the terminal, and Eliza's eyes scanned the tags on their rolling suitcases, spotting the FRA airport code on one. So these were Larry's fellow travelers, and he'd be here any minute now.

"Yoo hoo!" A voice cut through the noise of the arrivals gate. "Eliza! Over here!" Larry's blond curls were bouncing as he jogged towards her, a rolling suitcase in each hand. The suitcases bumped into the people he was passing, and Larry didn't seem to even notice the speed bumps. Eliza rushed forward to help him—and to take at least one suitcase from him, because the glares that were being shot in his direction suggested his fellow passengers might be about to stage a revolt against his loud, larger-than-life presence.

Eliza smiled and pulled Larry in for a quick hug. "Hi Larry, how was your flight? Welcome to Turkey!"

"Oh my God, it was awful!" he exclaimed. "I was trying to watch a movie on my phone, you know, so I wouldn't get bored, but then someone complained, I guess, and the flight attendant made me turn it off. Can you believe that?"

"Um...no, not really..." Eliza started. "I've never heard of them telling you what you can and can't do on your own personal phone." She hoped Larry hadn't been watching a raunchy scene while a family sat next to him in horror, but she couldn't really be sure...

"No, it wasn't anything like that," Larry assured. "Apparently headphones are non-negotiable. I tried to tell her that I can't wear them because of my delicate ear canals, but she was heartless. I had to sit there for hours with no entertainment at all. And then the food—ugh! I hope that wasn't an accurate introduction to Turkish food because, if so, I guess I'll be really hungry while I'm here."

Eliza tried to find something nice to say because she couldn't very well lapse into the "don't say anything at all," approach within a minute of her guest's arrival. "Did you get to see the sea out the window, though? When I first flew into Antalya, that first glimpse of the water took my breath away."

"Barely," Larry grumbled. "I was looking at it, and then the German guy in the seat next to me leaned over too and so I got annoyed and put the shade down. If he wanted a window seat, he should have paid for it."

"Larry," Eliza admonished. "A little generosity never hurt anyone. It's not as if you paid for your window seat—or that a window seat even costs more than a middle seat! It's all a matter of how early you register your prefer-ence—"

"I know, Eliza," Larry blushed. "I was just saying. Any-way, it's good to see you."

"I'm glad you're here," Eliza smiled. "Let's head back to my apartment now. You remember Crystal, right? Did Dr. Bennett tell you that we're roommates here, too?"

"He did!" Larry brightened. "I wish I had a friend like that. The two of you really stick with each other through everything, don't you? Maybe I can pick up some tips about how to keep a friend just by osmosis."

Was Larry alone in the world? Was his bristly exterior a layer of protection to keep people from hurting him? Or was he just trying too hard to get Eliza to like him because he felt like he didn't have a single good friend? Time would tell, Eliza supposed. Maybe this time in Antalya would do him some good, if she and Crystal could stay patient with him and be open to providing the help and guidance he needed.

Fifteen

Crystal was waiting for Eliza and Larry at home with a warm grin on her face. "I'm glad you're here, Larry," she smiled, patting him on the back. "You'll be sleeping on the sofa in the living room, so let's put your things over here. We didn't have a lot of warning about your visit, so I apologize that we weren't able to make the setup a little more comfortable for you."

"It'll be fine, I think," said Larry. "If the couch is too uncomfortable, we can go buy something different, right?"

Eliza and Crystal exchanged raised brows and looks that communicated many words. They weren't expecting their guest to stay long enough to *need* an improved sleeping situation, but it seemed like Larry might have different expectations.

"Um, Larry, if you don't mind me asking," began Eliza, "Exactly how long are you planning on being in Antalya?"

"I don't know, really," Larry said matter-of-factly. "Dr. Bennett booked me an open-ended flight, so it's really up to him how long I stay. I'm supposed to check in with him every day, and when he's satisfied with what we've accomplished here, then I guess he'll let me come back."

"*Let* you come back?" Crystal asked. "Goodness, Larry, it sounds like you've been banished here! Are you at least happy to be here, or is this like a chore Dr. B. has assigned you to do?"

"I guess I'm happy about it," Larry said, flopping down on the couch. "I've never been to the Middle East before, and I don't think any of my friends have either. So I'm pretty excited to be able to make them all jealous when I get back."

Eliza jumped in before Crystal's rolled eyes could speak for themselves. "Travel is great, isn't it? It opens us up to new ways of thinking, shows us how connected we all are. There's so much to learn from the people and cultures that we encounter. And Turkey is absolutely amazing; you're going to love it."

"That's right," Crystal agreed. "Making friends jealous is just a bonus perk. You get to experience so much history and beauty just by being here. I bet you'll have a great time. Now, what about going out for some food?"

"I'm starving!" Larry exclaimed. "The food on the plane was terrible—"

Not this again, thought Eliza.

"—so if we could find something remotely edible, I'd really prefer that. Are there fast-food restaurants here?"

"Larry, you're in Turkey. Don't you think you should eat Turkish food?" Crystal asked.

"Not if it's anything like the crap we ate on the plane. I asked for ketchup and they wouldn't give it to me." Larry pouted.

"There's a Burger King and a Popeye's Chicken at the mall," began Eliza, "But I agree with Crystal. We need to give you a proper introduction to Turkish cuisine. I don't think airlines ever do their country's food justice. Though actually, I was really happy with all the food on Turkish Airlines..."

"Maybe you just aren't as picky as me," suggested Larry. "I know what I like. What can I say?"

After a bit of hemming and hawing from Eliza and Crystal, they decided to take Larry to Kaleiçi for a drink on the coast before venturing to one of the many *kebap* and *dürüm* restaurants. *Perhaps after a beer or two, Larry will be a little more open-minded about trying new things*, Eliza thought with chagrin.

The bar they went to had the best view in the city. From their table they could look across nearly the entire beach-front in Antalya, and the sea was beautiful and calm that evening. Eliza never tired of the view, but she took the seat with her back facing it so that Larry could have the prime spot.

"Ugh, why are there all these stray cats here?" Larry yelped after a friendly orange tabby brushed up against his legs. "Why don't they do something about it? Go! Shoo! Get out of here, cat!"

A few heads had turned in their direction, and Eliza resisted the urge to shush Larry. Maybe he was afraid of cats...or allergic. There were plenty of reasons to react the way he had. No need for her to start correcting his behavior on his first night in the new city.

"So Larry, what would you like to drink?" Crystal asked as she opened her menu and handed one to him. "Efes is what most people drink here...I like the green one, the 'special series,' it's called."

"I guess they don't have craft beer, do they?" Larry asked. "Or an IPA, at least?"

Eliza rolled her eyes behind her menu. "No Larry, what's on the menu is what you have to work with. I'd recommend Efes too...I always like to try the local food and drinks when I go to a new place, rather than trying to find the things I prefer from back home. You might like it!"

When the waiter came to their table, Eliza used her basic Turkish skills to order for herself and Larry, while Crystal used hers to order some snacks for the table. Before the waiter could leave, Larry piped up. "Excuse me, do you have Wi-Fi here? What is the password?"

The waiter looked back with uncomprehending eyes.

Larry tried again, louder and slower. "WI-FI? PASS WORD? FOR ME?"

Eliza saw the color rise in Crystal's cheeks and knew her face looked the same. Crystal swooped in and asked the waiter to excuse their friend and if there was Wi-Fi available at the bar. When the waiter shared the password with her, she took Larry's phone from his outstretched hand and entered the password into it, not meeting his eyes. Eliza nudged Crystal's foot under the table, raising her eyebrows when her friend made eye contact with her. Crystal shook her head and looked away.

"So Larry..." Eliza began.

"Hang on a sec," Larry held up a finger, not looking up from his phone or ceasing his scrolling. "I've been offline for like a day. Can you believe they didn't have internet on the flight?"

Eliza turned to Crystal. "Wow, how times change. Do you remember that trip we took to Mexico with your mom in middle school? Of course, we didn't have smart phones at all, but we didn't even have a way to make international calls without paying through the nose. I think the hotel let your mom use their computer to let my parents know we made it, but that was it."

Crystal nodded, directing her eyes meaningfully at Larry. "Yeah, I remember that. I think it was good for us, honestly. The constant need to be connected and informed at all times to everything and everyone...it just causes stress. I think we could all do with the occasional day or week off of the internet."

"Not me!" Larry chimed in. "I can't and won't go without it. Too many people expect to see my Instagram updates and my tweets have been doing really well lately. I can't take too much time off or the algorithm will punish me. I've worked hard to get my reach where it is, and I can't sacrifice that."

"Gee, Larry," began Crystal, "Do you ever wonder if it's really worth it, though? That seems like a lot of effort to put into something that doesn't give you anything in return. Apart from a dopamine hit every time you get a few likes or a new follower, I guess. What would happen if you stopped posting?"

Larry shuddered, finally looking up from his phone. "I can't bear to think about it, so please don't make me. But I'll at least put my phone down for the meal, okay? I'm sorry. I don't mean to be rude."

Larry hung his head, and Eliza felt a twinge of compassion for him. "It's alright, Larry. Have you thought at all about what you'd like to eat for dinner?"

"What are my options?" Larry asked as the waiter appeared at his elbow with a tray of drinks. The waiter began setting down their beers and snacks, and Larry looked at the frosty mug in front of him with a grimace. "Excuse me? I ordered a bottle, not a draft beer."

"Larry, no, that's what we ordered," Eliza said. *What I ordered*, she thought, *because you didn't say a peep*. "It's fine," she told the waiter, thanking him with a nod and a friendly smile.

Larry wiped his hand down the outside of his mug and winced. "I just don't know if it's safe for me to drink this. What if they washed the mug with tap water and I get sick from it? I know it isn't the same as drinking the water or using ice, but I still have to be careful."

"Larry, Turkey isn't generally considered a country where you need to be careful not to drink the water—" Crystal began.

"Maybe *you* don't need to be careful," Larry jumped in, "but I definitely do. The last time I traveled to a third world country, I got so sick just from a sip of lemonade that had a few ice cubes in it."

"Well, there are a few things wrong with that," Eliza jumped in, off the look on Crystal's face. "But let's just start with not using the phrase 'third world country' in the first place, okay? There aren't really any perfect ways to describe the group of countries that you're talking about, but 'global south' or 'economically developing' are better descriptors than 'third world' any day. It's also not an appropriate label for Turkey at all..."

"Good to know," Larry said, raising his beer to his lips. "So are you also saying I can drink this without worrying I'll be hovering over the toilet later, wishing I hadn't?"

"Yes Larry, that is what I'm saying," Eliza responded through tight lips. She raised her beer to Larry and Crystal. "Here's to your first night in Turkey, the start of a great visit. Cheers!" They clinked their glasses together, and each took a long swallow.

"Yuck!" Larry exclaimed, wiping his mouth. "I knew it wouldn't be an IPA, but I didn't expect something that terrible. I may as well have ordered a Bud Light." He pushed his beer to the center of the table, oblivious to the eyes that his outburst had attracted to their table.

"Sorry you don't like it, Larry," said Eliza. She pushed the plate of bar snacks towards him, ignoring his wrinkled nose at the assortment of fried foods. "At least have something to eat."

After Eliza and Crystal had drained their mugs and Larry had finished offending the staff and patrons of Castle Bar, the three of them set off in search of a *kebap* that would meet Larry's dietary specifications. He had made his feelings about restaurant ambience and cleanliness, staff friendliness, and spice requirements abundantly clear. The two women had no doubt he would find fault with whatever restaurant they chose, but they could at least look for a place where they could sit far enough away from other people that Larry's complaints might not reach their ears.

As they made their way along İstiklal Street, Eliza heard someone call, "Eliza...is that you?" and turned to face none other than Cem, who had been walking in the same direction as them and jogged to catch up.

"Cem, hello!" Eliza pulled him in for a quick hug before Crystal did the same. Cem shook Larry's hand and welcomed him to Turkey, and for the first time in an hour, Larry was quiet, listening. Huh. Maybe all he had needed all along was a *man* to decide listening to others was worthwhile. Eliza tried not to think about that too much, or she knew the righteous feminist indignation bubbling up inside her would spill over and burst out all over Larry.

"We've been showing Larry around Antalya a bit; he just arrived today," Eliza explained. "We're looking for a restaurant now, taking him out for *İskender kebap*. Would you like to join us? And do you have a restaurant you can recommend?"

"I'd love to join!" Cem's eyes twinkled at Eliza. "And I know just the place. Come with me!"

Cem turned their group around and led them back in the direction they had just come from. Eliza hoped they wouldn't be heading right back to Castle Bar, despite a sneaking suspicion that Larry would be able to find much less fault with it now that Cem was leading the way.

She wouldn't find out, though, because before they could reach Castle Bar, Cem led them down another street, following a few turns in the road before they reached a small *kebap* restaurant. The four of them took a seat in the outdoor section, Cem and Eliza on one side of the table opposite Crystal and Larry.

While Crystal explained the menu to Larry, Cem leaned over and spoke in Eliza's ear. "I'm glad to see you again. I'd love to continue the conversation we started back in Kaş."

Eliza pulled back. Was he referring to the flirtation or to the bomb about Deniz that he had been about to drop? She eyed him warily and, finding no clue to suggest an answer to that question, asked him, "Which conversation was that, exactly?"

"I just can't bear the thought that you're spending so much time with Deniz without knowing who he really is. I don't want you to get hurt." The concern in Cem's eyes cut through Eliza's hesitation.

"Oh," she said. "Yes, I suppose knowing who I'm up against is important, isn't it? What happened between the two of you?"

"Can we talk after dinner? It's a long story," Cem explained. "And I don't want to be rude to Larry and Crystal. I can walk you home and maybe then we can sit and have a drink and talk."

"I'd like that," Eliza smiled. She felt the faintest of butterflies fluttering around her belly. It *had* been a long time since she had a heart-to-heart conversation with a handsome man who was interested in looking out for her safety.

She shifted her attention back to the dining table, in time to notice an epic eye roll crossing Crystal's face. Eliza started in shock, then asked her friend, "Is everything all right, Crystal?"

Crystal was no longer making any effort to camouflage her frustration with Larry. "I don't know what to do with this one and his eating habits. If I hear, 'that's not how we do it back home' one more time, I'm not responsible for what I do next."

"Sorry," Larry said, without a hint of apology in his expression or demeanor. "I don't think it's a bad thing to know what you like. And maybe people here would benefit from learning how we do things back home!"

"Larry!" Crystal cried. "America isn't the gold standard! We haven't figured out the *exact right way* to do every single thing, and you're going to make yourself miserable if you keep expecting others to live up to your desires. Would you at least consider trying to learn from others, rather than judging them as soon as you meet them?"

"What do you think, Larry?" Cem chimed in. "Turkey has some very old traditions, and some of the food we prepare has been passed down for centuries. I promise to only introduce you to the best of the best. Is it a deal?"

Larry zeroed in on Cem, ignoring the two women at the table. "I trust you, Cem. I don't know about Lizzy or Crystal, but I don't think they'll be happy with me no matter what I do. What do you recommend eating at this restaurant, anyway?"

Cem winked at Eliza. "Let's go classic for your first meal in Turkey. *İskender kebap* sound good to everyone? Now, Larry," he said, in response to Larry's open mouth, "You said you'd trust me, right? So let's put aside the concerns about ingredients and spices and whatever else you're thinking of and let the chef do his thing."

"Fine," Larry grumbled. "But if this doesn't go well, I retain my right to be as particular as I want to be."

The dinner was uneventful, thank God. When their plates of thinly sliced meat, tomato sauce, bread, and yogurt arrived, everyone tucked in. Eliza didn't eat *İskender* often, but she was feeling especially hungry and ate with relish. Conversation was minimal as they all dug in to the food in front of them, and even Larry seemed to be satisfied.

Until the waiter came to clear the table. "Excuse me," he piped up. "Have you ever tried a different sauce on that dish? The tomato was fine, but don't you have any other options?"

Eliza stared at him, her mouth wide open.

"What?" he exclaimed. "I'm just trying to help! Their menu isn't exactly offering a wide range of different dishes. I can't imagine a restaurant with so few options opening up back home. They'd go out of business before they even started!"

Crystal had been chatting with the waiter while this conversation unfolded between Eliza and Larry. She stacked all of their plates while reassuring him that Larry's exclamations were unimportant and not at all a reflection on the food, which had been *delicious*, she told him. Once he was gone, she turned back to Larry.

"What the hell, dude?" All pretense of politeness was gone from Crystal's voice. "Be more polite, and for the love of God, *keep your voice down*!" Larry hadn't seemed to notice that once again he was attracting a bit of an audience, and Eliza felt embarrassed to be sitting next to him.

Eliza had had enough. "Let's go home. We can talk about this there." They stood up, scraping their chairs on the floor as they stepped back from the table. Eliza walked ahead of the group, to the front of the restaurant, where the manager met her at the register. She thanked him and paid for their food, sending compliments to the chef for the delicious meal they had eaten. As they continued on their way, she couldn't help but notice that both Crystal and Cem thanked her for the meal, while Larry seemed blissfully unaware as he once again buried his nose in whatever was so damn fascinating on his cell phone.

Outside the apartment, Eliza touched Cem's arm. "Let's just sit out here and talk," she said. "If we go inside and excuse ourselves onto the balcony, there's no guarantee Larry won't join us. Clearly he can't take a hint."

"That's a good idea, Eliza," Cem smiled. "Larry, Crystal, it was nice to see you both. Have a wonderful evening. If you don't mind, I will steal Miss Eliza from you now for a bit. See you later."

Crystal waved and steered Larry towards the door, glancing back over her shoulder to wiggle her eyebrows at Eliza. Eliza laughed and shook her head. She'd catch her friend up later, but this wasn't a date...was it? It was an exchange of information, nothing more.

"So, Cem," Eliza began, sitting down on a bench outside the building and patting the seat next to herself. "It's time for the much anticipated story of you and Deniz. How do you two know each other again?"

"Well, we met at university, actually," Cem said as he sat. "We were both in the foreign language teaching department. I started one year after him, but we had the same course advisor."

"I had no idea!" Eliza was surprised. "But you're not teaching now…what happened?"

"Our advisor, Dr. Yılmaz, was the best. An excellent teacher, and someone who was so invested in her students, even in making sure they were able to find good jobs outside of school. That first year, it was clear that my dreams of finding a good job, doing the work I love…those dreams were in sight, for the first time in my life. You see, I was the first person in my family to go to university. And I wasn't sure that would ever happen. We aren't exactly an academic family. My parents did everything to help me succeed, but I never knew if it would be enough—if *I* would be enough. My scores…" He trailed off.

"What happened then?" Eliza asked.

"I think Deniz was jealous of the time I spent with Dr. Yılmaz, to be honest. Deniz had been the star student before I showed up, and I think Dr. Yılmaz had a soft spot for me. She saw herself in me, perhaps, or at least in my story. But the more time and effort she spent on me, the less she had for Deniz. I think that's why he did it, anyway."

"Why *who* did what?"

"Why Deniz sabotaged my future."

Eliza's mouth dropped in shock. "What? How? How could he?"

Cem cradled his head, elbows balanced on his knees. "He didn't like the attention I was getting, I guess. I was upstaging him, stealing his status as Dr. Yılmaz's golden child. One day, I was in Dr. Yılmaz's office, talking about my upcoming exams and a research project I was working on. Deniz barged in, and he didn't look happy to see me there at all, especially after Dr. Yılmaz asked him to leave. Anyway, the next day I found out that I was being kicked out of the program, out of the dorm. I had 24 hours to pack up my things and leave town. And I never *could* quite come back after that."

Cem was quiet as Eliza stared at him, slack jawed. "You mean he single-handedly ended your university career? What? How? How could he do that? I mean, *literally*, how could he do that? How did he have the *power* to do that? Not how did he have the heart to do it?"

"I never found that out," Cem said. "Dr. Yılmaz told me my position in the class was canceled and that she was very sorry, but she didn't tell me much more than that. She would barely even speak to me. I went back home. Helped my parents on the farm. Years later, I decided to try again to work in the teaching profession, like I'd always wanted. I moved to Antalya when I found a job that would let me use my English skills, at least."

"So you aren't teaching, are you?" Eliza asked. "I hope you know you can share with me what you're doing here, and that I would never, ever judge you. Especially knowing the opportunities that were taken away from you." She put her hand on his forearm, rubbing her thumb back and forth over his skin.

"Thank you, Eliza, I know." Cem said, his head finally lifting so his eyes could meet hers. "I suppose in a way I am still in the education field; it's just educating tourists about Turkey rather than teaching English to students who want to learn it."

"You're a tour guide?" Eliza asked.

"I am," Cem said. "A lot of it is really sales work...trying to attract in the tourists who are wandering around Kaleiçi, convince them that our company has the best tours. I spend a lot of time doing that, but when I get to show some Germans or Americans around and tell them about the history of the city, learn about their cultures and speak English with them...well, then it feels like it's all worth it somehow."

Eliza and Cem smiled at each other. "Thanks for telling me, Cem," Eliza said. "I'm sorry this happened to you. Of course I don't think less of you for it, though I hope you don't mind me offering that if there is ever anything I can do to help you get back into your intended field of work...I will be more than happy to do it."

Cem's eyes brightened. "Thank you, Eliza. You are more generous than I could have ever expected. It would be a dream to work at the Mediterranean School of Languages, even as an assistant or a secretary. I hope one day that could be a possibility for me again."

Eliza leaned her head onto Cem's shoulder. "I hear you, and I hope I can help." She sat back up, eyes once again on his. "I'm so glad we ran into each other tonight."

"Me too," he smiled. Did her eyes deceive her, or had his eyes dropped to her mouth? But now wasn't the time to make any romantic moves, not after a confession like that. Cem needed a friend, not a fling. But—

Eliza's thoughts halted as she felt Cem's lips brush lightly against her own. The soft pressure between them lasted only a second, and then it was gone. Her eyes fluttered open as he pulled away and got to his feet. He extended his hand and pulled her up to standing next to him. "Have a good night, Eliza. I'll see you around." He walked away, leaving her standing alone, watching his silhouette fade into the blackness between the streetlights. What the hell?

Sixteen

Eliza entered her apartment to find Crystal awaiting her arrival. "Well? What the hell was all that about?" her friend demanded.

Eliza dragged Crystal with her into her own bedroom, away from Larry who, despite his current state hunched once again over his phone, she had decided *never* to assume wasn't eavesdropping. Eliza closed the door behind her and turned to face Crystal, who met her with palms and eyebrows both sky high. "Tell me already!" Crystal exclaimed.

"Well, he told me the whole story with Deniz, and I'll catch you up on all of that..." she trailed off.

"...and?" Crystal asked. "What else? There's more, I know it."

"...and he kissed me." Eliza said.

"He what?" Crystal shouted. "Why didn't you lead with that? Amazing! It's about time you had your first hot hookup with a Turkish man. When are you seeing him again?"

"First of all, that in no way qualifies as a hot hookup. It lasted for maybe a second, and I wasn't even sure what was happening. I'm still wondering if maybe I imagined it." Eliza said. "And I have no idea when I'm seeing him. I gave him my phone number but I didn't get his, so the ball is entirely in his court at this point."

"I like it," said Crystal. "There's no opportunity for you to stress over whether you should text him or wait. No reason for you to think about next steps at all! Now we wait and see if he texts, if he calls...I'm happy for you! This is good for you."

"I'm glad you think so," said Eliza, "and that you seem so sure about it. I *think* I'm happy that happened tonight? I really don't know, though. It was so unexpected, and especially after hearing that whole story about Deniz, everything was just so surreal. I think I'll wake up in the morning convinced it was all a dream."

"Yeah, so what's the deal with Deniz, anyway?" Crystal asked. "Is he a total asshole, or are there two sides to the story?"

"Total asshole." Eliza shook her head. "Deniz really screwed Cem over...he got him kicked out of their program at university. Cem was never able to complete his degree, and he's working as a tour guide now when he always wanted to be an English teacher. Actually, we were talking about whether I could help him get a job at Med School when he kissed me."

Crystal grimaced. "Two things. One, yes, Deniz is the jerk in this situation, no two ways about it. I don't understand how he could even have that kind of power over another student. But two, did he really kiss you because you might get him a job? That's awkward."

"Awkward sounds about right," Eliza said. "That's why it was so unexpected. I made the comment about maybe it being possible for him to start as an assistant teacher or a secretary, in like an offhand way, but he took it really seriously. And then the kiss made me feel like I'd better follow up on it right away. I hope he didn't mean it that way. I really do like him, I think..."

"Hmm," Crystal paused, "Why don't you give it some time before you put your reputation on the line by suggesting Dr. Çelik hires him? Spend some more time together, have some fun...if it all feels right after at least a month, then go ahead and make the recommendation."

"Is a month the magic amount of time?" Eliza chuckled. "Where do you come up with these things?"

Crystal looked at her like she was a fool. "In a month, you'll have gone through your entire hormone cycle. I'm not sure where you are right now, but if you still feel like gambling your reputation on him when you aren't ovulating, then you know it's real."

Eliza laughed louder now. "I'm glad I have you, Crystal. You can always bring a perspective that I wouldn't think of on my own. I don't underestimate the wisdom of the hormone cycle, but without you here to remind me, it would never cross my mind."

Crystal hugged her. "You're welcome. I'm here to serve." She winked. "Now, shall we go entertain our visitor a bit? Or do you think he's even noticed we're gone?"

·❤·❤·❤·❤·❤·

Eliza didn't have to wait long to see what would happen next with Cem. The next morning, she was waiting to catch the shuttle when his first text came.

"Hi Eliza, it's Cem. Thanks for listening to me last night. Are you free after work today?"

Eliza smiled to herself and saved his phone number as a new contact in her phone before texting back. It was nice that he hadn't mentioned the potential job in his first text, and hanging out again *was* the task Crystal had given her to do.

"Hi Cem! Nice to hear from you. What do you have in mind today?"

His response was immediate. It was *also* nice that he wasn't playing the "wait a certain amount of time to text back" game. "I guess that means you are free. Let's go to the beach? Swim and then a beer?"

"That sounds perfect. Where should I meet you?"

"I can pick you up at Med School. What time do you finish?"

Eliza felt her stomach drop. She wasn't ready for him to come in to the university, to start making connections with her colleagues. She texted again. "I'm already on my way to school, so I'll need to go home to change before we go out tonight. Pick me up at my apartment at 6?"

"It's a deal. See you then!"

Eliza was smiling to herself as the shuttle pulled up. She plopped into the front seat next to Jack and started to fill him in on all that had happened with Cem last night.

"Oh boy, do I have some juicy news for you, Jack! Guess who kissed me last night?" She twinkled.

"Huh? Sorry...what did you say?" Jack looked up, and Eliza noticed the faraway look in his eyes and the dark circles under them.

"Jack, are you okay?" She asked. "I don't want to be one of those jerks who says 'you look tired' when you aren't, but...are you sick? Exhausted?"

Jack sighed. "Heartsick, I think. I'll be fine...what were you saying? Someone kissed someone?"

Eliza couldn't believe she was hearing the disinterested tone Jack used to ask his second question. Something was wrong with her friend, because normally he'd be the first to want to know any gossip, and now he was practically yawning while talking about kissing.

"That can wait." She said. "What is going on with you? What happened?"

"It's probably nothing. Maybe I'm just being dramatic. I just haven't heard anything from Barış since we got back from Kaş. I thought he was just busy with work, but I texted him yesterday and he ignored it all day. When I woke up this morning, he had written back and basically cut ties with me."

"He did what?" Eliza exclaimed. "What did he say? Is it possible it was a misunderstanding?"

"It's not a misunderstanding." Jack hung his head. "I had sent a message about going out on Friday evening, and his reply this morning said he's not going to be able to meet up for the foreseeable future. He apologized for it, but his tone was cold. Not at all like his normal self. I don't know what I did, Eliza, but I hate this."

Eliza pulled him in for a sideways hug in the bus seat. "Oh Jack, I'm so sorry! I can't imagine what you could have done, either. The two of you had been getting along so well and having so much fun together."

"Thanks, love," Jack gave a tiny smile. "I'll be fine, eventually. I just really liked him, and this really came out of nowhere."

"I just can't believe it," Eliza said. "It seems like there has to be a misunderstanding somewhere. A wire got crossed. I know! I'm going to have a small breakfast at the beach gathering on Sunday to introduce Larry to a few more people. Why don't I invite Barış to that and see if we can get to the bottom of it?"

"That sounds nice, Eliza," Jack said. "I'm not going to get my hopes up that he will come, but it would be a wonderful surprise if he did. And if he was happy to see me instead of avoiding me or freezing me out. Anyway...that's enough about me. What were you saying when you got on the bus?"

"Oh, right," Eliza said. "It seems kind of silly to be excited about it now, given the conversation we're having. I just had a rather unexpected evening last night, including a kiss!"

"Was it from Larry?" Jack wrinkled his nose. "I don't know him, but from everything you've told me, I can't imagine you'd be celebrating it if Mr. King Annoying planted a smooch on you."

Eliza laughed. "Oh my God, ew! Thankfully, no. It was *not* a kiss from Larry. It was from Cem...remember him? We met him in Kaş, but it turns out he works here, too."

"Oh yeah! Damn, good one, Eliza! He was hot." said Jack.

"Mmm hmm," Eliza agreed, "And he *still* is. And...I'm seeing him again today." She smiled.

"Look at you!" Jack cried. "It's about time, actually. Too much singleness isn't good for someone like you. You're too young and attractive to be spending every evening grading papers or eating ice cream with your roommate."

"It's a lot of work, though," Eliza said. "The last relationship I was in took up a lot of energy, especially when things went south. It's a lot easier to be just me. Just Eliza. Just Eliza is good at getting her projects done, staying on top of her responsibilities...What?" she cried in response to Jack's raised eyebrow. "I *do* know how to have fun, too...I just choose to do it in a way that doesn't require the constant attention to one other person's feelings."

"Sounds like you got burned in your last relationship," Jack observed. "What was his deal, anyway?"

Eliza sighed. "There were a lot of things going on there. We had fun together in the beginning, but he turned out to be more controlling and possessive than I could handle. After a few months of explaining myself, justifying my behavior, and even making some concessions where I was willing to, I realized it wasn't going to get any better. I miss having someone to come home to, someone to cuddle up with when things are hard...but I don't miss all the pain he caused me."

Jack leaned into Eliza and put his arm around her. "I'm glad you got out of it, then. You probably wouldn't even be here in Turkey if you were still with him, would you?"

There was no joy in Eliza's laugh. "No way. It's not like I miss Alec often, but it's always good to count my blessings. The things I wouldn't have if he were still in my life. And I can't imagine missing out on this experience. On getting to be friends with you."

"Same here, kid." Jack smiled, though it didn't quite reach his eyes.

"I'm here for you, Jack. Always," Eliza said. "And don't worry about figuring things out with Barış. I have a feeling it's all going to be resolved soon and we'll be having drinks on the beach Sunday morning."

"I hope you're right," Jack said. "I really do."

The first two classes of the day went as well as could be expected this late in the semester. Many of Eliza's students were feeling burned out on their studying schedule, even though the school's attendance policy—and the number of classes they had already missed this semester—required them to be at their desks during every single period until the exams were finished. The result of having every single student in the classroom, especially the ones who had been happy to skip classes on a whim earlier in the semester, was a marked drop in the overall level of participation, energy, and motivation. *Thank God for the students who were tuned in and engaged during every task we did today,* she thought. *Without them, I'd really be fumbling.*

Ahmad was one of those students, and Eliza didn't have to wonder why his motivation was so consistent and persistent. He had goals and a family that depended on him to achieve those goals. Eliza had been loosely supervising the group of students who were studying for their speaking exam, though they had soon shown themselves more than capable—and more determined and willing to study for long hours than she had ever expected. Her role as supervisor was entirely titular, put in place by the administration, and she often used their study sessions to grade her students' homework when she wasn't listening in on the answers the study group members were giving to their test prep questions.

One question that was included on the practice preparation list was, "Who has played the biggest role in influencing you—for positive or negative—in your life and/or studies?" The open-ended nature of this question and the many others on the list allowed the students to practice thinking of a compelling topic, preparing it for a mere 60 seconds, and then speaking about it in a rather off-the-cuff manner for two minutes. Questions like this one were Eliza's favorites to listen to. Students often talked about their parents or a teacher they had back home, but the ones who focused on who had the biggest negative influence on them were impossible not to pay attention to. They talked about politicians, military leaders...every answer was woven through with pain and struggle, like the cords in a piece of rope.

Today, Eliza offered a suggestion to the students for them to practice. The pain was compelling, but she knew it could easily turn into tragedy porn, with others listening and pitying and seeing the students in a two-dimensional way, devoid of anything but strife and struggle. "I know many of you have been advised by career counselors to lean into your struggle and 'milk it for all its worth,' and I know how uncomfortable that has made you. My reminder to you today—and the challenge I'm giving you to practice—is that you are bigger and more complex than your pain. It is a significant part of you, but it doesn't define you. The closer you can get to sharing your whole picture, the more you will be understood."

While the students were pairing themselves off to practice today's batch of questions, Eliza texted Barış.

"Hi Barış, I hope you've had a good week! I'm organizing a brunch on the beach on Sunday morning to welcome a colleague of mine to town. We're going to meet at 10 in Konyaaltı. I hope you can make it!"

Barış responded promptly. "Nice to hear from you, Eliza. I'm sorry to say I won't be able to come. I'm quite busy lately, so I don't think I'll be doing any hanging out for a while. I hope your friend has a nice time in Antalya."

The relative dearth of exclamation points in his message made Eliza's breath catch in her throat. She thought for a second before firing off another text.

"Sorry we'll miss you, Barış. If you don't mind me asking, is everything okay? I hope we'll get to hang out again someday!"

Eliza was saddened but unsurprised to see her last text go unanswered. Something was going on with him, and unfortunately, it seemed she wasn't going to be the one to get to the bottom of it. She checked the time and gathered up the materials she needed to take home with her. The last shuttle would leave in ten minutes, and she would rather wait on the bus than risk missing it.

Sitting in the front seat of the bus, engrossed in the email she was reading on her phone, Eliza didn't notice Jack getting on the bus at first. She had hoped he might have been on the earlier shuttle and that she wouldn't have to confirm his fears about Barış this soon after his text had delivered its shocking bluntness to her.

"Hi, Jack," she smiled with tight lips, knowing her expression was giving away her discomfort.

"Let me guess," he said, sitting down next to her, "You heard back from Barış and he isn't coming on Sunday. Or ever again. And he hates me."

"It's not *all* of those things, Jack..." she said. "But no, he isn't coming on Sunday. And he sounded cagey about when I'd actually see him again. Did something happen between you two?"

Jack sighed. "I've been asking myself that same question so many times this week, and I come up empty every time. We've had fun together, in so many ways. Our conversations are good, the attraction and chemistry is definitely there, we laugh a lot when we're together...hell, we even have the same academic interests! I mean, how common can that be?"

"I don't think it's common at all," Eliza agreed. "You two really do seem like a match made in heaven on all sorts of levels. Maybe it's really something about him...work stress or parental expectations...mental health? I mean, those are things that affect all of us and aren't always obvious from the outside. Try not to take it personally, and try not to give up on him just because you're feeling hurt and scorned. I know he isn't making it easy to be there for him, but maybe there's still some way you can do that."

"You may be right," Jack said, "And I don't want to add to his stress. I'll respect the space he's asking for, even though it makes me sad to do it. Making my problems his problems right now would only add to the anxiety and stress on his plate. Anyway. Thank you for being a friend...and please keep up the good work. I'm going to need some help filling up my time with fun and distraction so I'm not thinking about Barış 24 hours a day."

"You've got it," Eliza smiled, "And speaking of that, what are you doing tonight? I've got plans with Cem after work—don't look at me like that!—but we could meet up for a drink later. How about it? You, me, Crystal, and Mr. King Annoying?"

Jack smiled back at her. "It's a date!"

Seventeen

*M**aybe my uneventful weekends are over,* thought Eliza on the shuttle bus to the university Monday morning, *which is both a welcome break from monotony and overwork...and also utterly exhausting.* She had spent the previous 48 hours showing Larry around the city, her favorite restaurants, and the hiking trails and ruins within an easy bus ride. She had also spent that same number of hours reminding him to be quieter than he was naturally inclined to be, polite to the Turks who were showing him hospitality, and overall less unbearable. Her success had been minimal—in total, there had been approximately ten hours this weekend during which she hadn't wanted to slap or maim him, and he had been asleep during eight of them.

Seated at her desk for the first planning period of the day, Eliza picked up a compact mirror and dabbed concealer under her eyes to camouflage the exhaustion she felt deep in her bones. She needed another vacation again already...the trip to Kaş felt like it had happened a lifetime ago. A knock on the door startled her from her thoughts and from the makeup she was so diligently applying.

"Ms. Britt? May I come in?" Dr. Çelik's voice came through the door.

Well, that was unexpected. "Yes, please do!" Eliza cried, stuffing her concealer and mirror into the top drawer of her desk.

Dr. Çelik entered and sat in the seat across from Eliza's desk. "I know you're preparing for the classes ahead this week, so I won't waste your time. I need your help with a new project, partnering with Antalya Technical Institute's English department."

"Oh?" Eliza asked. "What's the project? I haven't heard anything about a partnership."

"I think it's something that'll be right up your alley, though that is an absolutely terrible expression," Dr. Çelik said. "We are combining forces to create an adult education program for the community in Antalya. The goal is to have English language programs available for those who never had the opportunity in school—whether they want to learn it because they work in tourism or because they are refugees hoping to have more professional or immigration opportunities doesn't really matter to us. Another goal of the program is to establish goodwill in the community, to develop the relationship between our two universities and between the academic community and the larger population of Antalya."

"Wow, this sounds fabulous," Eliza said. "I wouldn't have even considered creating something like this, but I would absolutely love to be a part of it. What role do you envision me playing in it?"

"I'd like you to be the representative of Med School in terms of public relations. I'm handling the administrative aspects myself, and I'll begin talking to the teachers who will be teaching the classes soon. But it's important to have public faces for the program, so we'll have you and your counterpart at Antalya Technical Institute do that. The two of you will host gatherings for prospective students, as well as orientations for incoming classes. And who knows, but you will likely end up on the brochures and billboards, too."

"That all sounds great," said Eliza, "But if these are beginning English classes, isn't it going to be a problem that I don't speak Turkish? I don't want to scare the students away before they've even started, but you know there's no way I can host any kind of meeting in Turkish."

Dr. Çelik waved her away. "Not at all. Your counterpart from Antalya Tech is someone named Deniz something...I can't remember his last name right now. But he's Turkish, so there's no problem with the language part at all."

Eliza blinked. How many Denizes could there be at Antalya Technical Institute? She knew Deniz was a common name—and a unisex one, at that, so it had twice the potential of being a stranger's name than a traditionally male or traditionally female name did—and yet she had a feeling that this Deniz was going to be a very familiar one. "Out of curiosity, how big is Antalya Technical Institute's English department? How many teachers are there? I'm just wondering if we'll be able to share the teaching load evenly or if it's going to fall disproportionately on one school or the other..."

"It's quite similar actually...we've got twenty English teachers here, and they have between twenty and thirty. But Eliza, you can leave the admin work to me. I assure you it's well in hand."

"Thank you, Dr. Çelik," said Eliza. "I'm more than happy to accept the opportunity, and I'm really looking forward to seeing how it unfolds."

Dr. Çelik stood. "I knew you would be a great fit. I'll go back to my office now and forward you the information I have about the program so far. There's a meeting scheduled for tomorrow afternoon, for the administrative team as well as you and this Deniz person. Take some time to read through the material today, so you'll be prepared for the meeting tomorrow."

"I will, Dr. Çelik," Eliza said as they shook hands, "And thanks again."

Alone again in her office, Eliza stared at the computer screen with unseeing eyes. What had she gotten herself into? The program did sound excellent, like such a good fit for her interests and skills...but Deniz? Could she stomach working closely with him? Especially after learning what he had done to Cem? There was only one way to find out, and it depended on them being able to spend time in the same room without going for each other's throats. Eliza knew she could be the bigger person...unless he tried to take the high road and be better than her, in which case she'd go for the jugular.

·♥·♥·♥·♥·♥·

At two o'clock the next afternoon, Eliza slipped into the conference room to claim a seat for the meeting about the new adult education program. The meeting was scheduled to begin in fifteen minutes, but Eliza liked to be early to claim a spot where she felt comfortable, rather than searching for a friendly face to sit next to like a new kid at lunchtime on the first day of school.

A mere moment later, the door opened again, and Deniz Aydem entered. *It figures,* Eliza thought, *that if anyone was going to have the same idea as me, it would be this asshole.* She smiled and returned to reading the papers in front of her, student homework that she had brought more as a security blanket than as something she would actually work on at the meeting.

Deniz pulled out the chair next to hers and sat down. "Eliza, it's nice to see you. How are you today?" He smiled warmly.

"I'm fine, Deniz. You?"

"Great, thanks! I was so happy to hear that you accepted the PR role. I asked Dr. Yılmaz to request you specifically, but I didn't know if you'd have the time or the interest to take it on. I'm looking forward to working together closely."

"You...requested me for the job?" Eliza asked.

Deniz's face showed the briefest flash of pink before he again steeled his expression. "Of course. Of all the teachers I've met from Med School, you seem the most capable. I don't want us to embarrass ourselves, you know."

"Ah yes, I understand that," Eliza said.

"And of course, the fact that we are friends already doesn't hurt, does it?" Deniz asked.

"We're...friends?" Eliza responded.

"Well, of course we are! We had a lovely time in Kaş, didn't we? I owe you for making me go out that last night. I haven't had that much fun since I was a university student."

"That's nice," Eliza said, looking pointedly back down at the papers in front of her.

Deniz didn't take the hint. "How are your friends Crystal and Jack doing?"

Eliza sighed. "Crystal is fine, and Jack...well, Jack is too, I guess." This might be an opportunity to get recon info about Barış and his feelings, but somehow exposing Jack's vulnerability to Deniz, of all people, felt wrong.

"I'm glad to hear it. I had a lot of fun with them both," Deniz said. "And I hope that we can all spend some more time together soon."

"Yes, well, I invited Barış to have brunch with us on Sunday morning," Eliza began, "But I guess he didn't pass the message on to you before he declined on your behalf."

Deniz looked startled. "I had no idea. I'd love to join you and your friends. What can I bring?"

"Don't you think it will be awkward without Barış there?" Eliza asked.

"Eliza, Barış is very busy with his work. He has to make choices about how he spends his time, and sometimes he needs me to remind him of what his priorities are," Deniz said. "But that has nothing to do with whether he would like to spend time with you and your friends or not."

"Yeah, right..." Eliza muttered. "It didn't seem that way from his text."

"Barış can be very single-minded when he is working on a project," Deniz explained. "Trust me, I've known him for a long time."

"As long as you've known Cem?" Eliza asked.

Deniz's eyes widened. "Cem? What about him?"

"I know the whole story. I heard what you did to him. And I can't help but believe you have something to do with Barış disappearing on Jack. Can you just not stand seeing other people happy? Is that what it is?"

"Eliza, I don't know—" Deniz began.

"Oh, spare me," Eliza said. "You act like you're my friend, but I know how you really feel about me and the work I'm doing here. And that's the least of my concerns, really. You stole Cem's only chance at success and happiness, and it looks like now you're doing the same thing to Jack. What is *wrong* with you?"

"Eliza, please let me explain," Deniz said. "I don't know what Cem told you, but it can't be the whole story if you're reacting this way."

"Can't it? Isn't it possible that I'm smart enough to know that there *are* two sides to every story...and that no matter what your side is, the results speak for themselves? No matter what he did, Cem didn't deserve to have his future taken away from him. And the fact that you can live with that, that you can *justify* it even...well, that's more than enough for me to make my decision about you."

Deniz opened his mouth to speak again, but at that moment the door to the conference room opened, and Dr. Çelik, Dr. Yılmaz, and two more people entered. Eliza and Deniz stood to greet them, then sat back down in their chairs, turning to face the others at the table and no longer looking in each other's direction.

"Eliza, it's very nice to meet you," said Dr. Yılmaz. "Deniz has told me a great deal about the work you are doing at Med School, and it was clear he was impressed by your efforts. I believe the two of you will make a great team."

Eliza fought back a grimace. Deniz had lied to Dr. Yılmaz about his esteem for her—why, she couldn't begin to imagine—and now it was being insinuated that the two of them were some kind of professional dream team. Not bloody likely.

"Thank you so much, Dr. Yılmaz," Eliza said. "I'm eager to learn more about this program and to begin working on it. With our two departments combined, I think we can create something truly revolutionary for the people in this city."

"That is the goal of the program," piped up Dr. Çelik. "And I think it's important for us to discuss both the vision of the program and our individual visions of our involvement in it. Let's make sure we're all on the same page. How does that sound?"

"That's a great idea, Dr. Çelik," said Dr. Yılmaz. "Why don't we start with Deniz?"

This ought to be good, thought Eliza. *How do you say "prestige and padding my resume" in a way that sounds nice and noble?*

"Well," Deniz began, "The idea for the program was born out of something Eliza said to me, actually. She was talking about the work she did, both in America and at Med School, working with refugee populations and the opportunities that language education opened up for them. It made me realize a two-fold goal for the ideal language teaching environment—students who are intrinsically motivated and committed to their education, as well as teachers who are passionate about what they are doing. I saw both of those things when Ms. Britt told me about the work she was doing. The students work harder than any others—especially than the ones who are only learning English to pass a test—and the passion that she felt as a teacher was evident. Inspiring. The program took shape in my mind naturally after that."

Everyone was looking at Eliza now. Why hadn't anyone told her this program was the brainchild of Deniz Aydem? Or that she was the inspiration for it? She felt her cheeks color, and her tongue seemed to swell in her mouth. "I...uh..." she began. "Well, it sounds like my view of a program of this nature has already been made quite clear. So...yes. What Deniz said, I guess." She looked down at her hands in her lap. Fumbling for words didn't feel good, but there was something else happening here. Something she couldn't quite put her finger on. Something she would have to work through later, without an audience.

The conversation continued, with the administrative team sharing their visions of the program as well. Eliza caught snippets here and there, but her primary focus was on keeping her attention directed straight ahead, rather than responding to the heat of Deniz's gaze boring into the side of her head. He wanted to catch her eye, that was clear, but she wanted to look anywhere but into the deep brown irises directed her way.

Was he trying to embarrass her? To put her on the spot in front of professors she respected and then watch her flounder? If so, job well done. Eliza had hoped to be composed and graceful today, selling herself as a professional who could be entrusted to be the public face of a program like this...and she had bumbled. She had blown it. She had spoken about as eloquently as a toddler trying to summarize the plot of their favorite movie. She needed to get out of here, and fast.

The meeting ended, and Eliza shook hands with the two directors, promising to be in touch soon with the initial promotional ideas they had requested. Deniz was occupied talking with Dr. Çelik, and Eliza bolted out of the room before he could succeed in catching her eye. Once she was in the hall, she power walked through the building as quickly as she could without breaking into a run.

She had almost made it to the front door when she heard the shout.

"Eliza! Wait!"

A breath huffed out of her as she rolled her eyes skyward. Without turning around, she raised her voice. "Deniz, what do you want?"

"I wanted to talk with you. Please. Why does it seem like you are ignoring me?

She whirled around. "Probably because I am! You embarrassed me in there. I was missing some very important information in that meeting, and I looked like a fool. This is *your* program? Inspired by *me*? Don't those seem like things I should know before I am put on the spot in front of *two program directors* who are expecting me to have a coherent thought in my head? To be able to string together a complete sentence about something I'm supposedly so passionate about? Deniz, you don't even like me. You certainly don't respect me. How dare you embarrass me like that by pretending to be inspired by me?"

"Eliza...I..." Deniz began, his features gripped by confusion.

"Spare me, Deniz." She said. "I'll work with you, and I'll even keep up your little charade. Friends who are mutually inspired by each other's ambition and hard work. But I don't owe you one single moment of my time outside of this program. And when no one else is around, I certainly don't have to be nice to you."

"Eliza, please listen to me." Deniz begged. "I *was* inspired by you. I *am*. I didn't want to be, and I still have my reservations about attaching my reputation to the other American teachers at your school. But you...no matter what I have done to offend or upset you, you have to believe me that I have always liked you."

"I don't know how you can possibly expect me to believe that," Eliza said. "When you have been so dismissive of the work I do, of my colleagues...maybe you just don't realize how you come across, Deniz. Some people have Resting Bitch Face, but with you, it's like Resting Bitch Personality. You're not exactly a teddy bear."

"No..." Deniz looked puzzled. "I'm not a stuffed animal, I know that—"

"I need you to stop trying to be friends with me." Eliza said. "I have enough on my plate right now, with my own work, trying to comfort Jack, getting Larry off my back, and helping Cem find a job. There isn't room for you, and even if there were, I wouldn't rent that space in my life to you, no matter what you were willing to pay. Now, if you don't mind, I really need to get out of here." She wheeled around and marched out of the building, but not before noticing the way Deniz's face fell. But that was his problem, not hers.

Eighteen

The apartment was quiet when Eliza entered. "Crystal!" she called. Then, reluctantly, "Larry?" No one answered, and she reached for her phone to text her friend. A message from Jack was waiting, and Eliza opened it first.

"Can you meet for a drink? I need a friend."

That poor peanut. He was having a hard time. "Of course," she texted back. "Where?"

While she waited for his response, she sent a message to Crystal. "Where are you? I had a rough meeting. Heading out for a drink with Jack now. Join us?"

Crystal's response came quickly. "In a meeting soon, I'll let you know when I'm available."

What meeting? Crystal had said nothing about a meeting this morning...and come to think of it, she hadn't had a meeting of any kind since she'd arrived in Antalya. But her friend didn't need an interruption dinging on her phone during her first meeting in Turkey, so Eliza left it alone. She'd find out soon enough.

Jack had responded while Eliza was lost in her thoughts. "Castle Bar, 10 minutes?"

Eliza let him know she'd meet him there, swept her hair into a ponytail, dabbed on some lip gloss, and stepped into her cutest, comfiest shoes on her way out the door.

Just under ten minutes later—also known as "right on time," just the way she liked it—Eliza walked into Castle Bar. She secured an outdoor table for two and ordered two beers while she waited for Jack to arrive. When he did, his attempt at a smile couldn't hide the pain he was feeling. She'd never seen her friend like this, and Eliza's heart ached for him.

She stood up to give Jack a quick hug before they both sat down. "Are you doing okay, Jack?"

He croaked out a laugh. "I know it's obvious that I'm not. I'm embarrassed by how hard I'm taking this, but I can't help it. I don't do well with being dumped. Do you?"

"That would be a 'no.'" Eliza said. "And it would also be the reason why I'm super single the vast majority of the time."

"I'm starting to think you might be onto something there. Maybe hookups are a better way to go, you know? No expectations, no attachment...it's safer that way."

"It's safer that way if that's how you're wired," Eliza said, "But *is* that how you're wired, Jack? I haven't known you long, but it seems to me like you're all heart. You're a romantic." She rubbed his arm as she said the last words.

"Yeah, and that's what's wrong with me. Maybe I came on too strong, too quickly, with Barış."

"Do you think that's what happened? That you scared him away?" Eliza remembered Deniz's words from earlier that same day, though she wasn't ready to share them with Jack yet. "Did you tell him that you loved him on the first date? Don't laugh; I actually did that once back in the day. *Huge* surprise when I never heard from that guy again."

"No, there were no proclamations of love in the time we spent together. But that's the thing. We spent *a lot* of time together. Maybe it was too much, and he just got sick of me."

"Who could get sick of you, Jack? No one worth spending any time with at all. I'm sure that's not it."

"That's enough of my sob story. What happened to you today? You looked like crap when I came in, staring out at the sea with that wrinkle on your brow like it broke your grandma's kneecaps."

Eliza laughed at that. "I had a weird meeting today, and I didn't know all the information about it beforehand. I got embarrassed. And by Deniz, of all people."

"Deniz?" Jack was surprised. "What were the two of you doing in a meeting together?"

"It's a long story, but basically there is a project we're going to be cooperating with Antalya Tech on. And that project is forcing the two of us to spend a lot of time together."

"And you're not happy about that?"

"Not at all! He was acting like he wanted to be my friend, but then he set me up. I made a fool out of myself in front of the entire administrative team because he withheld important information from me. And then there's the whole matter with Cem, which makes me wonder if Deniz is to blame for Barış ghosting you, and—"

"Whoa whoa whoa," Jack interjected. "Hold on. Back up. You're losing me. What's the deal with...Cem? And how does that have anything to do with me and Barış?"

Eliza sighed. "When I met up with him the other day...he had hinted at some bad blood between him and Deniz, and I finally got the story out of him. They studied together in university until Deniz got jealous of his connection with their advisor and got him kicked out of the program."

"What? How is that even possible? There must be more to the story!"

"Oh Jack," Eliza smiled. "Even when you're hurting, even when I'm telling you that this guy might be to blame for your own love story falling apart...you just can't help but see the good in people. That's why I love you. But no, I don't think there is anything redeemable about Deniz, no matter how you spin it."

"But how can that be? He and Barış are such close friends, and I know Barış has a good heart...morals...he wouldn't be friends with a monster."

"Maybe he doesn't know," Eliza shrugged. "And maybe he doesn't realize that Deniz is doing the same thing to him now."

"Why do you think Deniz is behind Barış ghosting me?" Jack asked.

"He's never been particularly kind about the American teachers at Med School. I'm guessing he doesn't want you to bring down the quality of Barış's research, and I doubt he realizes how deep the attachment went apart from the research."

"Eliza, you are a good friend and a total sweetheart to me," Jack smiled, "But you are paranoid AF where it comes to Deniz. Barış is an adult, and he is fully capable of making his own decisions. And if he isn't, and he just does whatever his little friend tells him to do…well, then it was never going to work out between us."

Eliza smiled at Jack and placed her hand on his. "How'd you get so wise, Jack?"

Jack shrugged. "A lifetime of living and learning?"

"No matter what happens, you're going to be just fine. And I'll be here for you, I promise. And I promise to keep my conspiracy theories to myself, okay?"

Jack stuck out his tongue at her. "You'd better. I've got enough on my plate managing my own runaway thoughts without having to rein in yours too!"

Just then, Eliza's phone buzzed with a text from Crystal. "Where are you right now? Gotta talk."

Eliza fired back the name of the bar and asked if Crystal wanted her to order a drink.

"Not yet. Let's talk first."

"Hmm, that sounds kind of ominous…" Eliza thought out loud.

"What's up?" Jack asked.

"I'm not sure…it sounds like something serious is going on with Crystal. And I think it involves me. I just felt my heart drop the way it does any time someone says, 'We have to talk.' I can't help but think I'm about to be in big trouble. But I'm wracking my brain and I can't come up with even the first idea of what this could be about."

Jack patted her hand. "Where has overthinking ever gotten you? She'll be here soon, and you'll find out what this is all about. In the meantime, you aren't going to *think* your way to a solution."

"Again with the wisdom, Jack," Eliza smiled. "And you're totally right. I may as well enjoy the sunset rather than wondering if it's the last one I'll ever see."

A few minutes later, a flustered Crystal turned up in front of them. "There you are!" she exclaimed, wiping a sheen of sweat off her brow. She asked the couple at the table next to them if she could take one of their spare chairs, and then she pulled it over, sitting down next to Eliza.

"What's up, Crys?" Eliza asked. "You didn't sound like yourself in your messages. Is everything okay?"

Crystal hung her head. "I'm making some changes. I accepted a job offer today, and I'm a little nervous to tell you about it...I'm not sure what you're going to think."

"Crystal, that's so exciting! Why would I ever begrudge you a job offer?" Eliza asked. "But wait...does this mean you're moving back to Michigan? Of course I don't want you to stay here on my behalf, but...wow! Whatever you need to do, I support you one hundred percent. I'll just miss you, but that's not the most important thing here—"

"Eliza, you're rambling a bit." Crystal interjected. "And I'm not moving back to Michigan. The job is right here in Antalya. I'm not going anywhere."

"Oh, that's great news! But wait. What's the job? Are you coming to work at Med School? Or are you joining the competition at Antalya Tech?"

Crystal lowered her gaze. "Actually, I'm going to be working with Mr. Collins. I accepted the director position."

Eliza's jaw dropped, and she worked quickly to make her expression blank. "That's...wow! I had no idea. I didn't realize you wanted a position like that. But with Mr. Collins? You don't mind working with him? I wonder if there's even room for you on the leadership team, between him and his massive ego taking up all the oxygen in the room."

"Eliza. This is exactly why I was nervous to tell you. I knew you wouldn't understand."

"No no no! I'm sorry. Help me understand. I want to be happy for you. I want to celebrate this with you. I want to be excited, if you're excited about it. So tell me why you accepted it?"

"Well, you know my work has been so stressful lately. The one-on-one lessons were really taking it out of me, and if I kept it up much longer, I'd definitely be cruising for a burnout. After you turned down Mr. Collins's offer, I started thinking. Just wondering what other roles are out there that might utilize my talents without demanding all of my time and energy. And then, the other day, I had a LinkedIn request and a message from Mr. Collins, and I agreed to meet with him today. The job sounds really good, Eliza. I know it wasn't a good fit for you, but for me...I think I could be happy. And I can't imagine something better coming along without having to start at the bottom and work my way up through the pecking order."

Eliza was silent, so Jack chimed in. He raised his glass in Crystal's direction and cried, "This calls for a toast! What are you drinking, Crystal? Let me buy you a beverage so we can celebrate this properly. Well done, you!"

"Yes, well done..." Eliza mumbled, as Jack flagged down the waiter to order Crystal a glass of wine.

"I know it's a big change," Crystal explained, "But I do hope you'll be able to be happy for me."

"I didn't realize that teaching was becoming such a burden on you. And of course, I would never want my best friend to have to live like that. I *am* happy for you, Crystal." She forced a smile. "Does this mean you're going to stay in Turkey forever?"

A laugh barked out of Crystal's surprised face. "I haven't talked about my retirement package, if that's what you mean. I am accepting this job today...for a yearlong contract. And I'll reevaluate after that. You don't need to make this a bigger deal than it is, dear friend. Even if I end up staying in Turkey, it's not like we won't see each other. Hell, who knows how long *you* are sticking around?"

"You're right," Eliza hung her head. "I know it's unfair of me to worry about where you're going to be when you're the one who moved halfway across the world for *me* in the first place."

"I think I just pushed your abandonment button," said Crystal. "Come back to the moment, Eliza. Be here. Right now. At this table, with your friends, drinking a toast to celebrate an exciting new job. Let tomorrow worry about tomorrow."

Surrounded by her two wisest friends, Eliza was a mess. She understood what they had both told her to do, intellectually, but she couldn't make that truth take root in her heart. She was dreading working on her new project with Deniz, preoccupied with what was going on with Barış, and anxious that she was about to lose Crystal to Mr. Collins. What was going *right*?

"I've got to go," Eliza stood up. "Sorry, I've just got too much on my mind and I won't be good company. I don't want to bring down your celebration with all my 'negative vibes.' I'll see you at home."

Her two friends gaped as Eliza fished a few bills out of her wallet and left them on the table. She couldn't look at their hurt faces, knowing that she was abandoning each of them at a time when they needed to know she had their backs. But she'd make it up to them later. And maybe they would find solace in each other. Maybe they'd find such solace in each other's friendship that they wouldn't even need her any more. Now *that* was a familiar thought. As a child, Eliza had always been afraid to introduce her school friends to her summer camp friends when they came to visit, confident that they would like each other more than they'd ever liked her and that she'd be irrelevant. Forgotten. Left alone on her birthday while her former friends went to the movies.

As she walked home, Eliza scolded herself. "You're over-reacting. Why do you have to care so damn much about this job? Or about stupid Deniz? Does any of this matter enough to consume your thoughts and keep you up at night? But let me guess...you're going to let it, anyway. No wonder you're better off alone. You can't even have a friendship without shitting on your friends' dreams and making everything about you. No wonder you were such a disaster in a relationship. Jack and Crystal will be better off without you—they deserve each other. Maybe that's the one good deed you've done so far in your life, introducing them to each other."

Eliza fished her keys out of her purse and was about to slide them into the door of her apartment when it burst open.

"Eliza!" Larry cried. "I was just coming to meet you. Crystal told me you all were at Castle Bar, and I was coming to celebrate her new job with you."

"Clearly I'm not there any more, Larry." Eliza spit. "But why don't you go on ahead? I'm sure Crystal will be happy to see you, even if you embarrass her by being a dick to the waiter."

Larry's eyes were wide. "Have I...been a dick to the waiters when we've gone out? I didn't..."

"Of course you have!" Eliza snapped. "Don't you realize the way you come across? You think you're so worldly, rubbing shoulders with the international teachers community, but you stick out like a sore thumb. You're the loud American stereotype, and we're all embarrassed by the way you act. In fact, I'm about to call Dr. Bennett and ask when the hell I can expect him to fly you back to Michigan, where you belong."

Larry was shell shocked. "I...I..." His chin quivered. "I'm sorry, Eliza." He steeled himself. "I didn't mean to embarrass you. I've always just wanted to be more like you, seeing how much Dr. B. respected you. But I can see you're never going to let that happen, never going to give me even a minute more of your precious time than you think I deserve. Well, I'll get out of your hair now. And I'll find someplace else to stay so you don't have to worry about me being such a *problem* anymore." He slammed the door on his way out.

Eliza crumpled onto the sofa. What the hell had happened to her tonight? She felt drained from the outburst. Justified in her frustration. Tired. She forced herself to her feet and into her bedroom, where she collapsed onto the bed and fell into a fitful sleep.

Nineteen

The light streamed in through Eliza's window, and she turned over on her pillow to get her eyes out of its path. She groaned as her body came back to consciousness.

"Ugh," her morning voice was an octave deeper than normal. "I feel like hot garbage." Her head ached like the morning after a night of heavy drinking, but that wasn't the cause of this feeling. It wasn't a hangover, it was a shameover. *Did I really snap at Larry? And oh my God, what about Crystal? Are we cool today?*

Eliza climbed out of bed and pulled on a light robe as she stepped into her slippers. She shuffled into the kitchen and boiled water to make coffee in the French press. There was no sign Larry had slept on the couch last night, and the apartment was too quiet for her to believe that Crystal was here. Had she come home last night? Left before Eliza had even woken up? While she waited for the French press to be ready to plunge, Eliza poked around the apartment in an effort to Sherlock Crystal's whereabouts.

By the door, she spotted the shoes Crystal had been wearing last night. So, she had come home. But had she gone out again? Crystal's keys were missing from the spot where they often sat, but that could mean anything; Crystal was known for misplacing her keys. Eliza wandered into the bathroom, and there she found her answer. The shower walls were wet, as was Crystal's toothbrush. Her makeup bag was on the counter by the sink...she was gone. Crystal was not one to get dressed up and ready to go unless she had some place to be. Eliza let out a sigh as she realized her friend was no doubt gone for the day, and the opportunity for the two of them to make peace would have to wait.

At this time of day, the balcony on the western side of their apartment was nicely shaded, perfect for enjoying a cup of coffee without feeling the brunt of the day's early heat. Eliza sat at the small table as she sipped her coffee and flipped through the day planner she had brought with her from home. Though it was Saturday, and she hadn't expected to have any work commitments—apart from grading—again until Monday morning, there was a scrawled note for this afternoon: *brainstorming meeting with Deniz.*

She gaped at the note, wracking her brain to remember when it had been scheduled. The picture came into focus as she remembered Dr. Yılmaz's email to the two of them, suggesting that they have a separate meeting on their own prior to the larger committee meeting scheduled for Monday afternoon. Deniz had replied to suggest Saturday afternoon, and Eliza had promptly scrawled it in her planner before firing back a one-word acceptance.

She groaned. That was just what this day needed—some one-on-one time with Deniz Aydem. If she didn't get her attitude right before they both turned up to the Keyif Cafe at two o'clock, she was liable to snap at him for ordering the wrong kind of coffee. Yikes. But what could she do to get her attitude right, apart from taking out her frustration on someone who deserved it? And who exemplified *that* more than Deniz?

"That's it," Eliza said out loud. "I can't imagine anything that would annoy Deniz more than me...just...ignoring his bullshit. I don't have to engage. I don't even have to talk to him outside of this project! I'm going to be professional, I'm going to do the best work I've ever done on this project, and I'm not going to react, no matter how he tries to provoke me. I can hate him and still work on a team with him. This is about the work we're doing, not about the two of us and our friendship—or complete lack thereof."

Eliza's phone buzzed then. Her heart raced as she anticipated a text from Crystal, but it was Cem's message waiting for her. "Hey you. Are you free for coffee?"

"Better make it coffee and breakfast. Where should I meet you?" she replied.

Cem responded with the name of a cafe near the cliffs, and Eliza hastily got herself ready and left the apartment to meet him. It was good to know there was still someone in this city who wanted to see her, even if he wasn't her first choice. Maybe a friendly face would help her remember that she and Crystal had argued and made up many times over the course of their friendship. There was no reason to believe the same thing wouldn't happen this time.

After locking the door behind her and exiting the building, Eliza checked the time on her phone. It had taken her longer than she'd expected to get ready, and she felt pressure to get to the cafe soon, so as not to keep Cem waiting. She increased her pace enough that she was slightly out of breath but not yet sweating, and she kept it up until she arrived at the cafe. The cafe where, surprise surprise, there wasn't a single familiar face waiting for her.

"Huh," she said, "I guess I beat Cem here." She took a seat on the patio and began looking over the menu while she waited for her friend to arrive.

"I'm so sorry I'm late!" The words interrupted her focused concentration on the menu. "Have you been waiting long?"

Eliza glanced at the time. "Just about five minutes. Nothing at all to worry about." She smiled at him. "It's nice to see you. What kept you?"

"On my way here I was stopped by a couple I took on a tour the other day. They wanted to chat about the places I had recommended to them, what they thought of it all...I couldn't get the conversation to end soon enough."

"That's sweet," Eliza said. "They must have liked you if they wanted to talk to you again."

Cem scowled. "Not exactly. It turns out they weren't impressed at all by my recommendations, and they really wanted to tell me all about it. I swear, this job is getting worse every day..."

Eliza felt the subject change coming before it did. "You're really ready to get out of there, huh?" she asked.

"It can't come soon enough." Cem confirmed. "Speaking of which, any news about hiring at Med School?"

"Nothing yet," said Eliza. "I checked our job postings the other day, and there isn't anything in our department. But...oh! I just had an idea. I'm working on a new program—with Deniz, unfortunately, but still—bringing English courses to the general population of Antalya. That program might need volunteers, and I'm sure working as a volunteer would be a great way to build that relationship..." Eliza trailed off as she saw Cem's nose wrinkle.

"Sorry," he said, "I know you're just trying to help, but volunteering? What is that going to do? You'll get a few hours of free work out of me here and there, but that doesn't solve the problem I'm having today. I need a new job, and I need a new job that uses my skills, my intellect...the degree that I should have."

Eliza collected herself enough to continue. "I understand that. Please don't think I was trying to get free labor out of you. I just thought that networking with the decision makers at the two universities in town might be a good way to establish some goodwill. It might move you to the top of the list the next time they're thinking about hiring. I don't know how much more I can offer than that right now."

Cem pulled his chair over next to hers. "Oh, come on, of course you know there's something else you can offer, my goddess." He picked up her hand in his own and brought it to his mouth. "What about going straight to the director to offer a recommendation? Hmm?" He raised his eyes to hers, his lips still on her knuckles.

Eliza pulled her hand back. "I wish I could, Cem. I just don't feel comfortable right now. I barely have a reputation here as it is, but if I stick it out for you, well—" She stopped herself off the look that crossed Cem's eyes.

"I see," he said. "Did Deniz get to you? Convince you I'm not such a great guy after all?"

"Screw Deniz," she said, biting back a smile as Cem's eyes widened in shock. "Don't you think I can form an opinion on my own? I haven't listened to a word he had to say about you, despite all of his efforts. I'm just speaking as a foreigner in an established department. It doesn't feel right for me to come in and tell the director how things should be done, like I'm overstepping my bounds. I hope you can understand."

"I do, of course," Cem raised his lips in a smile that didn't quite reach his eyes. "And maybe I will try your volunteer thing. See how that goes."

The two of them ordered drinks and breakfast, and Cem picked up his phone and started scrolling while they waited for their food to arrive. Eliza did the same after a while once she realized that there wasn't going to be much conversation happening.

Cem's attention shifted to Eliza. "What's going on with you two?" he asked, holding out his phone to her. On it was Larry's Instagram profile, and a recent photo of her with Larry and Crystal. He was pointing to Larry, and Eliza wasn't sure she liked the implication of his tone.

"That's Larry," she explained, as if she were talking to a child. "You can't be serious. For crying out loud, you met the man...did you really get the vibe that he and I had something romantic between us? The only thing between us is feelings of murderous rage, I can assure you. Not that I should *have* to assure you of anything, though. There's no need to get weird about a photo of me and a man. God."

Cem looked bashful. "Sorry. I just saw it was posted a few days ago, and I wondered if you were hesitating on helping me because something was developing there. It's not fair, I know."

"No, it isn't," Eliza said, "Especially considering that you and I *aren't* dating and that my personal feelings for you—or the lack thereof—are not the determining factor in whether or not I help you. What is wrong with everyone lately?" The waiter took that moment to deposit their breakfasts at the table, and Eliza focused her attention on putting her napkin in her lap, salting her food, and avoiding Cem's gaze.

"I'm sorry," he said, when they were alone again. "Really. I know I was being unfair. I know I overreacted. I just like you, and I have to remember that you're not Turkish. So maybe relationships and crushes don't work quite the same for you. I'll try to be better."

"I appreciate that," she said. "I'm really not interested in dating anyone, so I hope you'll accept my friendship. And I hope that you'll believe me that friendship is all it'll ever be. I just don't really do the dating thing...it gets too messy when I do. I want to be your friend, and I can't promise you anything more than that ever." It felt good to put that out in the open, and Eliza hoped it would make things less complicated between them.

"I appreciate you being direct," Cem said, "Even if I'm not used to it. And I think I can work with that. We'll just be friends and maybe colleagues one day." He winked at her. "And I'd like to spend some more time with your friend Larry, too. It seemed like he and I might have similar ambitions, and I wonder if we could help each other out."

"Hmm, that's an interesting thought," Eliza said. "I think Larry's a little pissed off at me right now, and justifiably so. I'll just connect the two of you via text message, okay? That way you can meet up with each other without me having to play third wheel." She fired off a quick group message then, introducing Larry and Cem and inviting the two of them to text each other if they wanted to meet up. It wasn't hard to imagine that Larry might enjoy having a fellow guy to hang out with, especially considering how much time he had been spending with her and Crystal.

A notification chimed on Eliza's phone then, reminding her she had some work to do before her meeting with Deniz that afternoon. God bless her disciplined weekday self, who had set that reminder, knowing that she would be doing anything and everything to delay her meeting with the ever-annoying Mr. Aydem. She looked up from her phone at her empty plate and then across the table at Cem, who was likewise engrossed in his cell phone.

"Cem, I'm going to have to take off now. I've got some work to do before a meeting this afternoon."

"On a Saturday?" Cem was incredulous. "Geez, maybe I don't want to come work with you after all."

Eliza laughed politely. As nice as that thought was, she was pretty sure Cem was just making a joke...and also checking that he wouldn't be required to take a weekend shift when—not if, *when*—he started working at the Mediterranean School of Languages.

"It's that extra project I told you about. I'm meeting with Deniz to talk over our role and see what ideas we can come up with."

"Oh. Right. Okay then, have fun, I guess." Cem stood and the two of them walked over to the cash register to pay for their meal. Cem pulled Eliza in for a quick hug before they parted ways in front of the restaurant.

Eliza walked just as quickly on her way home as she had on her way to breakfast. She needed to wow in this meeting with Deniz. She needed to show him—frankly, show *anyone*—that she had something worth contributing. Crystal's silence, and hell, Crystal's acceptance of a job Eliza had never actually wanted, hurt, and the need to prove her worth had felt intense ever since. "I'll show him...I'll show him...I'll show her..." was Eliza's mantra as she walked home.

Eliza heard music playing on the other side of the apartment door, and her heart pounded in anticipation of a confrontation, or even an interaction, with one of the people who had hurt her (and who she had hurt in return) last night. But by the time her fumbled key in the lock had gotten the apartment open, the living room was empty. The last sound Eliza heard before the living room's silence enveloped her was most likely the sound of Crystal's door slamming shut. Eliza sighed—now wasn't the time to force herself on her friend, who wanted nothing to do with her. She had work to do, and she wasn't going to let anything stop her.

·♥·♥·♥·♥·♥·

At two o'clock, Eliza was waiting in front of Hadrian's Gate for Deniz. She was prepared for this meeting, unlike she had been for the last one, and despite her dislike for Deniz, she felt excited at the prospect of getting to share her ideas with someone who, she hoped, would share her enthusiasm.

"Hi Eliza," said a soft voice behind her. Deniz had approached from the opposite direction that she had expected. She had been standing with her back to the Gate, looking for him on the street, when he had instead walked right through the ancient architecture. She wondered what he had been doing on the other side of it, but she decided not to ask. Best to keep things professional and moving along.

"Deniz, hello. Where would you like to go talk?"

"I was thinking...I'm getting a little tired of meeting for a coffee lately. It seems like all I do is caffeinate myself. What do you think about sitting in a park instead? We can find a spot with some shade, a nice view of the sea?"

Eliza did her best to hide her surprise. "That sounds...great, actually. Lead the way." She fell into step next to Deniz, admiring the shops they passed and the view of the Mediterranean as they reached the end of the brick road and turned left towards a large open area. As they approached the park, Eliza noticed one of the select few shady spots already had a large beach towel spread out under it. Deniz directed her to it and invited her to sit down, and she had her answer about what he had been doing in the old town while she waited for him at the gate.

Deniz smiled tentatively as he pulled out a clipboard and a pen. "I thought we could make a master list of all the ideas we discuss, so we can present a united front at our next meeting."

"That's a great idea," Eliza agreed. "Do you want to go first or should I?"

"What if we take turns? One of yours, then one of mine? And of course, I'll put our initials next to them so we know to give credit where it's due in the meeting."

Eliza smiled. "That sounds lovely. I'm not sure it's necessary, since we're working together, but I do really appreciate the gesture."

Deniz blushed. "Cansu—my sister—is always telling me about men talking over her at meetings, or repeating the same ideas she has shared and being treated like they're geniuses just for copying her. I don't want to do the same to you."

"You're a good brother, Deniz," Eliza said. "I'm sure just listening to your sister helps give her some hope that the whole world isn't full of men like that. What does she do?"

"She's in the hospitality business. Management for one of the hotels here in town." Deniz raised his eyebrows at the notebook in Eliza's hands. "Now, let's get started! I don't want to steal this entire afternoon from you."

Twenty

On Monday morning, Eliza dressed with extra attention and care. The collaborative meeting between
Med School and Antalya Tech was happening today, and
after her performance in their first meeting, she was determined to present confidence and professionalism today.
The work she and Deniz had done on Saturday had been
immensely helpful. They had come up with a list of over
twenty ideas, ranging in size from *"Media interviews—local TV, radio, podcasts"* to *"Hand out flyers on a one-on-one
basis."* In the two hours they had worked, they had fall-
en into a comfortable rhythm—not friends, but friendly
coworkers, at least. Deniz had texted her later that same
day with another idea, and the messages had been pinging
back and forth between them ever since...including a new
one this morning, she realized.

"What are you going to wear today?" Deniz had
asked.

"Um…why?" Eliza asked. How could that be relevant? Unless Deniz was just trying to keep the conversation going, Eliza couldn't think of one good reason he'd be asking about her sartorial choices.

"I was just thinking maybe we should coordinate. So they can start to see us as the public face of the program. Like we're TV ready, or something. It might be a dumb idea. Don't worry about it."

Eliza read the message again. Unfortunately, it seemed like Deniz might be onto something. Any ways that they could communicate their united front would be beneficial. And dressing like they might be pulled in front of a camera at any time for an interview would certainly qualify as dressing for the job you want rather than the job you have.

Eliza typed out her reply. "I think you're right. I'm wearing a black pencil skirt and a light blue blouse. What about you?"

Deniz's response came quickly, and Eliza was surprised to see it was…a mirror selfie. She smiled to herself as she took in Deniz's head to toe look. Starting from the bottom…those were nice shoes, very shiny…pressed dark gray pants…a blue button-down shirt, tucked in with a belt over his hips…but when she got to his face, she laughed out loud. Could Deniz possibly be feeling self-conscious? Unsure of himself?

"Very nice," she responded. "Though I'm wondering if my blue and your blue might clash. What do you think?" Then, before she could second guess herself, she snapped a picture in the mirror and sent it back to Deniz.

If he was going to be vulnerable, she supposed she could, too.

"It's perfect. See you this afternoon. Have a nice day!" replied Deniz.

Eliza smiled down at the phone in her hand, then caught herself. What was all this about? She knew better than to think she might—horror of horrors—like Deniz, but she had to admit that having someone in her life to have a friendly conversation with was a godsend. Things with Crystal had been icy all weekend, and Eliza felt embarrassingly starved for affection.

She stepped out of the bathroom and walked right into Crystal. The two women avoided each other's eyes at first, Crystal pushing into the bathroom as Eliza made her way out of it. Not so much as a word passed between them, and Eliza hated it. But she if she was going to be on time for work, she didn't have time to fix it right now.

It had been a week since Jack and Barış had stopped speaking. Jack's demeanor on the morning bus ride hadn't improved, but he was working harder every day to cover up the loss he was feeling. Eliza slid into the seat next to him and bumped him with her elbow.

"How's it going, bud?" she asked.

"Great!" Jack exclaimed. "I had a fun idea for my lesson today. We're reviewing grammar points before the exam, and I spent all weekend working on a Jeopardy-style game for them."

"Yikes, what happened to taking a day off? Or even an hour or two?" Eliza teased him. "I'm sure it's great, though. Did you get out at all, meet up with any friends?"

Jack's smile faded. "I just took it easy this weekend. I spent a few hours making video calls yesterday and caught up with all my family back home. I never thought I'd say this, but I'm kind of missing those people. Looking forward to when I can see them again in person."

Eliza felt a lump rise in her throat to match the emotion she heard in Jack's voice. She'd never been prone to homesickness, but in emotional times, the idea of being wrapped in her mom's arms and comforted by her soothing words always floated to the surface. When she was sick, when she'd gone through that last breakup...not that she'd ever let her mom see that side of herself, though. She kept the weak moments for herself, avoiding being with or even talking to her family until she could convey strength and groundedness. She wondered if Jack was the same way.

"Are you going home for a visit this summer?" Eliza asked Jack.

"I'm definitely going home," Jack began, "But I'm not sure if I'm coming back."

"What?" Eliza cried. "Why? Aren't you going to renew your contract? I'm sure they'd take you on for another year. You've always had great reviews from your students."

"It's not that, Eliza," Jack smiled sadly. "It's a great job, but things have been hard lately and it's making me reevaluate my choices. Maybe I want to be closer to my family—spend more time with my grandparents while I still have them, help my sister as she raises her kids, get to see those kids grow up...All of those things are hard to do from thousands of miles away. I haven't made a decision yet, though. I'm just thinking about it, so you can stop looking at me like that."

"Sorry," Eliza bumped into his arm again. "I know I'm being selfish. As your friend, of course I will support you no matter what you do. I just don't want to see Barış mess up the good thing you have going here in Turkey—"

"It's not about Barış," Jack interrupted, his eyes cold. "There was a time when he would have played into my decision making, but not any more. Whatever I thought was going on there...clearly, I was wrong. I'm not running away from him, but I'm also not staying *for* him."

"I know what you mean." Eliza rested her head on Jack's shoulder. "If you go, I'll miss you. But I only want you to stay if it'll make you happy. If you want to talk about it as you're making your decision, I'm here for you."

"Thanks, lady," Jack said, squeezing her hand.

After a full day of classes, Eliza walked with Dr. Çelik to the parking lot. The two women had agreed to drive together to Antalya Technical Institute for their meeting today, and Eliza was looking forward to the thirty minute drive and whatever uninterrupted conversation it provided. Dr. Çelik fastened her seatbelt, turned on the radio, and drove towards the university's security gates before Eliza could even stow her bag on the ground in front of her.

As she was about to ask about Dr. Çelik's day, the sound of a cell phone ringing reverberated through the whole car. The director's phone was ringing on Bluetooth, and she answered it promptly. The conversation was loud, but both Dr. Çelik and the man she was speaking with were speaking in Turkish, so Eliza felt secure that no one would think she was eavesdropping. She pulled out her own phone and scrolled through her messages to see if there was anything she had missed responding to, hoping against hope that maybe Crystal had beat her to the punch of making peace between them.

Naturally, her notifications were nonexistent. Eliza scrolled through their old messages, reminders of a better time in their friendship, and sighed as she shifted lower in her seat.

It was only then that she realized that Dr. Çelik's phone call had ended. Eliza wondered how long ago that had happened and decided it was better not to ask.

"Is everything alright?" Dr. Çelik asked.

"Yes, nothing serious," Eliza responded. "Just a bit of a misunderstanding with one of my friends, but I'll try to make it up to her later."

"Ah," said Dr. Çelik. "It never hurts to admit when you're wrong. If you were, in fact, in the wrong, that is. If you weren't, it's not always a bad thing to wait and see if the other person will apologize first." She chuckled. "That's the advice I give at every wedding I'm invited to, and I suppose it's true in all relationships, really."

"Really?" Eliza asked. This wasn't like any advice she'd ever heard before. It sounded a lot more calculating than anything she'd ever been told by her parents. They'd always encouraged sincere apologies and being quick to accept responsibility for your side of the street. Dr. Çelik's advice sounded like it would keep things a lot more interesting. And a lot more dramatic, too. "I'll try to remember that for the future, if I'm ever in a situation where I have some romance in my life again."

She had tried to keep any hint of scorn out of her voice, but Dr. Çelik reacted as if she hadn't succeeded. "Please don't take this the wrong way, Eliza, but I think you're too young to have given up on love in your life."

They were treading into unfamiliar and dangerous territory here with this subject. Eliza was determined to change the topic as quickly as possible. "Oh, you're right. I was just kidding."

"You may not like talking about this," Dr. Çelik continued, "But it's important to me for the members of my team to be well-rounded. To have work-life balance. If you are happy in your life, you'll be a happy employee for me. And love is a beautiful thing, something that makes people happy. Are you open to it?"

"I...I guess so..." Eliza stammered, feeling her face flush. "I suppose if I met the right person, I'd pursue something like that."

Dr. Çelik chuckled. "You sound like me when I was your age. Open your eyes, Eliza. That's all I can say. I believe you might have a friendship in your life with the potential to be something much greater, but that's just what it looks like from where I sit. I don't know your life, and I don't want to overstep."

A friendship with the potential to be something greater? What was Dr. Çelik talking about? The director had probably seen Eliza and Jack together often at work, but surely she couldn't think there was romantic potential in that friendship. What else could she be talking about? *Who else?*

Realization dawned on Eliza's face, and Dr. Çelik looked away from the road just as it peaked. "Ahh. You understood my meaning. Yes, I think your friend Deniz might be interested in you as more than a friend, if his glowing review of everything you've ever done is any indicator. I guess we'll see today how good of a team the two of you are."

Eliza could feel herself blushing, and she was grateful when Dr. Çelik turned the radio up and began to hum along, signaling that she had dropped the subject once and for all. She returned to scrolling through her messages and found a new one from Cem that had arrived while the awkward conversation had unfolded.

"Drinks on the beach?" he had texted.

She responded: "I'm heading to a meeting at Antalya Tech now, so I can't. Call me later?"

His response was a simple thumbs up emoji. It felt indefinite, but Eliza had learned not to expect too much from Cem and his communication skills.

Soon after, they arrived at Antalya Technical Institute, and Eliza followed Dr. Çelik inside the large front doors. The older woman seemed to know her way around the campus, parking near the foreign language building and steering the two of them to an unoccupied conference room. On their way down the hall, Eliza read the names on the office doors that they passed, and she recognized Barış and Deniz's offices, across the hall from each other. As much as she would have liked to pop into Barış's office and ask why he was ghosting Jack, she thought better of it.

Dr. Çelik would not be impressed by that, and she didn't want to do anything that would make Jack uncomfortable.

They made themselves comfortable in the conference room, and a moment later were joined by Deniz and Dr. Yılmaz. Once greetings had been exchanged, Deniz dropped into the chair next to Eliza and opened up his laptop, which was connected to the projector screen. He had taken their ideas from their Saturday brainstorm session and used them to create a PowerPoint—if Eliza hadn't already resigned herself otherwise, she would have developed a crush on him right then and there. From the color palette to the font he had chosen, their ideas looked professional, clean, and downright inspiring. She felt a thrill in her belly, something no group project had ever given her before.

"Eliza, would you like to introduce our presentation?" Deniz asked her, handing her the remote control that would flip between the slides.

"Er...yes, thanks," she agreed, her fingers slipping over his as she fumbled the remote onto the table. She could feel Dr. Çelik's eyes on her, and she wished they hadn't had the "girl talk" conversation in the car. She avoided Deniz's eyes as he again handed her the remote, afraid of what Dr. Çelik would see on her face if she made eye contact with him. Afraid of what she might feel, too, but that wasn't something she was going to let herself think about. Not right now, anyway.

"You've got this," Deniz said, patting her on the back and sitting down. The warmth of his hand on her upper back lingered even after he was seated out of arm's reach, and the warmth on her cheeks matched it. Eliza was grateful the lights in the room had been dimmed for the presentation so that the three other people in the room might not notice that her face, neck, and ears had all turned bright red.

"Welcome, everyone. We're here today to talk about the cooperative efforts of Antalya Technical Institute and the Mediterranean School of Languages in developing an English language program for adults in the community," she began, flipping to the next slide, which displayed the two university's logos along with the proposed name of the program. "Mr. Aydem and I spent some time together brainstorming the program, and this is what we wanted to share with you today: English for Everyone. Our slogan, 'Open the doors of your life and career with your language skills,' will, of course, be translated into Turkish for the majority of our marketing material."

"I like it," said Dr. Yılmaz, "But let's not settle on the name or slogan quite yet. Perhaps we can submit some more ideas and have a vote on it."

"Of course," Eliza agreed. "We merely wanted to have a preliminary idea so that we had something to talk about rather than always referring to the program as 'the cooperative education program between Med School and Antalya Tech.' It got a little unwieldy the more we talked about it."

Deniz smiled at her. It hadn't taken long in their working session before they'd both grown frustrated with the repetitive ways they'd been referring to the program. No matter what name they landed on, English for Everyone would have a bit of a soft spot for both of them, it seemed.

Eliza began to run through the ideas she and Deniz had come up with for the program, and he chimed in as needed to supply his perspective. They would share the role of being the public face of the program, with Deniz being the Turkish-speaking face and Eliza as his American counterpart. They played off each other as they explained, and by the end of the presentation, if the expressions on Dr. Çelik and Dr. Yılmaz's faces were any indicator, they'd succeeded.

Dr. Yılmaz spoke first. "Well done, you two. I can see we've made an excellent choice in selecting the two of you to head this program. I don't see any need for correction or input here, so you have my blessing to go ahead...as long as Dr. Çelik agrees." She raised her eyebrows to her counterpart, and Dr. Çelik looked up from her notes.

"I'm impressed, too, and I agree with my colleague. Eliza, I hope you'll take into consideration the things we talked about on the way here, but other than that, I have no suggestions to give."

Eliza's face colored again as Deniz and Dr. Yılmaz's heads swiveled in her direction. Had her boss just encouraged her to date her coworker? In code? Right in front of him? Life was weird as hell sometimes. "Thank you both. I think Deniz and I will come up with a schedule for working to-gether regularly and then we can get started on marketing the program as soon as you all in the administrative office give us the go ahead. When do you expect that might be?"

"We'd ideally like to start generating hype about the program before it's even open for enrollment. That will be happening at the beginning of the summer, so I think starting some slow promotion now and then really ramp-ing it up as summer gets closer would be just great." Dr.

Yılmaz said. "Now, if that's all for us today, I've got another meeting I need to get to."

They all got to their feet again and said their goodbyes. Once the two directors had left, Deniz and Eliza faced each other in the room. "I'll walk you out?" he offered.

"That would be great, thanks," Eliza smiled.

As they walked to the university gates, Deniz and Eliza debriefed their presentation. She praised his creative skills while he complimented her delivery.

"We make a pretty good team, huh?" she asked.

"Of course! Why do you sound surprised?" His eyes met hers and there was a bashfulness to them she hadn't seen before.

"I didn't think we were friends," she shrugged. "I think I jumped to conclusions too soon with you, though. Even if we aren't friends, it seems like we can be great coworkers."

"Eliza," Deniz began, "I hate to be the one to tell you this, but I'm pretty sure we're friends now."

Twenty-One

Eliza's first class the next day was a listening lesson, and her students were practicing with a lecture. She wandered around the room while they listened to the lecture once, then twice, observing the notes they took and nudging a couple of them who had put their heads down on their desks to "listen with their eyes closed." She noticed the pages of notes Ahmad had taken, smiling at him when he looked up. He worked so hard, and that was going to show when he took his placement test again at the end of the semester. If all went well, she'd miss having him in class again...but he'd be exactly where he wanted to be.

At the front of the room was the teacher's computer, where Eliza was controlling both the lecture and the sound system. A chime sounded that hadn't been there during their first time listening to the lecture, so Eliza walked over to the desk to check it out. A notification had popped up that there was a new email for her from Dr. Çelik.

She checked the lecture and, seeing that there were still five minutes left, she clicked over to her email to read the message.

> **From:** aylincelik@ms.edu.tr
> **To:** elizabritt@ms.edu.tr
> **Subject:** Vacancies + Recommendations
>
> Dear Eliza,
>
> As we are nearing the end of the school year, it is time to think about our staffing needs for the upcoming academic year. While it is not yet clear how many of our current instructors will be renewing their contracts for the following year, it is evident that we will need to do some hiring, regardless. I will be posting the positions publicly at a later date, but as the assistant director, I wanted to give you the first chance to make any recommendations. Your performance this year has been excellent, and we will talk about your future at Med School at a later date. Please know that any recommendations you make will be moved to the top of the applicant pile. That's not an offer I've ever made before—and certainly never in writing—so please don't let me down.

Sincerely,
Aylin Çelik

That was exciting news—Dr. Bennett would be thrilled, and throwing him a consolation prize in the face of his disappointment about Mr. Collins and the Collins Language School seemed just the thing to do. Eliza fired off a quick message to Dr. Bennett as the lecture finished, forwarding him Dr. Çelik's email and including a note: *"Dr. B, thought you might want to see this! Let me know if you have anyone in mind who would be a good fit."*

By the end of the workday, Eliza still hadn't heard from Dr. Bennett. With news like that, he would have normally been on the phone within half an hour, eager to scheme and plan and figure out the next steps forward. Acting on a hunch, Eliza called his office phone as she packed up her bag to go home.

"Dr. Bennett's office," an unfamiliar voice answered.

"Er...hello. This is Eliza Britt. Is Dr. Bennett available?"

"No, I'm sorry he isn't. Could I please take a message?"

"Could you tell me where he is, actually? Is everything alright? I sent him an email earlier today and haven't heard anything from him yet, which is so unlike him..."

The voice on the other end was cold and clinical. "I'm afraid I can't share any details about Dr. Bennett or his whereabouts. Would you like to leave a message?"

"I'm sorry. Who is this? I've worked with Dr. Bennett for years, and I've never heard someone besides Larry answer his phone. It just rattled me, that's all."

"I'm one of the secretaries here. Dr. Bennett had his calls directed to our desk, but I can't say more than that."

"Oh, you must work with Larry!" Eliza exclaimed. "I know Larry. Of course, Larry isn't there to answer the phone, because he's here! In Turkey! With me."

"Oh, right," the voice said, unimpressed. "You must be *that* Eliza. Anyway, did you have a message for Dr. Bennett?"

"Just ask him to call me back, please. He has my number."

When the call ended, Eliza couldn't shake the feeling that something was amiss. Dr. Bennett had never been unavailable to her, but she didn't want to jump to conclusions or assume the worst. He was an elderly man, that was true, but he'd always been in good health...hadn't he? He was probably just taking a day off. Or sitting in on a lecture. Nothing to worry about here.

Eliza's office phone rang then, startling her. "Hello?" she answered.

"Eliza, it's Dr. Çelik. I'm glad I caught you. Do you have a moment to talk? Could you come to my office?"

"Er...it's just...the last shuttle is about to leave, so..."

"I'll take you back to the city with me if need be, Eliza. It's important. Please." The urgency in Dr. Çelik's voice was a surprise, so she agreed and gathered her things. She locked her office door behind her as she set off for Dr. Çelik's office.

The door opened before her, and the director gestured to a chair, pulling her own next to Eliza's. On the table in front of them were a few documents, resumes and cover letters from the looks of it.

"I have to thank you," Dr. Çelik said. "I knew you were good, but I didn't know you were *this* good." She waved her hand over the documents.

"What do you mean?" Eliza asked. "What are all these?"

"I just sent you that email about the upcoming vacancies this morning. And here I already have a stack of applications, including two *very* promising ones with glowing recommendations from your Dr. Bennett. You don't waste any time! I think we'll schedule our first interviews by the end of the week."

"That's great news! I'm as surprised as you are," Eliza admitted. "I didn't realize Dr. Bennett would jump right into action like that, but I'm thrilled he has. Did you want to show me the resumes? Get my opinion?"

Dr. Çelik picked up the papers. "I'm not sure that would be appropriate. I have a feeling some of these are people you know personally, rather than professionally, and I wouldn't want to put you in a compromising position of having to offer criticism for one of your friends. I just wanted to thank you, actually. And perhaps to talk about your future here at Med School, if that's something you're interested in."

"Wow! I wasn't expecting that conversation to happen quite yet." Eliza's brow grew warm. "But I can tell you I've been very happy here, both in Antalya and at Med School. I'm certainly open to talking about extending my contract.

Though perhaps we could do it when I've had a bit of time to prepare."

"Alright, Eliza. Thank you again." She checked her watch. "Well, that was quicker than I expected. It looks like you can still catch the last shuttle if you leave right now. See you tomorrow."

Twenty-Two

A phone ringing in the middle of the night jolted Eliza awake. The red light from her alarm clock met her eyes, blinking 3:14 and letting her know it was an inappropriate time to be receiving a call. She fumbled for her cell phone and saw that Dr. Bennett was on the other end of the line. That didn't seem right…it had to be—Eliza did some quick math that wasn't quite as quick as it would be if she'd been fully awake—after seven o'clock. He couldn't be in the office, could he? And if he was at home—and if he remembered she was in Turkey, in a vastly different time zone—why was he calling her, or thinking about work at all?

Through the thin wall separating their rooms, Eliza heard Crystal groan. The sound of her friend waking up discombobulated and annoyed redirected Eliza's attention to the still ringing phone in her hand. She pushed the button to accept the call and raised the phone to her ear.

"Lizzy!" Dr. Bennett cried before she could even greet him. "Oh, it's just terrible! What are we going to do?"

The concern in his voice jolted Eliza further out of her slumber and nearer to crisis management mode. She cleared her throat, hoping to convey wakefulness in her response—though, as she thought about it more, why should she care if Dr. Bennett thought she sounded sleepy when he called in the middle of the night?—and responded to him. "What happened? What's going on?"

"Oh, it's just terrible! Someone has stolen my identity or hacked my emails…I don't know exactly, but it's terrible! I just don't know what to do, where to start. What do I do?"

"Er…slow down a little, please. It's the middle of the night and I'm not exactly following what you're saying."

"…Right. Sorry about that, Lizzy. I'm just so stressed I couldn't even think before I called you. I didn't know who else to talk to about it!"

"What happened? Did someone steal your wallet? You know you need to call your credit card company and report it. It'll all be okay. It's not a big deal; they help people with these kinds of things all the time."

"It's not that!" Dr. Bennett's voice raised. "I wish it were that simple. My wallet is right here in my pocket. No, it's…I don't know…my emails? My computer files? I just don't know what to do about it, but I think it's too late to fix it. Oh, poor Larry!"

That got Eliza's attention. "Larry? How is Larry connected to this? Did he do something? Did something happen to him? Can you start at the beginning, please?"

Dr. Bennett sighed. "Well, I got your message this afternoon about the email you sent. Only, there wasn't any email. No sign of it anywhere! And you know how scattered I can be, so I was searching for it, making sure it wasn't in the trash can or the spam folder, when all of a sudden a new message from Dr. Çelik of all people pops up!"

"Wow," breathed Eliza. "How long has it been since you heard from her?"

"Too long. I was pretty sure she thought I was a fool and had written off even a friendly working relationship completely. So I was very surprised, very happy to hear from her."

"What did her email say?"

"That's where all of this began. She was very kind, said she was so glad to hear from me and that she appreciated the time and attention I had given to her request. She was very impressed with the candidates I had recommended and would be moving forward with both of them. She thanked me again, expressed hopes that the two of us might connect at a conference in the future or collaborate on some upcoming research. I was flabbergasted. Completely and utterly flabbergasted..."

Putting aside the fact that Dr. Bennett apparently had a crush on Dr. Çelik, Eliza directed her attention to the part of his story that had made her stomach drop with a feeling of foreboding. "Could I ask...what email was she referring to? Did you send her an email? Refer some candidates to her?"

There was silence on the other end for a moment. "I didn't send anything to her, Eliza. That's why I think someone hacked my email. I even went through my sent emails folder, typed her name in the search bar, pored over all of it...no sign of anything."

Eliza felt her chin drop. "...and? What did you do after that? Did you...*tell*...Dr. Çelik that you didn't send her an email? That whatever she had received had been a mistake? A hacker?" *Please tell me you nipped this thing in the bud and communicated, for the love of God!* How many arguments, how much heartache had been caused in her lifetime by miscommunication—or lack of communication?

"I couldn't, Eliza! Whatever she received, clearly it impressed her! It impressed her enough to talk to me again, to break the vow of silence she seemed to have taken against me. It's not like she received a message requesting a Western Union money wire, or blasting her with inappropriate pictures. The message she got from me was something...good. Something she wanted to read. I don't think it was a love letter, either. It sounds like it was professional and helpful and like it connected her with people she was happy to meet. Maybe..." His tone was hopeful now. "...maybe, even if it was a mistake, maybe it's all working out in the best interest of everyone involved."

"You can't really believe that. This wasn't divine intervention! It sounds like it was someone behind the scenes, someone with access to your email pulling strings to get what they wanted. And you need to come clean about it. You can't let Dr. Çelik move forward with this. You can't let her think you're competent and capable and her professional equal when you can't even keep your email account secure!"

Eliza knew by Dr. Bennett's silence that she had overstepped. She had been too harsh with her words, but what more could he expect of her when he called her at three o'freaking'clock in the morning? If he wanted polite, socially acceptable Eliza, then he should call during the hours in which she was her human self, not the hours when she was supposed to be powered down and recharging for the next day. She sighed and spoke up again. "I'm sorry that was harsh. Wait..." Realization dawned, along with horror. "Why were you talking about Larry earlier? You don't think *he...*"

"I know it, Lizzy." Eliza could hear the sadness in Dr. Bennett's voice. "Even if you think I'm irresponsible and technologically inept, I do know *some* things about internet safety. There's only one person other than me who can access my email account, and it's Larry Smith. It must have been him. There's no other explanation. He must have read your email and responded to it and then deleted both messages, so I'd never know."

"Wow...that scumbag! I can't believe he—"

"No, dear." Dr. Bennett broke in. "Larry would never do something like this unless he was in trouble, I just know it. He's a good egg, responsible and conscientious. I just keep thinking about where he must be, who he must be with...the things he is having to do to get by in that strange city in that faraway, exotic land. I'm worried about him."

"Wait, you think Larry was *forced* to do this? By who?" Eliza was incredulous.

"Of course! He's mixing with the wrong crowd, just trying to stay off the street, stay safe...someone must have found out who he was and used that connection for their own evil gain. Poor Larry! Oh Lizzy, if only you hadn't driven him away! He might still be safe then…that poor child!"

Eliza had run out of things to say in response to Dr. Bennett's wails. Yes, she had been unkind to Larry, and she took responsibility for him no longer being safe and secure in her apartment, checking in regularly with Dr. Bennett. But she refused to believe he was all sweetness and light, that he had gotten swept up in some underground criminal network in Antalya with a soft spot for academic teaching positions. She may have just woken up from a dream, but even in that state, she was confident that no such network existed.

"What do you want me to do?" she asked. "I can try to track Larry down. And I can talk with Dr. Çelik, too. Maybe get a peek at the applications she supposedly received from you."

"That's a good start, Lizzy, thank you. I just hope it isn't too late for Larry. Oh, I do hope you can find him!"

"I will. I'm not sure how yet, but I will," Eliza said. "I'll keep you updated on what I learn. Try to get some sleep."

"Oh, I will! I'm sure it'll be hard, but I'll try…" Dr. Bennett hung up, and Eliza leaned back against her headboard. It still wasn't four o'clock yet, but she was too wound up now to go back to sleep. She was tempted to regret leaving her phone's ringer on last night, even if she knew that was futile. This crisis would have been waiting for her in the morning, even if she *had* been able to get a few more hours of sleep.

She shuffled out into the apartment's living room and flipped on the light. If she was already awake, she may as well try to get a bit of work done. There were lessons that needed planning, essays that needed grading, and a mystery that needed solving as soon as possible. The more of her regular work she could get done now, the more time she'd have to devote to that mystery during her work day.

"Hey! Wake up!"

Eliza woke with a start to see Crystal's face in front of hers, a cup of steaming coffee in her hand. She groaned and rubbed her hand over her face, stifling a yawn. "What time is it?" she asked.

Crystal shoved the coffee in her face. "You need this more than I do, I guess. It's seven thirty. Did you sleep out here last night?"

"Oh shit!" Eliza sat bolt upright. "I have to leave in fifteen minutes! Shit shit shit." She scrambled to her feet, swallowing gulps of hot coffee as she gathered the papers scattered around her and shoved them into her work bag. "I can't believe I fell back asleep!"

"What happened? Why were you sleeping on the couch, anyway?"

"Ugh, it's a whole mess and too long to explain right now. But it starts with Dr. Bennett calling me in the middle of the night to stress me out and ends with me waking up in a pile of essays and drool just about thirty seconds ago."

Crystal's eyes flashed. "He...called you in the middle of the night? What the actual..."

"It's okay," Eliza explained. "It wasn't, like, a typical Dr. B. freak-out about nothing. This actually warranted a middle of the night call. I just didn't think I'd be able to wind down enough after it to fall asleep again. I figured I'd sit on the couch, grading papers, until it was time to drink coffee and get dressed at a nice leisurely pace." She laughed a mirthless laugh. "I guess that's what I get for thinking I don't need an alarm clock just this once."

· ♥ · ♥ · ♥ · ♥ · ♥ ·

Within twelve minutes, Eliza was dressed with brushed teeth, unwashed hair pulled up into a ponytail, and the rest of her coffee poured into a travel mug. Her shuttle stop was a five-minute walk from her front door on a normal day, and she checked her watch now to confirm that she did, in fact, need to run if she was going to make it. Slinging her messenger bag over her shoulder, Eliza jogged down the street, ignoring the incredulous looks of the people she passed. In the months she'd spent in Antalya, she hadn't noticed many people running for exercise on this particular route, and she certainly hadn't seen anyone running in a pencil skirt and button down blouse. She swallowed any remaining pride and picked up the pace.

As she turned the corner, she saw the sight she had been hoping she wouldn't see. The shuttle bus was already there, stopped at the side of the road at the corner where she normally boarded. She was still a few blocks away, and her heart sank as she saw the bus lurch forward as the driver put it in gear and continued on his way.

"Wait!" she cried, her run turning into a sprint. She waved her arms, though it was futile. There was no way anyone on the bus would see her from this far away, especially if they'd already given up on the idea that she was going to work today. Nevertheless, she continued running, waving, and yelling until she made it to the empty street corner.

"Shit!" She pulled out her phone and called Jack. Maybe he could get the driver's attention and...what? She would run up the road after the bus until she got to it? So in addition to being late for work herself, she would make *everyone* else on the shuttle late, too? That seemed like a surefire way to turn any tepid working relationships into full-on enemies. It didn't matter, anyway—Jack hadn't answered his phone after four rings and Eliza had just heard an automated voice telling her his mailbox was full. She was on her own.

There was a taxi call button near where Eliza was waiting, and she thanked her lucky stars she was in Turkey, the only place she'd ever seen such a novel invention. Pushing that button would summon a taxi from the local taxi stand, and in her experience, it had only ever taken a few minutes for the taxi to arrive. No need to flail her arms around or learn to whistle with her fingers; just...push a button and wait. So she pushed. And she waited.

...and waited. And pushed the button again. Was this thing even working? Was there even a way to know that it was connected to anything? The anxiety Eliza had been feeling ever since she'd woken up on the couch this morning grew to its apex as she checked the time again. If she didn't get in a vehicle soon, she was going to be late for her first class. Late! Eliza Britt had never been late for a class, and, so help her God, she wasn't going to start today. She set off walking along the main road, searching for another taxi call button, a taxi stand, a familiar face that might be heading in the direction of the university...

And just when she was debating the merits of calling in sick to avoid the shame of being late for work, a car pulled up next to her and rolled down its passenger side window. Eliza kept walking, not in the mood for early morning flirtation or a Turkish language skill reality check as she attempted to help a lost person figure out how to get to their destination. As she quickened her pace, she heard her name being called.

"Eliza! Wait! Where are you going? Do you need a ride?"

With her back to the car, Eliza closed her eyes and swore under her breath. Of all the people to run into when she was sweaty, stressed, and on the verge of tears, Deniz Aydem was the last one she hoped would be here now. Showing up like a knight in shining armor...even if horsepower was the only thing standing between her and an on time work arrival. She gritted her teeth and turned around to face her would-be savior.

"Hi! I'm...about to be late for work. I've been trying to get a taxi, but—"

"Get in." Deniz leaned over and opened the door. "I've got time. I was heading in early anyway, so I can take you to Med School before I swing back to work."

"Really?" Eliza asked, but she was already sliding her messenger bag off her shoulder and stepping into the car, stowing her bag at her feet. "You don't have to do this...are you sure? Really?"

"I don't mind, I promise." Deniz checked his mirrors as he pulled back on the road and began to drive towards the university. "If you don't mind me asking, what happened this morning? It doesn't seem like you to be so..." He glanced in her direction, gesturing towards her appearance.

Eliza's cheeks colored, seeing herself through his eyes and the hot mess she was this morning. "I overslept...I busted my ass to get ready, ran to catch the bus, but I just missed it. And then the taxi button wasn't working, but I didn't know that until I'd already wasted another ten minutes waiting for it. I just...I've just been out of sorts ever since that phone call."

"What phone call?" Deniz raised his eyebrows. "Is everything okay back home?"

"No. I mean, yes...my family is fine, as far as I know. It wasn't any of them calling me in the middle of the night. It was my old advisor, Dr. Bennett. He called me at three in the morning, and there's this whole mess with his emails being hacked and some recommendations being sent that he didn't know about and he thinks his assistant Larry—my friend Larry, who's here in Antalya right now—had something to do with it, and...God. I don't know why I'm telling you all of this, I just..."

Deniz's brows furrowed deeper and deeper as he had listened to Eliza talk. As she trailed off, he spoke up. "What...what happened with Larry?"

"I haven't seen him in a week, and Dr. Bennett thinks he's been influenced by a bad crowd or something. Like there's an underground network of people in Antalya who are trying to get ahead in the English teaching business." She laughed, but stopped when she saw the seriousness on Deniz's face.

"Eliza, are you…" He steeled his expression before he continued. "Are you in contact with Cem?"

"No, why? I think he ghosted me, actually. No communication from him in…gosh, it's been almost as long since I heard from him as it has been since I saw Larry last."

"Do you think that's a coincidence or…?"

Eliza's eyes widened in shock. "Well, I *did* until right now! What are you suggesting? That there *is* some kind of underground teaching market and Cem is the mastermind behind it?"

"No, as far as I know, there isn't a network of teachers with no morals in Antalya. But I do know one person with no morals who wants the prestige and steady paycheck that comes from being a teacher."

"Prestige? Ha!" Eliza cackled, but Deniz wasn't joking.

"I know in your country you make a lot of jokes about the lack of respect that teachers get. I watch American TV programs, so I understand the humor. But here, for someone like Cem, for someone like me…it's different. We come from families that have had to work really hard to get anything in this world, and our parents desperately want to see us succeed. To surpass them. To know that we'll be able to provide for them, to take our turn as the caregivers."

Chastened, Eliza swallowed. "I'm sorry, I didn't even think of it like that, Deniz. This seems like a good time to ask what happened between you and Cem. If it's relevant, I mean."

"It's relevant, alright." He tightened his jaw. "Let me guess, he told you I had him kicked out of the program because he was outshining me as the teacher's pet?" Off her nod, he laughed without humor. "What a total ass. I might be petty, but I'm not *that* petty. No, what *actually* happened is that he had organized a scam in the English department, and when he asked me about it, I told our advisor. I knew our advisor, maybe even our entire department, would be at stake, and I didn't want us all to lose our chances."

"I'm not following exactly. What did he do?"

"He…he was so determined to succeed that he tried to game the system. Rather than putting his effort into studying, he spent all his time trying to figure out how to cheat his way into being at the top of the program. But then, he got greedy. He tried to systematize it, to profit off of other students. He was selling essays he'd stolen from one of our classmates, blackmailing the student assistants into giving him the answer keys…it was a mess. And our program was still new. Still trying to earn respect in Turkey, let alone internationally. Dr. Yılmaz was dead set on being accredited and having students from our program presenting papers and research internationally…and Cem put all of that on the line."

"Wow…I don't even know what to say…"

"But it wasn't just his future that mattered, you know? He wasn't the only one who was the child of farmers, the only one who was counting on their scholarship and this program to change the course of their family's future. It was all of us. There were thirty of us in that cohort, and he put everyone's future on the line. If it were just me, I wouldn't have said anything. I'd have dealt with it on my own. But the things he did to my friends, the way he blackmailed people I care about…I couldn't let it go."

"Of course not," Eliza breathed, fixing her eyes on the side of Deniz's face. There was tension there as he remembered that dark time, but there was something else too...relief, perhaps?

"I wanted to tell you that before," he said. "Because I wanted you to know who he was. But when you didn't want to know, when you didn't want to hear it, I had to respect that. And I hoped that maybe he had changed, that maybe he had grown up."

They were getting close to the university now, its gate just two turns away from where they were on the highway. Eliza started and blurted out, "Wait, do you think Cem is behind this thing my professor called about? Oh my God. Oh my God, what if he is? What if he's doing the same thing here that he did with your classmates? And Larry? Naïve Larry is going to take the fall for it?" She reached over and grabbed Deniz's forearm. "Is that what you're saying?"

Deniz met her eyes, and his expression was downcast. "That's the gut feeling I have. I can't tell you for sure, but I can help you get to the bottom of it."

"No, you've done more than enough. Thank you, Deniz. Really. I should have listened to you sooner, and I'm sorry I didn't. If you want to just pull over here, I can hop out so you don't have to deal with going through security at the entrance. Thanks again." Eliza opened her door and jumped out as soon as Deniz slowed to a stop, avoiding eye contact as she hurried out of the car, through the gate, and into the building.

Twenty-Three

There were a mere five minutes to spare before Eliza's first class started. She dropped her bag on her desk chair, rummaged around in it to find the teacher's books she needed for her first few lessons, picked up her attendance sheets off her desk, and set off for the classroom on the second floor. She smoothed down her hair with one hand, trying to ease the wildness she knew had been in her eyes ever since she saw the shuttle speed away this morning.

She didn't have time now to think about all that Deniz had told her, but her mind was a mess of swirling thoughts and feelings, regardless. She had been so harsh to him. She hadn't given him a chance to explain himself, and for some reason she couldn't begin to fathom now, she had given *Cem* the benefit of the doubt. His handsome face had no doubt played a role in it, as much as she hated to admit that to herself. But just look where it had gotten her.

In her classroom, Eliza fired up the computer. As the students filed in, she had a moment to log into her email and send a message to Dr. Çelik. If only she knew what to say to her...*Dear Dr. Çelik, Please let me see the applications you received yesterday; I have reason to believe there's an evil mastermind behind them.* No, that was too dramatic. But she needed to convey to her director the direness of the situation without, if possible, damaging Dr. Bennett's reputation in her mind. Damn him. Why did he have to go about complicating all of this? It should be simple—get the truth out in the open, regardless of how it impacted anyone's feelings.

Eliza sighed. It wasn't that simple. And she couldn't fault anyone else for their role in this mess. Not when it was all so clearly her fault. She had trusted Cem. She had even promised to help him find a job. She had alienated Larry. She had practically driven the two of them into each other's arms when she looked at it like that. How could she be so stupid?

Stupid and *selfish*, a voice in the back of her head chimed in. *Everything you've done, you've done to further your own career with no concern whatsoever for anyone who gets in your way. You hurt people again, just like always.* Eliza shook her head, trying to shut that voice up. This was a prime opportunity for her inner critic to speak up, but she didn't have time to wallow. Not when there was a classroom full of students awaiting their first lesson of the day. Well, "awaiting," was a strong word—there were a few eager beavers with books and pencils on their desks, but it was impossible to ignore the handful of students at the back of the room who were nearly asleep again. Not to mention all of them who had their eyeballs glued to their phone screens.

Rising to her feet, Eliza greeted the class. "Today, we're going to be focusing on grammar. You learned about the present perfect tense in our last class, so today we'll be practicing it." She turned to the whiteboard with her dry erase marker in hand and began to write.

I have been in Turkey since August.

I have been teaching for 4 years.

She underlined the words "since" and "for" and explained, "We use these words when we are referring to time. 'Since' is for the starting point of an action, and 'for' is for sharing how long something has been going on." Together, they came up with a few more examples using each sentence structure, and then Eliza turned the class loose to write their own sentences.

Walking around the room and peeking at what her students were writing, Eliza was pleased to see that, for the most part, they were using the two words correctly. This wasn't like the time they'd collectively struggled with the difference between "bored" and "boring." Though she had to admit, there was a certain charm when an out-of-sorts twenty-year-old announced, "Teacher, I am boring," in the middle of a lesson.

From the back of the room, she looked up at the board and read the sentences she had written again. "I have been in Turkey since August. I have been teaching for 4 years." *Only since August, and yet you managed to create a real mess. I doubt you'll be in Turkey much longer after you come clean with Dr. Çelik.* There was that damn voice again. But something about that phrase "come clean with Dr.

Çelik" had loosened something in Eliza's chest. She knew what she had to do now. She had to tell Dr. Çelik what happened, and she had to take the blame squarely on her shoulders. Yes, Dr. Bennett was involved and his reputation would likely receive some tarnish, but she, Eliza, deserved the lion's share.

As the students left the classroom, Eliza sat back down at the desk at the front of the room and wiggled the mouse to wake up the computer. Her email account was still open on the screen, including the blank draft message addressed to Dr. Çelik. Before she could lose her nerve, she wrote and sent the message that she knew would change everything.

Dear Dr. Çelik,

I'd like to schedule some time to talk with you today about the candidates you received yesterday. I believe there's been a serious mistake made, and it may be in the best interest of the university to go in a different direction. I know you were concerned about my ability to be impractical, but my concerns are professional, not personal, I can assure you. I apologize for any inconvenience caused by these applicants; please know that it is my mistake and not Dr. Bennett's.

Sincerely,
Eliza

After sending that message, it wasn't exactly easy to focus on her next lessons, but the students were a welcome distraction. Ahmad and several friends from the extracurricular group were in this class, and their dedication and positive attitudes always reminded Eliza of why she went into education in the first place. She'd miss this when she was gone from Antalya. Because she was sure she'd be gone from Antalya soon. She couldn't imagine Dr. Çelik hearing the full truth of how badly she had managed the hiring process and still trusting her to be her right-hand woman next year.

A lump of emotion rose in Eliza's throat and tears pricked at the backs of her eyes. She cleared her throat and swiped at her eyes. If she was going to melt into a puddle of tears about this, she would decidedly *not* be doing it in a classroom full of students. They didn't need to see that, and she didn't need to add any more black marks to her already tainted professionalism.

Eliza had always enjoyed teaching. From the first moments in front of a student teaching classroom during her college years, she had felt...something. A sliding into place. Like she was finally where she had always belonged. As a teenager, she had been awkward and uncomfortable in her skin, especially uncomfortable when attention was directed her way. Public speaking was a nightmare, and she'd feared those same feelings would crop up when she was in front of a group of students.

But it hadn't been like that at all. In front of a group of students, she had felt her nervous energy ease. She had spoken confidently and clearly, she had laughed and joked, she had loosened up into a version of herself she hadn't experienced since the innocence of childhood.

And she was going to lose that now. Breaking the trust of her director, in her first leadership role no less, couldn't be good. Dr. Çelik was a serious and stern woman and she took her responsibilities to heart. Eliza had gone so far against her wishes that the idea of her supervisor demanding that she take her things and leave today wasn't farfetched. Not at all.

There was no response from Dr. Çelik by lunch time, and Eliza's stress level had only increased. She went down to the cafeteria at noon, going through the motions of a normal day despite the fact that her appetite was nonexistent.

Jack was waiting in the cafeteria line when she arrived, and Eliza nearly crumpled to the ground at the sight of a familiar and friendly face.

"Hey you!" He smiled. Then, off something he detected in her expression, he asked in a lower voice, "What's going on?"

"Can't talk about it right now. It's a mess, though. Larry...Cem...I'll tell you later. After work?"

"I'll save you a spot on the shuttle home?"

Eliza didn't want to tell him she wasn't sure she'd be allowed to stick around long enough to take the shuttle home, so she tried a different approach. "Ugh, don't even say that word to me—shuttle." She shuddered, forcing levity and humor into her expression.

"Yeah...what happened to you this morning? I thought maybe you were sick or something. How did you get to school?"

"I certainly *tried* to take the shuttle. I ran after it for a bit, but nobody saw me, I guess. I tried to call you..."

Jack winced. "Sorry...I left my phone at home. I've been doing that lately, so I can't check it obsessively to see if Barış has miraculously started talking to me again."

"It's okay. I actually ended up getting a ride here from Deniz." She locked eyes with Jack as she delivered the end of her sentence, pleased to see his expression convey exactly the level of shock she had expected.

"Deniz?" Jack exclaimed. Then, lower, he asked, "Deniz? I thought you didn't even like him. What were you doing with him this morning? Oh my God, did you two hook up last night?"

Eliza could feel herself blushing. "Seriously, Jack! No, he was just in the right place at the right time. And don't wiggle your eyebrows at me! That wasn't a euphemism. There was no hooking up, I swear. He just pulled up in his car right as I was about to have a meltdown about not making it to work. And he drove me here."

Jack's eyebrows climbed nearly to his hairline. "Huh. What a gentleman. What an...unexpected gentleman. Sounds like a nice way to start your day."

"It was, actually. Better than taking a taxi and definitely better than being late for work."

Just then, Eliza felt a hand on her shoulder and turned to look directly into Dr. Çelik's eyes.

"Eliza, sorry to disturb you during your lunch break. I'm going back to my office now, and I'll have some time for you to stop by and talk before the afternoon lessons begin. Shall we say...half an hour?"

Eliza gulped. "Yes, that sounds fine. I'll see you then."

As Dr. Çelik walked away, Jack studied Eliza's face. Then he pulled her out of the line and away from the cafeteria. She started to protest, but he stopped her with a look. Once they had left the building, they began speed-walking to the other end of campus. Finally, Eliza turned to Jack and asked him where the hell he was taking them.

"Duh, for a walk. You're clearly nervous as hell about whatever Dr. Çelik wants to talk to you about, so lunch was going to be a real non starter. I've got a granola bar in my desk if you want it later on. Now...do you want to talk about what's going on, or do you just want to blow off steam until it's time for your little meeting?"

"Let's just walk," Eliza said with gratitude in her eyes. Jack squeezed her shoulder, and the two set off at a pace.

Twenty minutes later, Eliza's nerves had calmed enough that her hands weren't shaking when she knocked on Dr. Çelik's door. She took a deep breath as she entered the room and nodded in greeting to the director as she took a seat across from her.

"Eliza, thank you for meeting with me. Your email alarmed me, and I wanted to give you this opportunity to explain yourself."

"Thank you, Dr. Çelik." Eliza gulped. "I appreciate you meeting with me, and I won't take much of your time." Dr. Çelik nodded to her to continue, so she did. "When you shared the job openings with me, I reached out to Dr. Bennett, my former advisor and the person I trust the most in this field, and I did it in confidence. He has always had my best interest at heart, and I've never seen him do anything unprofessional."

"I believe you. I know Dr. Bennett, too, and I agree with your statement."

"That's good. I spoke with him yesterday, and I have reason to believe that someone else sent you that email from his account. That his email server was accessed by someone else—I think I know who—and that person sent you an email and deleted all evidence of it. So, I'd like to see the applications you received. To confirm if they came from the person I suspect is behind all of this."

Dr. Çelik's stony expression didn't give away much, but Eliza knew she had to be fuming inside. Eliza's incompetence had complicated what should have been a streamlined, professional hiring process. Hell, the hiring process hadn't even started yet. Her failure had messed it up before it had even begun.

"I'm deeply sorry, Dr. Çelik. Please don't be frustrated with Dr. Bennett. I know his email account should be more secure so that this never would have happened...but really, I never should have initiated this conversation with him in writing. I should have called him. I should have..."

"I understand, Eliza," the director interrupted. "I'll show you the resumes I received yesterday, and we can proceed from there." She shuffled through some papers on her desk and handed a small stack to Eliza. "Are you familiar with either of these candidates?"

Eliza thumbed through the pages and her heart dropped. In front of her were a cover letter, resume, and bachelor's and master's diplomas from Cem Demir, but...the same documents were there bearing Larry's name, too. As Eliza scanned the papers, she felt sick to her stomach. Larry and Cem had been elaborate in their forgery. The diplomas were professional, and the experience and education listed on both of their resumes clearly showed they were ideal candidates for the job. If only *any* of it had been true.

Looking up into Dr. Çelik's eyes, Eliza let the pain she was feeling show on her face. "I know both of these men. And I know these documents have been forged. Larry is a graduate assistant at Med School, and he has *not* completed his degree. And Cem...well, you should ask Dr. Yılmaz and Deniz about him."

Dr. Çelik narrowed her eyes and spoke. "This is most disconcerting, Eliza. I called the references listed for both of those men yesterday, and I heard glowing reviews about their past performances. I spoke to no fewer than three references for each of them, as a matter of fact. What you're saying now counters what I've been told by six people who are experts in their own fields."

Eliza couldn't believe her ears. "Who did you speak to? Was it anyone you know? How do you know they didn't fake it all?"

Dr. Çelik lifted her hand to stop Eliza from saying any more. "That's enough of that. I don't owe you an explanation, not when you've bungled up every contribution you've made to this program. As far as I'm concerned, sending these candidates my way is the one way you and Dr. Bennett may have almost redeemed yourselves for the chaos you've caused here. Even if you seem to have a personal vendetta against these two men, for some reason I can't understand. I couldn't help but notice you told me to ask *Deniz* about what he thinks about Cem. Letting our personal feelings get in the way of our work is highly unprofessional, Miss Britt."

"I understand," Eliza said. "And I'm sorry I brought this information to you this way. I wish..."

"That's enough," Dr. Çelik said. "You should go now if you're going to make it to your afternoon classes on time today. No need for another repeat of this morning."

Eliza felt her face flush. How did Dr. Çelik know about this morning? Of course there had been a report of her not being on the shuttle. And of course the security guards had noticed her getting out of a man's car. If that information had gotten back to Dr. Çelik, it made total sense she would come to all sorts of conclusions—personal, professional, or otherwise—about the nature of Eliza's relationship with Deniz. "I wasn't—I didn't—" she started.

Dr. Çelik held up her hand again. "I really don't need to know. But when your personal business affects your professional performance, it becomes a problem. I won't warn you again, Ms. Britt. Your future at our institution depends on the two of us having a solid relationship of mutual trust, and unfortunately, that no longer seems like something I can count on. "

Twenty-Four

Crushed. Devastated. Completely and utterly alone. Eliza stared dumbfounded at her desk, her eyes glazing over as she lost herself in a world of swirling, anxious thoughts. Dr. Çelik hadn't believed her. How could it be? How was it that *her ass* was the one on the line now, when there was real fraud going on right under their noses? And how could it be that Larry—naïve, clueless Larry—had been roped into something this serious, with this much potential to tank his professional reputation and take down others' careers along with it by Cem, of all people?

Because there was no way the truth wouldn't come out at some point. They couldn't get away with this, they just couldn't. But when the truth was revealed, both State University's reputation—for supposedly giving him a degree that he hadn't earned—and Med School's—for hiring someone entirely unqualified over other far more deserving candidates—would be tarnished. Eliza started as another thought entered her mind. Med School's English program was new. Was it already accredited? What if the same thing was in danger of happening here that Deniz had prevented all those years ago when he was a student?

She needed to speak to him. Deniz. She knew that, but she felt her phone repelled from her hand like a powerful magnet with the same pole. Admitting all of this to him would be so embarrassing. Embarrassing didn't even begin to cover it—it would be humiliating. All the esteem he had given her, it was undeserved, and she didn't want to be the one to make him realize that.

Because it wasn't just the fact that her career was on the line that hurt so much. No, the truth of all of her many failings confronting her at once was excruciating. "I'm a garbage human being," Eliza sobbed to herself as she dropped her head to her desk. "I managed to tank the most precious friendship I've ever had in record time, to alienate the one person who's always had my back. Who moved across the ocean just to keep me company, for crying out loud. What am I even going to have left when this is all over? No career, no friends, no one who even wants to get within five hundred feet of me if I'm this much of a hot mess."

The way this day had begun should have been interpreted for what it clearly was—a sign that nothing good was going to happen and she should have stayed in bed. From the first moment she had woken up on the couch this morning, things had gone from bad to worse to the unthinkable. The job she hadn't even been convinced she'd wanted…well, now that she was about to lose it, she could see how she really felt about it much more clearly.

She had barely had time to think about whether she'd want to renew her contract or not. This year had flown by so quickly that she'd hardly had time to eat, sleep, and breathe—never mind think about the future. But now, as she was staring down the barrel of potential unemployment, one thing was evident. Jobs aside, she wasn't done with Turkey yet. She'd barely seen anything outside of the Antalya city center. The trip to Kaş had stirred up her desire to explore and enjoy, but the stress of her job had kept that from happening. Or rather, her obsessive focus on her job and all its accompanying stress had kept that from happening.

But she wanted to walk around Sultanahmet in Istanbul at prayer time and hear the chorus of calls to prayer coming from at least ten mosques in the immediate surroundings. She wanted to go to Cappadocia, wake up at the crack of dawn, and spend way too much money on a tourist trap hot-air balloon ride. She wanted to take the time to learn more than the embarrassingly small amount of Turkish that she knew and meet more people than just the colleagues and students she'd spent all of her time with. She wanted to try actually *living* here, not just give up and slink home with her tail between her legs.

An uncomfortable feeling pricked deep in her stomach. She didn't want to do all of those things alone, either, as hard as it was to admit it to herself. She imagined herself in Sultanahmet Square and when she closed her eyes to visualize it, she was…holding hands…with Deniz? That couldn't be right. But there he was again, in Cappadocia, laughing with her in a hot-air balloon as it rose over the unique rock formations and the sun just crested the horizon.

A sob shook loose from Eliza's throat. None of that would happen, not the way things were unfolding right now. She'd been unkind to him from the beginning, and he'd been impossible to read. They'd started off on the wrong foot by all accounts—Eliza wasn't inclined to superstition, but regardless, she wondered if there had been an evil eye or two pointed in their direction at their first meeting. Could all of this have been avoided if she'd just slipped on the *nazar boncuğu* bracelet Crystal had given her to congratulate her on the new job? Thinking like that wouldn't help now, anyway.

A soft knock on the door jolted her out of her dark thoughts. "Eliza?" Jack's voice called. "Can I come in?"

"Yeah..." Eliza sat up and wiped her eyes. The joy she felt at the sound of her friend's familiar voice was matched only by the sight of his kind face, and her eyes overflowed with tears again.

"Oh my God," Jack rushed to her side, wrapping his arms around her. "What's wrong? What happened?"

Eliza told him everything. Any attempt at restraint was overrun by the sheer force of her emotions. Once she started spilling all that she had kept inside, it was like a dam had burst and there was no putting it back together.

Jack's disgust at what Larry and Cem had done—and at what little regard Dr. Çelik had shown for her concerns about it—mirrored her own. Before she could continue, he interrupted.

"Wait a second. Have you even talked to Crystal yet? Don't give me that look. I know something's been up with the two of you. You need to fix things with her first."

"You're right, Jack. Of course you're right. What would be the point of fighting for any of this if I didn't have my best friend to celebrate it with?"

Jack gave her a squeeze on the shoulder as he stood to leave. "It's going to be okay. You know that, right?"

Eliza laughed through tears. "No. Not even a little bit. But I'm glad to see you're feeling so confident."

"Call me later, okay? When you need me...when you and Crystal need me to help figure out how we're going to clean up this mess. I'll be there."

Before her work could be done that day, Eliza had two important emails to send. She sat down to write the first one to Deniz, and the words poured out.

To: denizaydem@at.edu.tr
From: elizabritt@ms.edu.tr
Subject: Thank You

Dear Deniz,

I don't know if I said it strongly enough this morning, but thank you. You rescued me when I was in the middle of a very stressful situation, and I am so grateful that you were there. That you didn't just drive on past, even when you would have been fully justified in doing just that.

I haven't been kind to you, I certainly haven't been a friend to you, and I wish that I had realized that sooner. I wish I could have been deserving of your kindness and friendship, but it's too late to change what has already happened. I'm sorry, truly, for not taking the time to get to know you sooner. I admire your strength of character, and it's obvious to me now, even if it's too late, that you are an exemplary human being.

To put it briefly, today was a disaster. Cem has struck again, and if I'm not able to stop the momentum, he will likely take down my friend Larry in the process. Perhaps even the Mediterranean School of Languages and my alma mater, State University, too. It's an absolute mess, and I'm sharing that with you because you know him. You know what he's capable of, and you've stopped him once before. I'm not asking you to help me fix this — this is my mess, I created it — but if we could, I don't know...talk about it? If you have the time, if you have the energy, I would really appreciate that.

Thank you, again. For helping me this morning, for telling me the truth about Cem, for being a friend even when I wasn't one to you. I really mean it.

Yours,
Eliza

P.S. How is Barış? I hope he's well, and I hope
he's happy. Jack has been miserable. I didn't
want to tell you that before because I wanted
to appear strong more than I wanted to be
honest, but that's the truth. I just wanted you
to know.

The second email that she had to write proved more
difficult. She opened a new "compose" screen and typed in
Larry's address, staring at the blinking cursor as the words
didn't come, the sentences didn't form. With a sigh, she
dove in, her own words to Deniz coming back in a new
form — better to be honest than to appear strong.

To: lawrencesmith@state.edu
From: elizabritt@ms.edu.tr
Subject: I'm sorry

Dear Larry,

I'm so sorry. I was a terrible friend to you.
No, I wasn't even a friend. I don't deserve
that title. I can't explain, and I won't try to
justify why I was such a total jerk. But it
was never about you, it was always about me.
Even when I was frustrated with something

you were doing, it was really just something I saw in you that reminded me of myself.

But you're not me, so that wasn't fair. You are a good person, Larry. You're capable and you're dedicated, and you're brave, too. I just wanted you to know that. That I'm sorry and that I really do care about you. I just want you to be safe and happy and living a good life. Okay? Would you write back and let me know you're okay, please?

xo,
Eliza

Rolling her shoulders in an effort to release all the tension that had accumulated during that day from hell, Eliza readied herself for the journey home. Walking down the hallway out of the building was such a commonplace action, she normally didn't give it a second thought. But after the conversation she'd had with Dr. Çelik today, it felt like she was walking the gauntlet. The fear of running into the disapproving director seized her, along with the panic that there might be others in the building who were aware of what had happened. Before she could talk herself out of it, she shoved her laptop into her messenger bag and left the office, locking the door behind her.

She had nearly made it to the door when a familiar voice made her skin crawl.

"Eliza, what a nice surprise." Her nose wrinkled in disgust at the sound of Cem's boasting tone.

"Cem," she said, without turning around. "What do you want?"

"My goodness, is that the welcome you give your new coworker?" He asked, as he stepped around her, into her line of sight. "With that kind of attitude, I'll be surprised if they keep you around for another contract. Not much of a team player, are we?"

"Why are you doing this?" she asked him.

He stepped closer and lowered his voice. "I'm just taking what's rightfully mine. And I love to watch you try to stop me and fail miserably. You can't take me down, sweetheart. I'm too good."

His cockiness had charmed her once, and now it disgusted her. "We'll see," she said, forcing her tone to stay as neutral and monotone as she could. "Good night, Cem." She left the building before he could get the last word, forcing herself to walk at a measured pace to the shuttle and not sprint out of his line of sight.

Twenty-Five

On the ride home, Eliza tried to keep herself calm and collected, she really did. But the smug expression on Cem's face combined with the disappointment she had seen in Dr. Çelik's eyes and she found her emotions rising the closer she got to her apartment. She had to do something, even if it meant watching her own career opportunities blow up in the process. She couldn't sit back and watch the Mediterranean School of Languages put its accreditation and its very existence on the line by hiring Cem.

Pulling out her phone for some aimless social media scrolling, hoping it would give her at least a temporary reprieve from her obsessive thoughts, Eliza noticed a missed call from Dr. Bennett. She hadn't spoken to him since the wee early hours of the morning, and there was a lot he needed to know about all that had unfolded since then. A quick text message reassured him she would call as soon as she was home—this was not a conversation to have on the crowded shuttle bus, where any number of people could overhear the juicy details.

At the apartment, Eliza felt her heart leap to find Crystal home. "I need to talk to you," she said, stomach in her throat. She couldn't bear the thought of another rejection just now, but even that fear couldn't stop her from making this right. "Do you have a minute? Please?"

Crystal had already stood to leave the room at the sound of the door opening, no doubt to keep up the status quo dance of avoiding each other the two roommates had been doing. "I guess so," she said, turning to face Eliza and crossing her arms over her chest.

Eliza stepped closer to her friend. "Crystal, I miss you. I'm sorry. I was a jerk. I've been a terrible friend to you lately, and you don't deserve that. I've been so focused on myself and my career and I just...I didn't see you. Not the way you needed to be seen. The way you deserved to be seen. Can we be okay again?"

Crystal's eyes met hers, and Eliza could see that they were wet. "I'd love to be done fighting," she said, "And thanks for the apology. It's been really shitty not talking to you, you know. I've missed you, but I just couldn't bring myself to be the first one to break the silence."

"Nor should you have been," said Eliza, pulling her in for a hug. "This was all my fault, and I'm so sorry."

Before the friends had too much time to make peace, there was a knock on the door. Eliza opened it to find Jack, a bag full of takeout food in his hands. "I tried to wait for you to call me, but I got bored." He pushed past Eliza into the kitchen, setting the bag on the counter. Finding

Crystal there, he greeted her. "Good, you're here. Did the two of you figure your shit out already?"

"We did…" Crystal trailed off. "What's going on?"

Eliza groaned. "There's so much to catch you up on, Crys. It was a big day and not in the good way."

Eliza filled Crystal in on all that had happened while the three of them arranged their food on plates and moved to the couch. "I don't know how this all happened at once like this," she said. "I feel like the drama surrounds me, but maybe I attract it somehow."

"That could be," Crystal said, pausing before she dug into her Adana dürüm. "Though I don't know how you could have predicted all this. Cem did a great job hiding his psychopathic tendencies at the beginning, and I certainly never imagined him and Larry joining forces for evil."

It was Eliza's turn to laugh. "Okay, you might be overstating that ever so slightly. Talking about evil psychopaths does help me put the events of the last 24 hours into some perspective. But I mean…if I had listened to Deniz sooner, maybe I could have avoided all of this." Eliza had filled Crystal in on Deniz's experience studying at university with Cem, and her friend's reaction had been similar to her own.

The three of them talked for an hour. By the time they'd cleared their plates, Eliza's tears had dried, and she had a renewed determination to right the wrongs she had caused. The only thing she hadn't shared with her friends were her feelings for Deniz and her sadness over the impossibility of anything developing between them. Saying it out loud would make it too real, and she wasn't ready for that yet.

Eliza took each of her friends' hands in her own. "I've been so focused on my work lately. I lost sight of you both, of life outside of building my career. What a joke that feels like now. I'm so sorry for that, and I'm so grateful for you being here for me today. You saved me, both of you. I'd still be a blubbering, hopeless mess if not for the two of you."

Jack and Crystal squeezed her hands back. "You're never a mess," said Jack. "You're human. And you were really brave, being vulnerable with us today. I hope you know that's always the right path to take. That even if you get hurt by it, being vulnerable with the people you love is always the brave choice."

After they were all fed and Eliza's tears had dried, it was time to figure out a plan. Crystal had gotten up to track down a notepad and pen when another knock on the door interrupted her return to the sofa. At the sound of her surprised squeak, Eliza called out, "What? Who is it?"

But it wasn't Crystal's voice that responded. It was a deep voice, one she had heard over and over in her head today, repeating the words he had spoken to her just that morning. "It's me, Eliza," Deniz said. "I hope you don't mind me coming here."

Eliza jolted to her feet, hurrying to meet Deniz and Crystal near the door. "Of course I don't mind! Thank you for coming. I...really appreciate it, actually."

"How did you know where we lived?" Crystal asked. "That's what I can't figure out."

Deniz looked bashful. "I should have asked you. I spoke with Jack today, actually, and he gave me your address."

"You spoke to Jack today?" Eliza was confused, throwing a look at her friend, who raised his arms in exaggerated confusion. Had those two men ever had a one-on-one conversation before? Not as far as she knew, but Deniz's expression had closed with discomfort and she didn't probe further. "Why are you here?"

"I read your email," he said, stepping closer to her. "I wanted to help. I wanted to see how you were doing. It sounds like Cem put you through hell today."

Eliza groaned. "I wish it were just Cem putting me through hell. At this point, I'll be very surprised if Dr. Çelik even lets me stay until the end of my contract."

Deniz frowned. "What?" he asked sharply. "She can't fire you, not over something like this, and not without evidence of wrongdoing. It's your word against his, and that isn't enough."

"Maybe she won't fire me, but she can make my remaining months so hellish that I quit, can't she? If she doesn't want me there, then maybe I shouldn't be there."

"I think you're getting ahead of yourself...surprise, surprise," Crystal interjected with a twinkle in her eye. "Deniz, why don't you come sit with us? Shall I make some tea?" She gestured towards the couch while she went into the kitchen and began filling the kettle. Deniz's attempts to protest at the unnecessary hospitality were unheeded and waved away. Within a few minutes, all four of them were stirring varying amounts of sugar into their tea, taking sips of the hot liquid in the hourglass-shaped cup.

"So..." Crystal began. "Why don't we talk about the elephant in the room? What are we going to do to take down Cem and potentially save Eliza's job?"

"I saw Cem today," Eliza cringed. "He practically admitted to all of it. I wish I'd had a recorder in my pocket, then we'd have him on tape and that would at least create reasonable doubt about his innocence."

Crystal was shaking her head. "That isn't good enough. There's got to be more, something concrete..."

Deniz cleared his throat. "I could...I could speak with Dr. Yılmaz. I didn't want to involve her until I knew it was alright with you, Eliza." He locked eyes with her as he said her name. "But she must have some evidence from Cem's university days. Transcripts or lack thereof, I mean. Official paperwork from his dismissal. I don't see how Dr. Çelik could deny that."

"That's amazing!" Eliza cried, surprising herself with her enthusiasm. "Dr. Çelik respects Dr. Yılmaz more than anyone. That would change all of this, I know it."

"Unless..." Crystal spoke up. "Unless she continues with her whole 'Eliza and Deniz are in cahoots and plotting against me' train of thought." Eliza blushed and shot her friend her most convincing "shut the hell up" look. "Oh, don't look at me like that. Maybe you didn't tell Deniz about everything she said, but he needs to know. Especially if it involves him."

Deniz's expression was quizzical and concerned. "What involves me?"

"Dr. Çelik thinks this is all personal, of course...and she thinks you and I are in on it together. She's...observant, let's say. She noticed the way you talked about my work and your respect for me at the meetings, and she talked to me about it. About the potential for something...romantic...developing between us. I tried to shut her down, but she wasn't having it. I swear, she's making up something that doesn't exist, but even if that's the case, it still matters. She's so convinced that we're a team, a united front, that she won't accept anything that comes from you as being from a neutral third party."

"And maybe not anything that comes from Dr. Yılmaz either, since the two of you are so close," Crystal threw in.

Deniz's face had lost its color. "Your boss talked to you about our relationship? Was she threatening you? Offering you advice? Why didn't you tell me sooner?"

Eliza laughed mirthlessly. "Come on, Deniz. It's not like we were on the friendliest of terms before, well...today. And talking with you about an imagined relationship between us isn't exactly my idea of fun."

"Huh. Alright. Well, that's all the more reason to look for additional support for our case. Anyone else got anything to add?" Deniz was avoiding Eliza's eyes now, and she couldn't help but wonder what had caused the change in his demeanor. A minute ago, he had been warm and friendly and now he was detached and clinical. That was a mystery she'd have to save for another day, though.

The four friends—it was strange to think of themselves as friends, but it felt appropriate for the first time—continued to chew in silence, each lost in thought as they brainstormed their plan of attack. Suddenly, Eliza perked up. "Oh! I totally forgot. I promised to call Dr. Bennett." Deniz and Crystal deflated as she finished her idea, whatever hope they had felt that she'd solved the problem at hand extinguished.

Dr. Bennett answered the phone on the first ring. "Lizzy! I'm so glad you called."

"Hi, Dr. B!" She tried to make her voice cheery. "I've been thinking of you today. How is everything?"

"Well, I've confirmed the worst, Lizzy. It's not good news, and it breaks my heart, but I know now that Larry sent that email from my email account."

"What? How do you know that?"

"You know I'm not exactly a technological genius, I know...but I work at a university with all sorts of experts in all sorts of different fields. I had the thought this morning that maybe there was someone over in the IT department who could help me get to the bottom of this. So, I carried my computer over to the building and I asked just that. 'Is there anyone here who can help me figure out if someone sent and then deleted an email from my account?'"

Eliza held her breath. "And?"

"And sure enough, they did it, Lizzy! There was no email in my trash folder, you know, but they found it...something about the servers, I think. You know I'm not good at understanding this kind of thing. I just smile and nod. But they found the sent email in a file on the server, and they printed it off for me."

"Wow...what did it say? How did you know it was Larry?"

"Oh, he is clever, that boy. I'll give him that. The email sounds just like me. In fact, if I hadn't been so sure of where I was at 6am when it was sent—of course you know I was still deep asleep then, Lizzy, I never wake up a moment before 7:30—I would have doubted myself and thought I actually wrote it. But the attachments were files I'd never even seen before, resumes and transcripts for Larry and for someone named...Cem? Is that right?"

"Yeah, that's him. Is there anything else? Any other way to prove that it wasn't you who sent the email?"

"That's it, Lizzy. Why? Do you need more? Who wouldn't believe that?"

Eliza sighed out her disappointment and then filled Dr. Bennett in on all the doubt and grief Dr. Çelik had expressed. When she was finished, it was Dr. Bennett's turn to sigh.

"My God," he said. "She has you in a hard position. But then I guess she's in one, too. She wants to believe these two new, wonderful teachers have just fallen into her lap, and I'm sure she doesn't want to lose you, either."

"Don't be so sure of that," Eliza said. "At this point, I think she sees me as a loss. I've done nothing but let her down."

"Don't say that! You've done a lot of great work there, Lizzy. You're just so focused on what you haven't done yet that you can't see it."

That hit home. When was the last time she had reflected on her accomplishments rather than looking ahead towards her never-ending to-do list?

"Oh, there is one more thing..." Dr. Bennett began. "I forgot to mention it before when I told you about the email."

"Yeah? What's that?" Eliza asked, not daring to get her hopes up again.

"The IT guy that helped me said something about an I...P address? I think that's what it's called. The email had some kind of address attached to it to show where it was sent from. And would you believe? It wasn't sent from Ann Arbor, like all of my other emails are. No, it was sent from Antalya, Turkey. Imagine that. What are the odds?"

"Yeah, I don't think that's random chance," said Eliza. "Could you send me the copy of that report from IT? It's going to help me put a stop to this nonsense once and for all."

"I'll ask my assistant to send it to you. You know, I don't even know where I would begin to do that; I'm no—"

"No good at technology, right?" Eliza interrupted. "But actually, that's not true. You and your technology skills may be just the thing that saves my job and saves Med School from a very unpleasant future."

She ended the conversation with Dr. Bennett and turned to face Deniz, Crystal, and Jack. "We've got him. With Deniz's evidence of Cem's past misconduct and this additional proof that the job application originated in Antalya, there's no way he's getting away with this. Now let's come up with our plan of attack..."

Twenty-Six

The next day began before the sun rose, with Eliza leaping out of bed after a restless night's sleep as soon as her alarm sounded. Jack and Deniz had stayed until midnight, and Crystal and Eliza had retired to bed soon after they left. The hours they'd spent together had been consumed with phone calls and emails, documents printed and copied, collated and highlighted within an inch of their lives. All that hard work had been interspersed with just the amount of laughter and lightheartedness that Eliza had begun to feel the stress of the day—of the week—eke out of her body. Her shoulders, which had been inching up around her ears, relaxed as her friends lifted the burden off of them and shared it among themselves.

Still, when she had climbed into her bed and closed her eyes, rest hadn't come. Her mind was a veritable merry-go-round, each questioning thought visiting her in turn, one after the other. *What if Dr. Çelik doesn't believe me? What if I lose my job? Is this going to make things weird between Dr. Yılmaz and Dr. Çelik? What about Dr. Bennett—is he ever going to be able to hold on to the fleeting respect that anyone gives him? Is Dr. Çelik going to make this personal, about me and Deniz, again? What if Cem is telling the truth?* That last thought stopped her in her tracks—his gaslighting skills were so proficient that now she was even doubting reality and her interpretation of it.

She had drifted off into a light sleep hours later, and the alarm had roused her easily. She silenced it with a flick and leaped out of bed, adrenaline already coursing through her veins and eliminating any trace of tiredness.

In the kitchen, coffee was already brewing, and Eliza heard water running in the bathroom. "Good morning, Crystal!" she called through the bathroom door, making her way back to her bedroom to choose her clothes for the day while she waited for her turn in the bathroom—and, of course, her first cup of coffee.

The confrontations demanded by this day were going to require an appropriate outfit, of course. Eliza opened her wardrobe and flicked through the hangers inside, searching for the right outfit to convey the "I'm a serious boss bitch and you'd do well to listen to me once in a while" look. Within minutes, her bed was covered in pencil skirts, blouses, blazers, dresses, and pants. She rearranged them to form different combinations, opting for a black pencil skirt and a button-down shirt. Now if only she could decide on *which* button-down shirt would be best...

"That one!" came Crystal's voice from the doorway, where she was patting moisturizer into her freshly washed face. She was pointing at the emerald green shirt on the left side of Eliza's bed. "It's a great color on you, and…let's be honest. Choosing a dark color on a stressful day is definitely the boss move." Off Eliza's confused expression, she explained. "Pit stains! Duh. Are you really going to walk in there in a white button down? Please! By ten o'clock this morning, you're going to be keeping your arms glued to your sides to hide the fact that you're stressed the hell out. And no one is going to fall for it. Wear the green shirt."

By the time Eliza left for work, she was feeling grounded (thanks to the hearty breakfast Crystal had insisted she eat), jittery (thanks to the two cups of coffee and counting she had drunk so far), and confident as hell (thanks to the skirt that was professional *and* form fitting and the blouse that brought out the flecks of green in her eyes rather than the exhaustion-induced bags under them).

She greeted the driver as she entered the service shuttle and walked back to her usual spot next to Jack. He looked up at her approach and a smile spread across his face. "Yes! That's what I'm talking about!" he cried. "Why don't you dress like this more often? And are you *so* ready to get some sweet, sweet justice from Cem?"

Eliza felt herself blush at Jack's exclamation. "First of all, I hardly think I look like a slob on a normal workday. Maybe there's a little more makeup today, and yeah, I guess I don't wear this blouse often, but…"

"Stop with the excuses and justifications. You look hot!" Off her expression, he added, "And very professional. Duh!"

Eliza continued, as if she hadn't been interrupted. "And second, I'm ready for justice to be served. I don't want to destroy anyone, but…yeah. Justice would be nice."

"It's going to be the best. I wish I could be there to see it!"

"Same to you, bud. I wish we could do all of this together, but...divide and conquer, right? That's the way it's got to be."

"And there will be time for stories over drinks tonight." Jack winked. "You won't miss a thing, and neither will I."

The plan had been settled that Jack and Deniz would address Dr. Çelik, and at the same time Eliza and Crystal were going to confront Cem. Unfortunately, though the plan was solid, it wasn't one that allowed for immediate action. Eliza knew Cem would be teaching a demo lesson at three o'clock, and so until then there was nothing to do but go about her business as usual, ignoring the pit in her stomach that came along with impending confrontation.

In her two morning lessons, her students were practicing the writing portion of the upcoming final essay. That meant they would have forty-five minutes to brainstorm, outline, and draft an entire opinion essay, choosing their topic from a selection of three. It was one part of the exam that gave students the most anxiety, so Eliza had opted from the beginning of the semester to have them practice it once a week. Though they groaned whenever the essay writing lesson rolled around, Eliza could see the progress they'd made over the past months and she knew her students were feeling more and more confident about their odds of passing the exam.

If only today weren't essay writing day, she thought to herself as she sat at the front of the room, staring at her classroom full of students feverishly writing on the papers in front of them. She walked around the room to ensure they remained on task, but they had taken her previous admonitions—"The teacher can't help you during your exam, so read the topics carefully and then get to work. Any question you ask, the teacher proctoring the exam is probably going to say, 'I can't answer that,' and keep on walking."—to heart and no one needed her help. It was...nice...not to be needed, in general. But not today. Today she could use a distraction, she thought, as she checked the time again. It had only been three minutes since she last looked at the clock.

By the time lunch rolled around, Eliza felt like she could bench-press a Volkswagen. She met Jack outside his office, and the two of them walked to the cafeteria together. Once they were settled into their table, digging into the lentil soup that was on the menu today, Eliza started speaking. "How's your day going so far?" she asked her friend.

He smiled back at her. "You're nervous, huh? Everything is going just fine. Deniz texted me before we came down here, and he's going to be here by two thirty. He's still planning on picking up Crystal. Have you heard anything from her?"

Eliza shook her head. "I'm going to call her after lunch just to make sure nothing has changed. I wish I could confirm Dr. Çelik's schedule today...what if the meeting time changes and we don't know it?"

"We'll figure it out. This isn't going to slip away from you just because of a schedule change, Eliza. It's all going to be okay."

Eliza should have known that her worry about schedules changing was a premonition. She paced in the entrance hall of the language building, waiting for Deniz and Crystal to arrive. Cem had showed up early, and he was in Dr. Çelik's office now with the door closed behind him. She and her friends wouldn't have any time to regroup before they'd need to jump into action.

A familiar face rounded the corner of the pathway leading to the main entrance of the hall and Eliza felt her heart trip over itself. She had never been happier to see Deniz, that was certain. Next to him was her oldest friend, and watching the two of them walk side by side, easy laughter flowing between them as they talked, Eliza glowed from within. They had both shown up for her, and gratitude at that reminder flooded her with emotion. She'd always known Crystal had her back, but seeing Deniz there too stirred up a wistfulness within her. In another reality, maybe it could be like this.

But now wasn't the time to think about that. She flew to the door and met them at the threshold. "He's here already!" she hissed before they could recover from the shock of her sudden appearance. "We've got to move now!"

Deniz nodded at her. "It's okay, we're ready." He held up his briefcase. "I've got everything in here for Dr. Çelik, including a personal letter Dr. Yılmaz wrote. As soon as Cem is out of sight, I'll slip into her office and ask for a moment of her time. There's too much evidence in here, Eliza. She won't be able to deny it."

"Thank you," Eliza said, reaching out to grasp his wrist. "Really. It means a lot to me that you're helping with this. I know you're not doing it for me, I mean…I know putting Cem in his place is important to you too, but…"

"Eliza," he interrupted her. "I'm doing this for you. I'm not here for revenge or even for justice. This is important to you, and so it's important to me." Her ears flushed with heat and she was thankful she had worn her hair down today as he walked purposefully towards the administrative offices.

"You ready?" Crystal asked, as she laced her arm through Eliza's. Noticing the color on Eliza's face, she laughed. "Yeah, we'll talk about that later. You didn't tell me you had a little crush thing going on…" She elbowed Eliza in the ribs, needling her.

Eliza rolled her eyes and jerked Crystal down the hallway in the opposite direction Deniz had gone. "Come on!"

They arrived at the empty classroom and peeked through the door to be sure there was nobody else inside. When Eliza's eyes landed on him, she let out a gasp. "Larry?" she cried as she pushed the door open.

Larry stood, eyes darting to the door. "What are you doing here?" he questioned the two women. Crystal was already striding across the room toward him with her arms opened for a hug.

"What are *we* doing here?" Eliza demanded. "What are *you* doing here?"

Larry had dodged Crystal's hug and was pacing like a jaguar in a cage. Crystal pulled Eliza into the seats closest to the door, leaving space between them and Larry. "It's okay, Larry," she said. "Sit down. We're just here to talk to Cem, and it's good that you're here, too."

"What do you want with Cem?" Larry asked.

Before either of them could give an answer, the door opened again, and Cem strode in, papers in hand. He marched to the teacher's desk at the front of the room and set down his papers before he looked up, saw the two women seated where they had been out of his eyeline behind the door, and blanched. "What the...?" he trailed off.

Crystal stood in front of the door to block his exit. "You weren't expecting us, huh? Well, your demo class has been indefinitely postponed, thanks to a little help from a couple of friends of ours. But now that we've got you here, you're going to listen to us."

"You're going to listen to *me*," Eliza said, stepping forward. "And Larry, I'm glad you're going to hear this. You need to know who you're dealing with."

"Don't believe a word she says," spat Cem. "You know what she's like. You know how selfish she is."

"That's enough, Cem," Eliza continued. "My colleague Deniz is showing the evidence to Dr. Çelik right now about how you tried to cheat your way through university, nearly taking down the program and robbing it of its accreditation. You were dismissed from the program for fraud, not for any ill will directed your way from your classmates. You're a liar and a cheat, Cem...not a victim.

And after all the lies you told me, I can't even imagine what you told Larry to get him to help you with all of this."

"Cem?" Larry spoke up now. "Is this all true? You told me you were qualified...that nothing we were doing was wrong, really. That you were just taking advantage of an opportunity while it presented itself, but you'd make it all right later."

"Not just *me*, Larry. *Us.* You and I are in this together. Did you really think I asked you to come here today just for moral support? You simple, stupid boy...you're in this with me. I sent application materials for both of us, so if you try to take me down, I'm afraid you're going to be taking yourself down, too." Cem's expression was smug as he watched Larry take in this news.

"You...what? I was just trying to do something right for once. To help you..." His face lost its color as he turned to Eliza. "Oh my God...Eliza...am I in trouble too? I didn't know..."

"That's going to be between you and Dr. Bennett, bud." Eliza gave him a small smile. "He might be so happy to have you back that he forgives you right away...but there might be some penance you have to serve, too. I don't know." She turned back to Cem. "But *you*...you're never going to get away with this again. You'll be blacklisted so thoroughly I imagine you'll be grateful if you can find a tour agency willing to hire you. That'll serve you right for looking down on the honest work you *used* to have."

Cem was left gaping like a fish out of water, as Eliza and Crystal strode out the door with Larry close on their heels.

Twenty-Seven

They were only a few steps away from the building when Larry stopped Eliza with a hand on her arm. "Wait." He said. "I need to say something to you."

Eliza turned and gave him an encouraging smile. "It's okay, Larry. I was a jerk to you. You getting swept up in all of Cem's bullshit is at least partly my fault. You don't need to explain or apologize or do anything. I see the turmoil on your face, but...I promise you. It's unwarranted." She prepared to continue walking to the parking lot with Crystal, but Larry wasn't following them.

"Thank you," he said. "Thank you for not giving up on me, for forgiving me...for all of it. I didn't show you nearly enough appreciation while I was staying with you, and it took being away from you, being in Cem's world, to realize what an ungrateful guest I'd been. To you two...and to Turkey. This trip has been amazing, this city is beautiful, and all I've done is compare it to 'back home' and criticize it. I'm going to shut up for a while, I think. Do more listening and learning than speaking and screwing things up."

Crystal laughed, and she started off towards the car, waiting for them in the parking lot. Deniz was already behind the wheel, and Jack was riding shotgun.

"Come on, Larry," Eliza grabbed his wrist. "What are friends even for if we can't mess up in front of each other, call each other out on it, and spiral into shame and feeling like a failure? No one is perfect, and no one *deserves* all the good people—or all the annoying people—in their life. We just...we hurt each other, and we help each other, and we try to learn to do more of the latter and less of the former with the passage of time. That's it. You and I...we're good. We're friends again. I promise."

The tension in Larry's shoulders visibly relaxed, and he smiled at Eliza as the two of them started to jog towards Deniz's car. Crystal held the back door open, and Eliza slid into the middle seat while Larry went around to the other side. Deniz turned back to her with a questioning look in his eyes, and she grinned back at him in answer. For the briefest of moments, the closeness in the car made it feel like grabbing him by the ears and planting a kiss on his face would be the most natural thing to do, but she dismissed the thought with a toss of her hair.

"Well?" she asked Deniz and Jack. "How did it go? You can clearly see,"—she gestured to Larry sitting next to her—"that *we* were successful. How about the two of you?"

Jack spoke up first. "I ran great interference, thank you very much. I mean...you already knew that, since no one wandered into that demo lesson who you didn't already know was going to be there. I had to tell Ayşegül that there were free pastries in the teacher's room to distract her, and I'm pretty sure I'm going to pay for that particular lie later. But it was worth it if we got the job done. Deniz?" He wiggled his eyebrows at Deniz, encouraging him to chime in.

"Yeah Deniz, what happened?" Crystal leaned forward.

He let out his breath with a sigh. "She didn't make it easy, that's for sure. Dr. Çelik didn't want to believe what I was saying about Cem. Especially since it all aligned with what she had already heard from you,"—he looked at Eliza—"but the documents from Dr. Yılmaz, the official records from the university…the more papers I laid in front of her, the quieter she got. By the end, she thanked me and said she'd deal with it."

"…did you ask what she meant by 'dealing with it'?" Crystal asked. "Was that like a 'dealing with it by sweeping it under the rug' or…?"

"I asked." Deniz said. "I told her the story of our university days and all that was at stake for the program, emphasizing that the same could be true for Med School if she goes forward with it. She knows all that. She won't hire him, I'm sure."

"Actually, I can guarantee it." Jack's eyes were wide as he pointed out the windshield. Two security guards were walking across the grounds in front of them, escorting Cem in between them. His head was held low, and the guards' pace was brisk.

"Yeah." Deniz's voice was quiet. "I wonder what he'll do now."

"That's not really our problem anymore, though, is it?" Larry spoke up for the first time, and there was steel in his voice. "He might look humble and innocent there now, but that guy doesn't need our sympathy." The others turned to him, surprised by his tone. "What? I'm not trying to be a dick. I just don't think we should let him looking a little sheepish harsh the buzz of our celebration. Anyway. Where are we going?"

Eliza spoke up for the first time. "It's definitely time for a celebration. I'm thinking maybe—"

"Actually," Deniz interrupted, "I've got someplace in mind, if that's alright with all of you. Shall we?" He started the car and looked at the faces of his passengers. Seeing their nods and looks of confusion, he began to drive.

Crystal raised her eyebrows and mouthed, "What's up?" to Eliza. Eliza shrugged back. Deniz's plans were a mystery to all of them, and there was nothing to do but go along with the ride. He turned the radio up, blasting pop music as he took them from the university in the direction of downtown Antalya.

The mystery was solved as soon as they got to the entrance of Castle Bar. Seated at a table with five empty seats around him was none other than Barış. They all stopped in their tracks at the sight of him, and Deniz turned to Jack. "I'm sorry for my role in keeping the two of you apart. When Barış needed encouragement to take your relationship more seriously, I didn't realize it and I steered him in the wrong direction. When I understood what I'd done, I told him he needed to give you another chance. Or at least stop freezing you out." He squeezed Jack's shoulder and pushed him toward the table.

Falling into step next to Deniz, Eliza spoke quietly. "Thank you, Deniz. For all of it. I know I gave you a hard time about so many things, but...wow. It looks like you made all of them right today. I don't even know what to talk to you about now." She smiled.

He smiled back. "You'll figure something out, I'm sure. We could try being friends...and I'll try not pissing you off again. But no promises." He winked.

At the table, Jack and Barış were grinning as they reconnected. They had seated themselves next to each other, and Jack—in a rare move of demonstrative affection—had his arm around the back of Barış's chair. Barış was talking and laughing, and the smile spreading across his face was contagious. Eliza felt her heart lift as she watched the reunion unfold from her seat across from them. Crystal was seated to her right, across from Larry, and Deniz was to her left.

After they had ordered drinks and caught Barış up with all that had happened today, they raised a toast. "To making things right," Deniz said.

"To friends and forgiveness," Eliza added.

"To starting a new chapter," chimed in Barış.

The night stretched ahead of them, and they filled its hours with laughter, food and drink, and the lightest feeling Eliza had felt in weeks. Even her exhaustion from the past 48 hours evaporated in the presence of the joy, relief, and belonging she felt sitting at this table with these people. There was Crystal, her oldest and most reliable friend. There were Barış and Jack, the very picture of the blossoming of new love. There was Larry, reminding her with every word and look they exchanged that connection and redemption could be found even in the friendships you'd judged as impossible from the first day. And there, by her side, was Deniz. She didn't know quite what to make of him yet, but the comfort she felt sitting by his side, so close she could feel the vibrations when his laughter rippled through him, was an unexpected feeling.

Her reverie was interrupted by Barış. "Eliza, you've been awfully quiet." His eyes twinkled. "But it's been a while since we last saw each other, and I just have to ask. We know Jack is going to stay for another year if he can renew his contract, which he will *easily* do because he's an outstanding teacher." He said that last part while squeezing Jack's knee and nodding with every word. "But what about you? Are you sticking around? Are we going to get more time to be friends properly, or are you going to vanish into thin air?" He pouted as he finished speaking.

"I'm...not really sure yet," Eliza admitted. "Of course, being here with all of you is a huge perk of working here...and the thought of leaving Antalya when I've explored so little of it makes me feel sick. But, the job itself has been a bit of a disaster. I have serious doubts that Dr. Çelik would even ask me to consider staying, honestly. Between this whole Cem debacle and the hot mess that my professional development program turned out to be, I imagine she'd like to start over again with a blank slate." She took a deep breath to strengthen her resolve. "And maybe that's what I need, too. Maybe the lessons learned here are just what I need to do a decent job at my next role, wherever that may be." She shrugged, looking down at the table.

"No." Deniz was the first to speak. "I'm sorry, I don't mean to dismiss your feelings, but...frankly...you're wrong. You're focusing on all the things that have gone wrong, but...Eliza, you've done so much here. The cooperative program that we're working on together is going to change the adult education landscape for this entire city. You can't leave it." Something about the way he said "it" felt like he meant "me," but Eliza dismissed that as wishful thinking, wondering what might have been.

"It's too soon to say, Deniz," she smiled. "I'll seriously consider staying if the opportunity presents itself, okay?" She looked at Crystal now. "And I promise to *at least* sleep on it before I make any decisions. Now, enough of the serious stuff. Let's get back to the fun!"

An hour later, the adrenaline that had been keeping Eliza alert the entire day had vanished without a trace. Exhaustion crept in on silent paws, and she was stifling yawns while the rest of them continued to celebrate. Deniz leaned in to her side and spoke into her ear. "Come on," he said. "I'll take you home."

Before she could protest, he had pulled her to her feet and made her apologies to the group. She told Crystal and Larry—he was sleeping on their couch again, tonight and for the foreseeable future—that she'd meet them at home and let Deniz steer her off of the terrace towards his parked car.

He didn't let go of her hand, even when there was no longer a crowd to direct her through making it necessary. Eliza became increasingly aware of the heat in between their palms and the potential for sweatiness. Just as she was about to pull her hand away, he spoke.

"I'm glad to have a minute alone with you, Eliza. I...I just need to say this." He turned to face her, taking her hand in both of his. "I care about you. I like you. Not just as a colleague or a friend, but...This,"—he gestured between them—"There's something about this that feels so right to me. It's too soon to say what it is, and we've barely spent any time together ever since we realized we could be friends, but...I'd always regret it if I didn't at least tell you. I'm not asking you to stay for me. I'm just asking you to add me to your pro/con list." He laughed. "I won't even tell you which side of the list to put me on."

Eliza was silent as she took in his words. This man was *good*, that much was clear. The kindness he had shown her, the support he had gone out of his way to give her, and the humility he had demonstrated in righting the wrongs between Jack and Barış...she was in awe. Hearing him confirm that he, too, felt the spark of potential between them stirred up bubbly feelings in her stomach she hadn't dared to feel since well before her last relationship took a turn for the worst. She hadn't let herself believe in the magic of possibility since her heart had been ripped out and stomped on, and that had been just fine for a long time. No one had even tempted her to reconsider giving magic a try. No one had asked, no one had offered, and no one had even caught her attention.

But Deniz had caught her attention from the very first moment, she thought now. She had noticed him, been intrigued by him, and she wouldn't have taken his initial snubbing so personally if neither of those things had been true. Criticism from a random asshole was easy to ignore, she had learned, but criticism from someone you had a crush on could be devastating. Was that what had happened?

Naturally, she had said none of this out loud. And judging by the discomfort on Deniz's face before he said "...right." and continued to walk towards his car, she needed to.

"Wait." she said. She grabbed his nearest hand and pulled, turning him back around to face her. "Thank you. For admitting that. For being brave."

"You're welcome, Eliza," he smiled sadly. "I just couldn't handle you not knowing. And I hope I didn't make you uncomfortable. Come on, let's go."

"No," she continued. "You didn't let me finish. Thank you for being braver than I am, for doing what I couldn't do. I've been so hard on you, never let you feel secure in believing that we could be friends...but something changed. Not just today, when you saved me...but for a while now." She could see the uncertainty and confusion traveling across his face, telling her it was time to stop talking *around* the topic and say what she damn well meant. "I like you, too. You're definitely in the 'pro' column of my list...near the top even. And I really hope we get a chance to see what this,"—now it was her turn to gesture to the rapidly shrinking space between them—"is."

The space was nonexistent now, as Deniz pulled her toward him, one hand on the small of her back and one hand on her neck. His eyes met hers, dropped to her lips, and then back up with a question written in them. She gave the briefest of nods before she closed her eyes and leaned in to his kiss. Their lips met, and all the things they'd been saying to each other, all the puzzle pieces they'd been placing on the table slotted themselves into place. Their words had gotten them part of the way to the truth of what was brewing between them, but this, this physical connection between them, expressed a greater level of understanding and connection than they could communicate with their limited vocabularies.

The kiss deepened and shifted, mouths opening to further exploration. Eliza felt the warmth of Deniz's arms and chest surrounding her, the firmness of his back muscles under her hands, the pounding of his heart so near to her own. When the kiss broke, they came up for air, once again finding each other's eyes. This time, a laugh escaped from each of them in turn, along with the new color on both of their cheeks.

"Well," Eliza was the first to speak. "I guess *that* was a long time coming."

"It was," Deniz agreed. "But the next one won't be." He winked at her and took her hand in his. "Come on for real now. Let me take you home. That's enough making out in the streets of Kaleiçi for today."

Twenty-Eight

A week later, that night was the memory keeping Eliza warm in the cold cabin of her transatlantic flight back to Michigan. Larry's time in Antalya had come to an end, and Eliza had decided to join him since her semester had ended early, when Dr. Çelik announced her plans to "go in a different direction with the department next year." She wished she had been able to spend more time with Deniz—the two of them had seen each other every evening, right until the day her plane left, though they were "taking things slow" with the physical aspects of their budding relationship—but the long conversations, the meaningful stares, and of course the make-out sessions were by far the most valuable things she was taking with her on this journey.

"You still haven't told Dr. Bennett you're coming, right?" Larry asked. "So, I definitely shouldn't tell him...right?"

She smiled. "Right. This will be a pleasant surprise for him, having his two favorites in the same room. Did you invite him for lunch like I suggested?"

"Yes, we're going to meet tomorrow at the O'Brien Pub at eleven. I'll make a reservation just to be sure. Sometimes they're crowded on weekends."

"Sounds great, Larry," Eliza patted his knee. She turned to her phone and opened her text messages.

There was, as she had expected, a new one from Deniz. He had dropped her off at the airport this morning, and he had been sending messages every hour or so ever since. She checked the time. She expected the messages to drop off at some point—the man had to sleep after all—but so far they were still going strong.

"Can you bring back some peanut butter? I've tried all the imported stuff I can find here, but I'd like to compare it with the real deal. For science."

Eliza laughed before she wrote back. "Of course! Now here's the real question: crunchy or smooth?"

His text bubble popped up and disappeared a few times before the next message came through. "I have no idea what that even means. I'll do some research and get back to you."

Eliza smiled to herself. There was so much comfort knowing that she was on the first part of a round-trip journey. She and Deniz weren't in a long distance relationship, or at least they weren't going to be in one for any longer than the ten days she spent back home. She'd be back in Antalya before the end of the month, and she would have plenty of time to enjoy the summer *and* get ready for her new job in the fall.

Because even though Dr. Çelik hadn't renewed her contract—a fact that was disappointing but in the long run unsurprising—Dr. Yılmaz had been quick to extend an opportunity Eliza's way. Eliza had questioned Deniz about it, suspecting he had had something to do with it, but his denial was firm. Dr. Yılmaz had been impressed with Eliza since before they had even met, and her program also had teaching spots that needed to be filled for the fall. The position would be a full-time teaching post, and Eliza was ready to hang up her administrative hat and get back in the classroom where she belonged. She had gotten into teaching for her love of the craft, and the work she had been doing at Med School had nearly robbed her of that love. Everything was falling into place.

At eleven o'clock the next day, Eliza was already seated at the table at O'Brien Pub, her back to the door so that Dr. Bennett wouldn't know it was her until he had already been shown to the table. She sipped her water and was replying to Deniz's latest text when she heard a familiar voice behind her.

"...just a fabulous menu, you know. Larry, you *have* to try their fish and chips. I know, you're probably thinking fish and chips, how special could it be, but...wait, there's someone at our table? Oh Lizzy, my dear girl!"

Eliza was pulled to her feet and engulfed in Dr. Bennett's arms before she could even put her phone down.

"Hi, Dr. B!" She laughed. "Hi, Larry." She smiled over Dr. Bennett's shoulder at her friend.

"Lizzy, what are you doing here?" Dr. Bennett asked as they all took their seats. "Getting homesick? Missed me too much? Are you going back?"

She patted his hand. "Well, of course, I *did* miss you and my family, so I'm here to soak up all the good times I can."

"And…?"

"And I'm also going back. Dr. Bennett, Antalya is amazing. So beautiful, and there's still so much more to see and more to do there. I'm really glad I'm not done with it yet."

Dr. Bennett placed his napkin across his lap and picked up his menu. "A little birdie told me,"—he glanced at Larry—"about what happened with Dr. Çelik. And after you helped her clean up the mess with that Cem character! Did you talk her into letting you stay on?"

"I didn't," Eliza said. "And I wouldn't want to, not really. Don't get me wrong, the Mediterranean School of Languages is doing great things, and I'm very pleased to have had the opportunity to develop and shape that program. But…administrative work isn't for me, Dr. B. I missed being in the classroom. Even though I was still teaching some classes, all the time I spent working on professional development programs and coordinating teacher schedules…it sucked the life right out of it. I couldn't do it anymore. And I've had a job offer from Dr. Yılmaz at the Antalya Technical Institute, a teaching job. I've accepted it already, and I'll head back later next week to get started."

Dr. Bennett sighed and smiled. "It makes me so happy to hear that, Lizzy. I had a feeling from the beginning that admin work wasn't for you, I really did. But I wanted you to find that out for yourself. This role was the perfect learning opportunity for you, and I'm very glad you took it. And that you learned so much about yourself in the process!"

"Thank you," Eliza smiled. "Now tell me, what's new with you?"

"Oh, that's an awfully long story, Lizzy," Dr. Bennett smiled. "Let's order first or else we'll all starve to death!"

"That's an excellent idea. What's good here?" she asked as she opened her menu.

For the first time since they greeted each other, Larry spoke up. "I heard the fish and chips is excellent," he said with a twinkle in his eye.

They ordered their meals and relaxed into easy conversation. While they ate, Dr. Bennett regaled them with stories of the last school year, the students he had taught, the papers he had written, and all the drama involved in both. Eliza and Larry laughed along with them, pleased to see their advisor, who had been so stressed and worried over the phone, was in his element again, storytelling and entertaining like the natural that he was.

After their empty plates were cleared away, Dr. Bennett pushed back his chair from the table, leaned back, and folded his hands over his belly. He looked at Eliza over the top of his glasses, which had slid down his nose ever so slightly, peering with a newfound intensity.

"Er...yes?" She asked, discomfort rising to the surface.

"Lizzy, I think there might be something—or some-one—else that's got you so excited about going back to Turkey." He said. Off her expression, he rushed to clarify. "Larry didn't tell me any specifics, I swear. But in all the stories I've heard, I couldn't help but notice some rather gentlemanly behavior dedicated in your direction. And I must say, it's about time."

Eliza's blush deepened. Dr. Bennett had been there right after Alec had dumped her, and she had cried in his office more than once during that first traumatic post-breakup week. Ever since then, she had resolved to keep her personal life and professional life separate, and she had done a fine job of it. Until now.

"I'd really rather not..." she began.

He waved a hand in her direction. "I'm not asking for any details. That's your business. I just...I'm glad to see you're happy. Lighter, somehow. Like maybe some hard edges are starting to soften up a bit. Maybe." He smiled sheepishly. Clearly, her discomfort with this topic was contagious.

"Thank you, Dr. B." she said. "I'm happy, and I'm taking a chance on someone for the first time in a long time. It feels good."

"Just remember," he said, "It's not just about taking a chance on another person. It's about taking a chance on yourself, on happiness, on trying something new. No matter what happens with this young man...it'll be worth it. You'll learn, you'll grow, and maybe you'll even get your happily ever after."

"Amen!" cried Larry, raising a glass.

Eliza smiled at them both and raised her glass to meet theirs. "Cheers to that. I've got a really good feeling about this one."

Author's Note

Eliza and Deniz's story will continue in *Sense, Sensibility, & the Mediterranean Sea*, which will be published in 2023.

Thank you so much for reading this story through to the end. It was a lot of fun for me to travel back to Antalya, my first home in Turkey, through the pages and to spend time with my literary queen, Jane Austen herself, as I studied her work and the genius ways she wove her stories together.

I love a good enemies-to-lovers story as much as the next reader, but as this one was ending, I faced the classic struggle that comes after pages and pages and pages of "will they or won't they?" questions, only for the couple to get together at the very end: Eliza and Deniz's story didn't feel like it was over yet. Eliza has experienced a transformation in the world of her career and her single-minded focus on it. But what about Deniz? What about his family?

How would they feel about things getting serious with his American girlfriend?

Therefore, the sequel for this story took form before I'd even finished the first draft of this manuscript and it's why this story had to end with a "happy for now." Have no fear, the "happily ever after" is coming for Eliza and Deniz. We're just going to take a few more twists and turns and laughs along the way before we get there.

This story, like everything I write, is informed by my experience. I see pieces of myself in my characters and pieces of the people I love in them as well. This story holds a special place in my heart because Antalya, Turkey, holds a special place in my heart. It was there that I got my first job teaching English at a university (though of course both schools in this story are 100% fictional), and it was there that I met my husband.

To stay updated on other works in progress, please visit my website at kcmccormickciftci.com. I've got a free story waiting for you there, and I send out regular updates on upcoming releases, books I'm loving, and other recommendations.

If you loved this book, please consider leaving a review, as that is one of the best ways to support indie authors like me. Reviews left on major retail sites (wherever you bought this book is a great start!), Goodreads, and Book-Bub will help other readers discover this book, too.

Acknowledgments

This book took quite a journey to find its way into the world, and I'm grateful to everyone who played a role in that.

The idea, the character names, and the sheer nerve to believe I could write a full-length novel all came to me on a spontaneous trip to Michigan's Upper Peninsula with my brother. Thank you for inviting me along on that work trip, for all the laughs and good conversation, and for unintentionally fairy godmothering this book into my world.

Many of the words found their way onto these pages in my parents' house and in my aunt Mary's house. I only stayed hydrated, nourished, and focused because of the support received in both of those places, so thank you to my mom, dad, and Mary. Thank you for being excited with me, for asking all the right questions, and for reminding me to keep my dreams.

I'm fortunate to be in a family full of readers and writers. I have fond memories of "helping" my aunt Karen type the index for one of her books, and now in a full circle moment, I get to read drafts written by my own nieces and nephews. Keep telling your stories, and keep reading the ones that you love.

To my friends, both the in-person ones and the online ones, thank you. Life would be so much less rich without you, and I am grateful for you. Even if I'm not great at communicating when I'm spending all my words on writing, you're in my heart.

Thank you to our family in Turkey for the roof over our heads those first few months, for homemade cheese, yogurt, and bread, and for all the love, acceptance, and support.

There are definitely more stories set in Turkey to tell, and I know some special Turkish cats are going to find their way into them. Sis and Bıyıklı, you have made our lives so much more fun, and I am obsessed with you both.

None of this would have happened if not for the job that brought me to Turkey, the friendships that made me stay for a second year, and the wonderful human I fell in love with. Your support has made this possible, but even more importantly, I would be completely unqualified to write a love story if not for your existence in the world and your presence in my life.

About the Author

KC McCormick Çiftçi is an English teacher turned romance writer. She spent the majority of her twenties living and working abroad, collecting the experiences that inform the stories she tells. She enjoys telling multicultural and international love stories through romantic comedy and women's fiction. She and her Turkish husband split their time between southeastern Michigan and southwestern Turkey.

Prior to diving into the world of romance, KC published two self-help books for intercultural couples, *Lov-*

ing Across Borders and *The K-1 Visa Wedding Plan*. Both are available wherever books are sold.

For updates on upcoming releases, behind the scenes news, and all my favorite book recommendations, visit kcmccormickciftci.com (or just point your phone camera at the QR code below).